P9-CQN-369

THE HOUSE ON MAJOR STREET

THE WORKS OF CHEKOO

# The House
# on Major Street

## A   N   O   V   E   L

# Leon Rooke

The Porcupine's Quill

Library and Archives Canada Cataloguing in Publication

Rooke, Leon, author
  The house on Major Street : a novel / Leon Rooke.

ISBN 978-0-88984-419-3 (softcover)

  I. Title.

PS8585.064H585 2018      C813'.54      C2018-906289-4

1   2   3   ·   21   20   19

Published by The Porcupine's Quill, 68 Main Street, PO Box 160,
Erin, Ontario NOB 1TO. http://porcupinesquill.ca

Readied for the press by Chandra Wohleber.
Sketches throughout the work are by the author.

Represented in Canada by Canadian Manda.
Trade orders are available from University of Toronto Press.

We acknowledge the support of the Ontario Arts Council and the Canada
Council for the Arts for our publishing program. The financial support of
the Government of Canada is also gratefully acknowledged.

John Ehle
*In memory:*
*great friend, great writer*
1925–2018

And Rosie and Jennifer

## Notes and Acknowledgements

The 'Mayan love charm' is from the book entitled *Mayan Love Charms* by Petra Hernandez, translated from Tzotzil by Ambar Past and published by Taller Leñateros, Chiapas, Mexico, 2007. Authors whose work is quoted in this book include Anton Chekhov, Eugene Ionesco, T.S. Eliot, Aldous Huxley, Marguerite Duras, Samuel Beckett, and (perhaps) James Joyce. Lines from these authors receive attribution in the text. An unattributed line ('Behold, the hour is at hand') is from Chekhov's short story 'Ionych'.

Characters from Chekhov's 'Lady with a Lapdog' and 'The Kiss' are herein dispatched to new ground. Sophia Tolstoy's stated reservations regarding certain Chekhov stories are—more or less—paraphrased from her diary entries. Opera lovers will recognize 'Fiuto! Razzola! Fruga!' from *Tosca*. The Mavis Gallant line, somewhat altered, is from her short story 'His Mother'. Robert Browning's fondness for referring to Elizabeth Barrett Browning as 'his own little Portuguese' (herein quoted) likely has as original source the 1900 edition of *The Complete Works of Mrs E.B. Browning*, Charlotte Porter and Helen A. Clarke, editors.

Living presences—real people—stroll these pages. The author takes deep pleasure in enlisting among them three friends: Rare-book specialists Steven Temple, David Mason and the late Richard Landon. Permission to use Richard's name was granted by his widow, Marie Korey (herself a radiant light in the rare-book field). Both Steven and David, in their letters (which see), express (profound?) discontent (astonishment?) with the author's use of the word 'dishevelled', in description of them (Richard would have as well). That the author is himself frequently so perceived is no defence, and thus I—me, the novelist, this very minute—disavow the word's relevance to these remarkable individuals.

There are more real people than these to whom the author owes an endless round of thanks. Chandra Wohleber has now served as my editor through three Porcupine's Quill books. *Served* is hardly the appropriate word. The unsavoury truth is that the older I get the harder the editor must work. Torture, yes. But is she ever 'dishevelled' by this? No. Maybe. If so, she has only screamed silently, in the tradition, perhaps, of many brilliant guidance officers. Then there's the tech-whiz/typist Allegra Robinson whose major task it was to translate into readable English 3,000 long, thin book marks on which the author had illegibly written what he madly proposed to be 'a novel'. Again, pure torture. But she did it. Even was nice about it. Advice to authors: Use standard paper. Preferably typed. In the wings has been the Porcupette. By name, Stephanie Small. Stephanie has been in my midst a good while now, working on projects both under and above ground, by which I mean Steph has accomplished deeds a more astute author would himself have done. Thanks, Stephanie. Thanks to the work of Jennifer Dickson, which inspired the name of the hospital where Zan recovers, that is, the Hospital for Wounded Angels. The Ontario Arts Council bestowed upon the author, through their Writers' Reserve program, a welcomed grant for which all my lenders are grateful. Me too. Despite this being my sixth (seventh?) book with Tim and Elke Inkster's exquisite Porcupine's Quill, their 'Still in Business' cry continues to resound. 'Holy catfish', remarks the languishing author who has never once made back his Quill advance.

❖

*I want him to come*

*On a new road*

*So his white clothes*

*Won't get dirty.*

*I don't want him*

*To fall in the mud.*

*Don't let*

*A bad snake bite him.*

—Mayan love charm

Early in the morning a lady with a lapdog showed up at the house on Major Street. She said she was looking for a former cavalry officer, Ryabovitch by name, whom she understood had struck up a friendship with a young boy presumably residing at this address. Ryabovitch was in fact upstairs at the time, contemplating flight through a window. He had heard the yapping dog. He could leap to the porch roof, possibly without breaking a leg, and make his escape. Romance had not come easily to him. It surprised him that it had come at all. That Anna Sergeyevna was a glorious woman he had no doubt. But intense, my word!

Emmitt Haley, father of the young boy, answered the woman's anxious summons. He wore only pajama bottoms, his feet bare, the day brutally cold, boasting a sombre blue cast. Rainfall, intermittent. It took him some time to understand what the harried woman was saying. Her accent was unfamiliar, her manner troubling. Sorry. What? Who?

Ryabovitch. I know the snake resides here.

A snake?

Da, and a snivelling rat.

Finally, Emmitt comprehended that this snake, Ryabovitch, Ryabovitch the pig, had trampled on this woman's heart. How distressing. But it was difficult to concentrate on her words. An icy wind was blowing. His feet were numb, fingers getting there.

But, but, but. Now rain was falling harder. Icy pellets striking his toes. The visitor appeared not to notice the rain. He was trying to tell this berserk woman that no one bearing the name Ryabovitch lived in this house. Friend of my son? This minute upstairs in bed, comatose, and conceivably never to emerge! Not possible. Lady, you have the wrong house. But his tongue was tied. He ached with cold. He ached to say to the woman, Lady, I am not up to this ordeal: a bad, sleepless night after so many. You come at a bad time.

At that moment the woman let out a shriek. She had seen, inside the house, a speeding blur. Descending the stairs. A speeding blur.

*There he is!*

Such was her shriek. Shrieks. An instant later, she was scrambling to get past him. To get through the door.

*Lady!*

A variety of shouts, random noises—pandemonium—brought Emmitt's wife, Daisy, to the door. She had been in the kitchen dully watching eggs boil in a pan of water. It could be admitted that she had been watching this boiling water for some duration. Sooner or later those eggs will find their way into the garbage. She was partner to a pill-induced slumber, let's say. Xanax, perhaps. Lorazepam. What else? She has her secret stash. She has her reasons—her beautiful son may never again waken to the real world.

So here she is, on this cold wet morning, shoving her husband aside. Actually punching him—hair not yet combed, dingy gown about to fall off her—a slattern! What has this once-attractive woman done to herself? A professor of English literature, for God's sake! On medical leave, just now. Appalling developments here at 2x8 Major. She, too, is yelling: '*My God, Em, why are you making that woman cry? Have you lost your senses? My God, Em, let the woman come in!*'

For some minutes, the dog had been yelping. She was a nervous dog, strongly opinionated. Pomeranian by appearance. Not that Emmitt or Daisy knew a Pomeranian from a sheep dog or any other. The Pomeranian dog could have told everyone the scoundrel Ryabovitch had been in there. She hadn't seen the blur, but had smelled him. Now he was gone. The whole business had been a waste of time. Her mistress always fell for rotters. Consider that rotter husband back in Russia, for instance. A flunky, a lackey. Consider that dolt Gurov she succumbed to in Yalta. Such has been her whole life's story. The Pomeranian loved her mistress, but God knows Anna Sergeyevna did not make this loving easy. No more than did that other dolt, Chekhov, when he set out to write the true-life story of a good dog. And got everything wrong. *Sitting in Varney's pavilion, Gurov saw, walking on the sea-front, a fair-haired lady of medium height, wearing a beret, a white Pomeranian dog running behind her.* A lie. The few times she'd allowed herself to run behind Anna it was solely so she could nip at her heels. Hurry her along. The time the lazy author was writing about she'd been splashing through blue waves, chasing a seagull. *Never trust an author* was the Pomeranian's motto. In fact, in her estimation a wise Pomeranian— herself—while the most sociable creature on earth, trusted no one.

What might an erudite scholarly wag say of this hodgepodge lacerating 2x8 Major?

*Help, help!*

Ours is a house occupied by the blind, the deaf, the mute, the totally help-less! We are lame, we are crippled, we are maimed and tormented, socially inept, bunglers of the first rank, mental midgets bereft of hope! We crawl about on hands and knees, we cry out (*help, help!*). We crouch in dark corners, entreating our captors: *What have we done? Why are you doing this to us? Mercy! Mercy!*

Hurry, friends, with news of our desperate plight. Inform the police, the military, the press, the very topmost, exalted despots of our great country. Barons of the left, moguls of the right, pillars of the very centre-most centre. Our dye is cast, our pigment set.

Oh, help us.

Forget latitude, longitude, write down this address: two-x-eight (2x8) Major, a stone's throw from Bloor Street's best. Heart of the heart's heart. A scholar's digs. Known land of the Mississauga Anishinaabeg, Haudenosaunee and Wendat peoples. Turn where you see the Bloor SuperSave. You have passed Trinity Church. Go back. One two three, how many doors south. Red brick house (renovated not, and no plans to). Lacy windows, how many bodies buried in the basement, beaten shrubs by the front walk, rubbish today swirling, snow a mile high. Rain, intermittent.

You can't miss it. Extreme measures are called for, don't even think negotiation. Too late, too late! Beseech our liberators to arrive with tanks, flame throwers, scud missiles, pots and pots of chicken soup; have phantom jets strafe our house and thousands of enraged crusaders lay siege to our door. Be warned, bad news awaits ...

Be cool.

Hang easy.

Save us. We perish by the hour.

❂ ❂ ❂ ❂ ❂ ❂ ❂ ❂ ❂ ❂ ❂ ❂ ❂ ❂ ❂ ❂ ❂ ❂ ❂ ❂ ❂ ❂ ❂ ❂

The one window of Tallis Haley's second-floor room looks out over an exquisite garden. In this garden stands a fine sculpted fountain, erected overnight by unseen hands. So it seems. Because when Tallis Haley—*The comet, man! Weird light. Watch that little freak go!*—was removed from Children's Hospital and restored to his own bedroom, the site greeting his closed eyes was a rubble-strewn field. Memory is sticky tar, but he remembers this clearly. Now there are rolling hills, trees, swollen streams. Getting past his own infancy is a hurdle—*strange territory*—though a boy must try. Teepees. Muskrat and chipmunk, buffalo!

From a high limb, or hanging like a bug to a wall—you could—*he* could—see all the way to Winnipeg. Turn a snitch and there is ... well, what is that? A shimmering surface of blue. Could that be the Great Lakes?

Another century. He hasn't even been born yet. He's over the hump.

Each night now, in the sticky black tar of a blue haze, no less than a dozen schoolgirls perambulate, with elaborate cries of ecstasy and considerable expertise in the charm area. A dream. Oh, it's a dream, by anyone's account. Bewitching, yes, a joyful ceremony. And every night, you understand, which is hard on a boy in the comate status.

Fantastic events unfolding here at 2 x 8 Major.

Ask Daisy, ask Emmitt. Inquire of anyone.

Chekhov is rumoured to abide here.

These girls frolic, they dance, they weave the spell of divine and harmonious rites. Even in the cold, even in softly falling snow, they come. They relieve themselves of negligible encumbrances—backpacks, purses, school books: under heavy coats, thick hats, cumbersome boots, they cavort about the cascading fountain, as if exorcising themselves of daredevil demons, of weights carried for centuries. Girls in overdrive.

Phantoms, Tallis might think, from the innocent beyond. No males allowed. No means no. Keep your distance, Jack.

Later in the night, they form a chain of hands and snake away, fade like white sheets floating on a gentle wind. Going, going, gone.

The sight of so many girls elates Tallis Comatose Haley, shivering under a blanket, his face smeared to the frosty glass. How does he come to be at this window? He is bedridden. He cannot bestir his limbs. He cannot speak. He dares not rattle finger against pane. One false move, one tuck of the brow, one scratch of his nose, and might not everything disappear forever? His body sweep into the deepest, blackest void.

Save us, save us!

Woo us, fine maidens, into the nimble, heathery hereafter. Bind us with the invisible strands of your invisible net flung from the great beyond. Dancing girls, grazing buffalo.

*Help! Help!*

Earthwork. In his deep sleep, his dark coma—why is it so black in here?—Tallis Haley hears giant machines, massive backhoes, front hoes, jackhammers, raucous drills at work beyond his window. His walls quake, the floor vibrates. His bed quivers as though aloft on springs. They are destroying the city. Has it come to this? Soon, archaeologists will swarm over the ruins. Crickets will tweeter. Vultures abide on high, stark limbs. Black water oozes around possums dead in frozen muck. Frogs harrumph throaty approval as they barter with time.

Then utter silence to prevail.

Eternal darkness.

## BLIP!

Ho, boy. Back to the womb, the tomb. Back where I started from: a plain, soft-spoken boy, running to fat, as he tides the hours from his 2x8 stoop, thinking of lunch. The stoop. Where he was.

Early November. Somewhere around then. But what was the year?

What was it got his new pal Ryabovitch so jacked up? Where did he go?

❂ ❂ ❂ ❂ ❂ ❂ ❂ ❂ ❂ ❂ ❂ ❂ ❂ ❂ ❂ ❂ ❂ ❂ ❂ ❂ ❂ ❂ ❂ ❂ ❂ ❂

Take this down ... Daisy, we worry about you. Comb your hair. Trash those ratty slippers, the dingy gown. Ten in the morning. You've got that woozy look. How long did you intend to boil those eggs? Water all gone. Another pan ruined. Don't tell us you've dropped another Xanax.

'*Please, don't harp at me. Why would you not let that upset woman inside the house? I rather liked her. I believe we will become good friends. Frankly, Emmitt, your demeanour, on many fronts, alarms me. Don't talk to me now. I have business to conduct with ...*'

*60 Minutes*—the full story, the news in depth—is on the scene. Cut to Lesley. Lesley is covering this patch. Lucky us.

Lesley is slam-bang beautiful. Dynamite smart. 'I'm on it, okay,' she's heard to say. 'Give a woman a break.'

While in town it's hoped she'll hop by Holt Renfrew to pick up an outfit. Celebrities, they do that the way Emmitt stops by the Hardware to buy a new paintbrush or replace a light bulb. He hasn't done so lately, though bulbs at 2x8 constantly go blip. *Blip*, there goes another one. The house is old, must be the wiring. Commodes not that efficient either, if you must know. Water pressure in the upstairs bath a mere dribble, but must you know that? What if next week we wanted to sell?

Always something.

The southside eavestrough has come down. Did you want an example? Just to mention what homeowners face.

Lesley says, Daisy, our viewers will not be interested in your eavestroughs. Let's talk turkey about that coma. About the desperate situation here at ...

A snowy, rain-softened day, weeks ago, Tallis Haley, sixteen, was sitting outside on his front steps, listening to Tina Turner's 'Proud Mary'. On the Sony Walkman. Next up, 'Little Girl Blue'. The trumpet guy, singer, Chet Baker's 'Little Girl Blue'. But not listening that intently. Why not? Because he's immersed in a book received in the morning mail. A Chekhov story, 'The Kiss'. *At eight o'clock on the evening of the twentieth of May all the six batteries of the N—— Reserve Artillery Brigade halted for the night in the village of....* The boy knows this story. It is a favourite. The officers are invited to a party. Women will be present. A few pages further on, Tallis Haley will meet again his old friend Ryabovitch, the doddering fellow who never has known a woman's love. At this point the boy, reading, might be expected to moan. To say, 'I haven't either.' Soon, in a darkened room, a scented, unidentifiable woman will kiss this Ryabovitch. Usually, and without the least difficulty, it is Tallis Haley in receipt of the kiss. He hopes this time to fully embrace the mystery and deliver his own firm kiss upon the inspiring lips.

It is not to be. Cruel fate intervened & smacked the little hot-shot flat.

A young cyclist crashed through the hedge and spiralled through the air to land directly on top of Tallis Haley. Noggin to noggin. He has been in a coma since that hour. So, too, for a brief time, the girl.

Does this girl have a name?

Who is asking?

A reader. I don't normally pick up books like this. If I do, I quickly throw them down.

Zan is her name.

My son fought valiantly to ... the weeping mother told this reporter, before succumbing to grief.... See inside story for full details.   ➤

Not dead yet. Help! Help! Help! Help! Help! Help! Help!

Call in to 911:   ➤                    ( Did I not call you earlier? )

911 has its own problems. *People call us, wanting whisky delivered. Wanting a backrub. They have a flea infestation. The upstairs toilet has sprung a leak. We are human beings here, you know. The phones never stop ringing. Yes, there was a major catastrophe at 2x8. That's resolved now.*

Let's talk about the accident imperilling the lives of two young people, Lesley says.

*Two?* It strikes me, Lesley, that the entire neighbourhood is imperilled.

Okay. Let's talk about that.


Before that, emerging from the limo, tottering on her heels under blast of strong wind, softly spinning snow, Lesley is intercepted by a madman. Name's Ormsby, pleased to make your acquaintance. You want the low-down on Nixon? I've got the low-down on that staunch Republican. Lesley has nothing against people who live on the street. Whenever at work she runs into Mike Wallace she's reminded of them. All the same, she says, Go away, please. I thought I was in a civilized country. You can't prove it by me, replies Ormsby. You smell of pizza, Lesley says. It happens I've eaten. Listen, my good woman. When your president, ex-president, that crook, erupted from the womb he had dirt under his nails. Finger and toe. Dirt in his ears and packing his nose. His mother, looking at him, sobbed to the rafters, saying in her harsh way— every spade a spade—'Don't try telling me that's blood. Just don't try.' And all those women, young and old, extinguishing the lamps, pitter-patter, the shuffle of worn feet, grind of knobby knees and calloused hands. The bowed heads. The appeal to a higher deity, it ever there gnawing within their soppy brains, all circling away from the mother's bed with murmurs of shame, following which every one of them carries the flickering candle or smoking lamp or lit match—they were that stupid, you see—each thinking: 'No luck in this place. Not in this house. Never a twitch of what you could call good news. He will not be a happy man. Hold on. Somebody stole Mama's pizza sack. You want the low-down on Nixon's school days at Dook—Duke University to you—you've come to the original Deep Throat.'

Lesley's driver, a flock of others, hustle the goon away.

Background, a man wearing a pink hat says: No show without background. Colour, pageantry. Maybe slice that nut in.

*60 Minutes* has pull. The full block has been cordoned off. You're going somewhere, take another route. It's a maze of one-way streets out there anyway. One block this way, the next block that way. You'll wrench your wrist making those turns. *But I've got to git to the Harbord Bakery. Fifty years I've been picking up my goods at Harbord Bakery.* So. Fine. Do that. Just avoid Major Street. Today, *60 Minutes* owns that street.

Such is what the Russian Ryabovitch is this minute attempting to convey to Tallis Haley. Something going on out there ... is his actual comment. He's not up to date on the film business. Wires, cables, strung all over. Big trucks, vans, people. Busy, busy. *60 Minutes* hasn't properly done Canada since the 1979 Iran hostage crisis.

Someone has pulled Lesley aside. The production manager is upset. We can't find the girl, he says. We have her bike, or *a* bike, said to be hers. And a rider for it. In event the authentic shmoo eludes us.

Shmoo?

An old Al Capp word.

Who he?

Before your time. You young chicks. Youngster named Osteen will pile into the dummy on the porch. Immersed in fucking Chekhov. Fuzzy. Cameras screened. All hunky-dory, given this mucky snow. The establishing shot, I'm talking about. Then cut to screeching ambulance. Scurrying feet. Stabilizing calm as you fade in with the raw data. Got it?

Sure thing. Lesley has it. Only ... why are you telling me this now? I have the parental issue to think about.

I see the whole thing, beginning to end. All six min.

Excuse me. I'm scripted for fifteen.

A lie. She gets nine max.

Lesley is no powder puff. These production people, they think they rule the world. Find the girl, demands Lesley. No stand-in lookalike, please.

We have no segment without the actual Zan.

Zan. Christ. Who names these people?

Lesley casts a wicked eye his way. They do not get along that well. She's argued for twelve. Minutes, we are talking about. They've allotted a provisional nine. Will be pleased with seven. Wiped to zilch, with no girl. A routine accident, is that all we've got?

Let's admit this: Emmitt is mesmerized by Lesley's beauty and proficiency. He's tongue-tied each time her face bevels his way. She doesn't often make that turn. Daisy pokes him: Stop making a fool of yourself, she tells him. Maybe it's Lesley's short skirt compounding the situation. Lesley is zeroing in on Daisy. Daisy can't sit still; will she have to be chained to the chair? Lesley thinks she might like to be in a coma herself. Sometimes she's thought that. She's pretty well convinced that she's seen men thinking *If that pretty woman was in a coma I could* do *with her whatever I wanted to. Were I a knave. Did I forget myself. Were we not a nation under one God. Did the Divine Entity desert me. Were I to follow in our Founding Fathers' footsteps. Did I falter in my path to sainthood.*

*Why did they ever get the vote?* She's seen that too. In youth she was quick to blush. Since then, she's seen stuff that would scare another woman to death. What woman hasn't, come to that.

A sizeable crowd has gathered out front. Everyone wants to see Lesley. So what if she's U.S.? She's still Lesley. Lesley Who? Why is this Lesley on our street? A policeman is keeping them back. He's big and burly, taking no crap. That's the kind of policeman he is. What, some loudmouth says. You got something against policemen? You want to do something about it? Here now, says the burly policeman, you two stop that.

Move along there. Put a sock in it.

Wait. There's the production wizard. He wants shots of the coma boy's upstairs window. Go up and Windex the bastard. Does it open? See if it opens. Pan the street from up there. Zan was going to the SuperSave. Get a shot of the SuperSave. We will monkey that bastard in somehow. I want her falling off the bike. Once, twice, three times falling. The crushed bike. Spinning tires, whirling limbs, the startled face. Bike and girl flying through air. *Smack!* The boy! He's horsemeat! A fucking Darryl F. Zanuck production. Got it? Shake a leg, please. Lesley is tired of whittlin' her nails. Her feet hurt in those heels but have you once seen her wince? Does she have ballerina feet? You're asking me?

We have the girl.

What girl?

The assaulting party. The assailant.

X?

Not X. Zan. Don't you have her name on the Crib Sheet?

Where is she?

Hell's bells! She's slippery as a tufted titmouse.

Lesley: Are you relaxed?

Daisy: Heck yes. I'm relaxed as a worn-out door mat.

You look jumpy to me.

I'm jumpy as a...

Tufted titmouse?

It's the warm-up stage. Lesley is good. Daisy is good enough, though she would say only so-so. Maybe those pills? She has found herself hoping Lesley is a solid feminist. Diane Sawyer, a Lesley forerunner, same network, she's convinced, isn't. A Nixon disciple, old Diane. Daisy has little patience anymore with those who've become lukewarm, and none for those ignorant of or in denouncement of the Movement. It's shattering that so many young people have never heard of... well, anyone.

Lesley: Daisy. You have been firm in the belief that your son has a good life, even possibly a happy one, despite his coma.

I've seen his footprints. He moves about at night. He goes places. Does things. And there are consequences. Last week Anna Sergeyevna showed up at the door. Mad as hell. Are you familiar with Anna Sergeyevna?

The lady with a lapdog. Yes. That is to say, I've seen the movies.

I was unaware there were movies.

One, a 1960 black-and-white Soviet Union classic. The other, in colour, a lesser Italian. You saw this lady in the flesh?

We all did. That is to say, the well-known romance novelist Sheila Shott—an old family friend—chanced to drop by. We had a long chat with Anna. Emmitt put together a nice lunch for us. Avocado on croissant, I believe it was. Do you know Sheila's work?

Romance? Please, Daisy. Be kind.

Break! the director shouts. Lighting, where are you? Git that shadow off Daisy's face.

Lesley, at the kitchen table with Daisy, has removed her shoes. Everyone who can is gawking at her pretty feet. Emmitt is in the grip of joyous delirium. The camera people are of course blasé. Get a shot of those feet! the director cries. For the museum!

We don't want morbid. We want hope.

Everybody says this.

We want morbid supplanted by hope.

Everybody repeats this.

Faces appear in the upstairs window. Is that him? people say. Is that our boy? No, it's merely the Windex crew.


The production manager is on the phone, wringing out Research. I want a perambulating Chekhov, he tells them. Perambulating. Like, taking a stroll. Surely they had film in his day. He consorted with actors, actresses, you know. He wasn't a stay-at-home recluse.


*60 Minutes* is distributing Mama's pizza on Major Street. They had no intention of doing so. It's just that here came along a seedy-looking guy conveying a pouch full. He was pounced upon. A hoorah went up: Let's have pizza! The fella had no choice. Mob rules.

The fella's name is Ormsby. This is his first and last day delivering Mama's pizza. Already Mama has received complaints. Hello, Mama. Mama, my pizza arrived cold. Hello, Mama. My pizza had a slice missing. Mama, my pepperoni pizza had been picked of all the pepperoni. Olives gone too. Also, Mama is slack-jawed from listening to Ormsby speaking of the evils of Richard Milhous Nixon. Ormsby rarely speaks of anything else. Somewhere in Mama's catacombs exists a raft of letters sent Mama by one Tallis Haley. I can vouch for the honesty and durability of Ormsby, these letters affirm. He is a man of considerable character. I have known him to feed stray cats. He washes infrequently. He combats alcoholism. Do not let this dissuade you from employment.

Mama is out the sixty-two dollars owed her for these pizzas. *60 Minutes* will not cough up the dough. Nor will Mama ever see again the warming bag.

First thing you know, *60 Minutes* will have that boy lying in state.

No they won't.

He'll be like prince or president, lying in state.

No he won't.

People will line up to view his remains. Our little fat prince, they will say.

Will not. I can't conceive of that.

It was *Finnegans Wake* Daisy left out in the rain. Fourteen days she left it out there. She gave that book a good soak.

I majored in history, Lesley said. I never picked it up.

It rained day and night. Steady drizzle fritzing into ice. Claimed she forgot it was out there. On the petite green table she enjoys her tea.

What kind?

Lapsang souchong.

That's a good tea.

She's had *Finnegans* drying on a shelf two years. Now lost. Won't purchase another copy. Seeks a free desk copy. Thrifty. You might say.

You read it?

Not that copy. I was dying to see how it turned out. Any hayseed can write a story in simple chronological sequence. Anyone doing so may be considered a quack. I mean, hack. That's a Joycean quote by way of Beckett, Samuel.

A dire view. You've lost me, Daisy.

Daisy leaps from her chair, shattering Lesley's composure. Excuse me. I've got to … take something. Away she scoots.

Ormsby is waylaying loiterers whose curiosity has dispatched them to the street where now they must dodge laid cables, Ormsby, and frown belligerently at unknown people hurling salutation, accusation, or pithy comment in their direction. Surely from this mob Ormsby may snare a dime or two. Food. Every human on earth requires food. He will be the provider. As ideas go, this one, his latest, after cataclysmic thought, is pure unforeseen brilliance. Free daily delivery to your door of eggs and bacon, he tells potential subscribers. Five dollars. Sign here.

Where do you get these eggs, this bacon? some clown dares ask.

The question prompts Ormsby to spin on his heels, to totter against a fence, to pound his brow, until the lodging quarters of the answer, any answer, comes to him. Finally, it does.

Farmers, he says. See that dotted line? Sign above it. Brown eggs or white?

The call in the street is for Zan. Where did she get to? As for that, who is she?

We need X. Zan by any other name. She prefers X. She signs school papers X, teachers know who she is. Zan, no way. Lots of freefall ethnic groupings in that Free School. Give X an A plus, give that Zan freak a failing mark, we know who X is. Well, we did, till they said forgit marks. Forgit. Admen actually wrote that in a memo. So I forgit. You were asking about Zan? Forgit Zan. Focus on X.

Tell me about her.

A mystery is X. Hell of a bike rider. Mouthy.

I hear she was in a coma also.

I know nothing about that.

Are you not the author?

The author is off to Saskatoon for the day. Our world is in upheaval, he says. Charlatans on every street corner, he says. Governments in collapse. Half the earth driven mad by war, famine, irresoluteness, apathy, incivility, religion, each other—the catastrophic ordering of love and hate.

Are you serious? You can't be, surely.

How right you are. I can't be. Even so, I take no responsibility for how these locals conduct themselves.

Zan regards the happening on Major Street with a sense of self-annihilation. She's to blame. I did it, she's constantly saying. I sent Tallis Haley whirlwinding into instant coma. Don't try telling me different. Different *lee*. I'm not stupid.

You and all your classmates in this school are stupid.

Just because you dislike us and hate teaching doesn't mean you have to be rude.

Young lady, are you mouthing off to *me*?

That transpired at Let's All Tuck-In with Stupidity Day at Free School. A resounding success. In truth, in these times, when Zan the X girl gives in to speech it is largely to herself.

She regards the bewixing Major Street display with angled face displaying narrowly deployed eyes above tightly compressed lips. This vamped-up Major Street business is not to her liking. No good, no good. She tells herself this, lips tightening. Talking to yourself is not a good sign. Talking to yourself means your brain is composed of little chopped-off sticks constantly criss-crossing, like a camper, lacking tools, attempting to ignite a flame under a wet pile. Talking to yourself is an inevitable force bearing down on your tender frontal lobe. *60 Minutes* is itchy to get you. They got her, they lost her. Me, I'm visiting my sister, I'm in for the day from Port Hope. *60 Min* is on the prowl. I was you I'd hit them up for moolah, an acquaintance advises. Perfect strangers have repeated this. Sixty minutes is one hour, that's what X knows about sixty minutes. Sometimes less, sometimes more. There is no *60 Minutes*, and little else, in her home abode. Forgit TV, an uninvited guest. Purveyor of insanity, that's the tube. How else to explain the sad hollowness of what is meant to be funny? Did we raise you for this? In consequence, she's been denied the delights of *Sesame Street, Big Frog, Mr Rogers, Captain Kangaroo, The Fall of the House of Usherettes*. Of whatever. The blissful education voided. Thank God for her current enrolment at the Free School, where anything goes. I ask you, Zan, through crossed wet sticks: Who knows how to raise, let's say, a standard fine upright child? One who could never, let's say, maim, crush, render insensible, an innocent boy. Say I'm the parent, I'm asking: how would I raise *me*? I'd be lost. For that reason, I give the parental unit leeway on …

Certain parental action she may not, will not, cannot possibly ever forgive. Her mom's habit, for instance, every morning of leaping from her bed shouting *Fiuto! Razzola! Frugo! I sniff, I rummage, I seek!* Yanking the pillows beneath any sleeper's head, madly yodelling *Sniff, rummage, seek!* I married Chig, she's been known to say—'as any woman would say'—only to daily chastise him, punish him, in the hopeless effort 'to remake him into the better man I know in my heart he will never become.' At these and other like remarks, Chig obligingly smiled, rising to pour his beloved another wine. If her shoulders chanced to be bare, he kissed them. She liked telling the pair of them every incident occurring during her work day, chortling wildly over encounters Zan found dull, idiotic, misjudged, pathetic, and often plain disgusting. If Chig failed to laugh—he was good at pretending to—Motherhood moped. Tears sparkled like precious diamonds beneath pleading eyes. She was a headstrong woman, which often led to folly. Driving, she found herself pointing eastwards when a western destination was intended. 'These roads!' she'd cry. 'The city does this to us intentionally! They want us to be lost. It's the democratic ideal. Sometimes I can't even find my own house.' She seemed to like driving their sneezing blue Renault into snowbanks. 'Bent bumpers have appeal,' she said. 'They emphasize and advertise the riders' character.' When these two adults met after extended absences, at airports, they wept out of pure joy, their kisses exclamatory, their embraces enduring through the gruelling minutes Zan stood by in disbelieving watchfulness, her toes cramping. Wicked, she thought. Wicked to display wild abandonment before a wide-eyed scandalized child. She voiced the supposition to psychic companion Glandola that these sightings were all hallucination on her part. Glandola said, 'Nonsense. My mother claims it is entirely within the range of possibility that married people may through the years retain love for each other. Not everyone laughs because they hear something funny. Loving makes for humour, happiness, a positive attitude. Don't be such a scaredy-cat.'

'What makes you think you're so smart?' was Zan's snivelling response.

'Many believe they will dance into the Hereafter.' Pudgy Glandola laughed, running on ahead as though bees swirled about her.

Such is the rubbish flitting through Zan's head as she flees the encroaching arms of *60 Minutes*. It's an entire screw-ass army out there. Thank goodness she doesn't lack friends. Hide here. Hide there.

And what blitzy creature is that walking her bike? Who is that saying, 'Got it! Snowy day, car pushing my ass, a streaking cat—I fling myself into Nowheresville. Camera zooms in on me flipping through air. Got it. Piece of cake. I was an aerialist with Cirque du Soleil, you know.'

She's old. At least twenty. No way that stand-in can be construed as me.

Is it time to reconsider? Let *60* have me?

Or *run!* Cite, as the parental unit might say, Deuteronomy. Cite Romans. Cite the epistles of St Paul. Or, in a pinch, that mastermind Luke.

This is what she will tell that woman Lesley. My psychic friend Glandola, privy to my love, can levitate normal mortals. She will lift Tallis Haley straight up from the bed.

She will unite us.

Has it been reported that this girl Zan was herself for weeks in a coma? She was.

It may be argued she still is. Her own mother, wonderful woman, hints as much.

Daddy Chig—heart gladdened—abstains. Day of the accident, Zan wasn't as attentive as she might have been. He can admit this to himself without believing it. Go to the store, Zan. Return with kitty litter. Here is the money. I want to see the change, please. He provided the mission. Is himself, therefore, partway to blame. As was the icy roadway, the streaking cat, the speeding car—the boy for simply being there. What *wasn't* to blame … is what he, Chig, asks himself. The whole g-d world shares the blame. That is what he thinks. Okay, the argument smacks a bit of existentialism, it is not an argument he would repeat aloud, but it is what he believes. A thing like that occurs, your whole brain goes wonky. That much he will say aloud. And often does. To no one's admiration. It is also true—he has been witness to this trait a number of times: his little girl is a bit hung up on the boy. Love's bug may be no larger than a tiny insect, but the bug has got its teeth into her. Every hour it has crawled in for another bite. Still more reason to think she might have been inattentive to the cat, the ice, the car—the whatever. Zan was inclined to daydream, if you wanted the strict truth. Quick explosions of temper in his previously mild-mannered even-flowing honey of a problem child. Protestation, prevarication, outrage: *What was all those phone whispers about?* What whispers? Leave me alone. *Who is that boy you keep talking about?* What boy? I don't know any boy. What business is it of yours anyway? Do I intrude every second into your life? Quit pestering me.

As an example of Zan's thinking process, let's back up a few months. The accident has not yet happened. It is a Saturday in November, eleven a.m. A truly dull, inconsequential day, was how she regarded that day. I am a study in boredom, she told herself. I think I will stroll over to Sally Bird Park. Now if you were of a mind that day to visit Sally Bird, we hope you did not go. In the first place, by noon the city will be in the embrace of a freak storm: bone-chilling winds, heavy sleet succeeded by blinding snow. Driving and walking will be treacherous. You will wish you had remained where you were. In addition, Zan, this minute on her way to Sally Bird, has a strong preference for solitude. She has things to think about. Modes of conduct to consider. She hopes you have decided to stay away. You do not want to get involved in this.

There she is now, bolting from the house. Her mother stands in the open doorway, yelling, *Button your coat!* Parents, Zan thinks. They simply do not know how to speak to a child. What bad manners they have. How loopy they are. Even when happy, which hers most of the time are, some confusion of intellect has them perpetually telling you what you can and cannot do. How tiresome they are. Avoid having children is the lesson Zan draws from every such demeaning episode. Have a child and you'll end up batty and bossy as these parents are. Haul yourself off to Paris at the first opportunity—is what she thinks. Live the life of that fucker, Riley.

On a day this doomed, Zan decided, the best thing to do, the only solution, was to set herself down on the one bench in Sally Bird Park and twiddle her thumbs until she fell in love. With the first boy chancing by. Because why waste time? This thought made her amazingly happy for about three seconds. But look what happened. Here, poking himself along, his head in a book, was the boy she already loved. Tallis Haley. Fancy that! How extraordinary! Her day was saved. No way she will admit it was the hope of sighting him that brought her to Sally Bird in the first place. Her psychic friend, Glandola, had so advised her: *Plop yourself down at Sally Bird at eleven on the Saturday, and your beloved will appear. Have I ever been wrong?*

*Yes.*

*My mother confirms the vision. She sees him in a Blue Jays cap. I didn't see what was on his head.*

*Heck of a psychic you are.*

Zan had in mind a 'benefit' performance: as he passed, she would cross her legs. Yes. Perhaps emit a famished chirp. Droop her shoulders, glaze the eyes, like one in a trance. She would not declare herself, or so much as speak. Unless he did. In all likelihood, he didn't know her name. He probably wouldn't even like her. Blue Jays? Would she now have to bone up on baseball?

Here he came. Bouncing along like one atop a horse. Were those new shoes?

He passed, offering no more than the quick glance he'd give any girl.

Heartbreak. She'd as soon have stayed at home.

Snow began falling; wind picked up—a tempest; in minutes the Sally Bird grounds, the trees and streets and rooftops whitened, as did Zan's head and shoulders. The entire city seemed at once to have fallen into perfect silence. Utter somnolence under the fall of lovely snow. How utterly utterly beautiful. What a world. What need had one for love, in this beautiful universe? She was shaking with cold, however. Her very eyelids were icing up. Her fingers were too numb to button the coat. Her ears soon would crack away.

How quickly everything changed. Spring lay ten years in the future. Not that she had one.

The parental unit was at home, flopped out side by side on the giant parental bed. Outflanked by weather, her mother said. Consumerism is dead, Chig said. Liberalism next. Me too, Zan said, if I don't soon get warm. Crawl in, they said. We will pretend you are our own wee baby found on the doorstep.

How utterly utterly strange it was that she found herself agreeing to do so. And how lovely and instantly warm she found it to be, once she stretched out between them. And from this bed what a nice view one had of the falling snow. Your father has been reading to me, her mother said. I believe he fancied himself within the embrace of a romantic spell. Do you want silence? Or your dear father in his best Paul Robeson voice reading aloud to us?

Reading what? Zan said, alarm stealing in. Paul Who?

He was zipping along with *Sonnets from the Portuguese* when we heard you crashing through the door.

Sonnets?

From the Portuguese. Mrs Browning wanted to call them *Sonnets Translated from the Bosnian*. But Mr Browning liked calling Mrs Browning his 'own little Portuguese'. Thus the title.

That man sounds mean and bossy to me.

They had a deal. Don't show the other your work. He all the time of course unloaded his on her. She, never. Then one day to quietly slide this sonnet packet into his pocket.

You married people are awfully peculiar.

Shh. Listen.


*Mercy me. Our dear papoose is crying.*


❂ ❂ ❂ ❂ ❂ ❂ ❂ ❂ ❂ ❂ ❂ ❂ ❂ ❂ ❂ ❂ ❂ ❂ ❂ ❂ ❂ ❂ ❂ ❂ ❂


Emmitt Haley, normally a down-to-earth, everyday sort of fellow—how he sees himself—rarely bossy—at times falls prey to flights of fancy.

I'm putting in your call to God right now, sir.

Don't want him. Want my son.

He's not receiving now, sir.

Keep trying. Okay, put me through to the other party you mentioned.

He's on another line now, sir.

Try Tallis again.

Sorry. His line is busy.

He's talking to someone?

It would seem so.

Who?

I can't tell you that, sir.

Why not?

It's a privacy issue. How would you like it if I opened your private conversations to any nosy Tom, Dick and Harry?

No skin off my back.

There are regulations, sir.

Hook me up to another party up there.

Give me a name, sir.

How would I know who is up there? Inform me anytime he is receiving, please.

Who? I can't read your mind, sir.

My son.

I wouldn't know your son from Adam, sir. If a son refuses to converse with his father it isn't my affair. All families have these difficulties now and again. My husband, for instance, often claims I shut him out. Yet to my mind every door is open. He could come through a window if he wanted to. But do I want you or some other party interfering in this stalemate? I think not. Maybe one day your son will take your call and maybe he won't. Maybe he's mad at you.

I'm sitting right here looking at him. He's not mad at anyone.

You don't have to snap my head off, sir. I'm the innocent recruit here.

Daisy shuffles softly into the dimly lit room, dressed in a dingy house robe, mangy slippers loose on her feet.

Tired? I'll relieve you for a while. Didn't I hear you talking to someone?

Muttering to myself.

He looks harried, doesn't he? Must have had a bad day.

All our days are.

No need to snap my head off. Why haven't you shaved?

2x8 has its bad days. Enter this in your calendar. ANOTHER BAD DAY AT 2x8 MAJOR. DATE NOT RECORDED. What accounts for these bad days? UNKNOWN. Should you not wake up through a long stretch of days yours might fairly be called ANOTHER BAD DAY. If your limbs have not stirred, your eyes have not opened, if you sleep like the dead, it might be optimistic to claim, as some in this household do, that this boy is on a journey. He is not among those who may legitimately declare the day is bad. Someone in this household may say yesterday was a bad one, the whole week was, but not this boy. Not you. Your limbs have not stirred, a glaze would be upon your eyes should they dare open. One prepared to surrender an honest evaluation may be forgiven for concluding this body is dead. This person is no longer among us. This person has given up the ghost. This person has gone to his reward. And he was such a good boy. Such pleasure, such joy, he brought to all who knew him.

Such remarks might indeed compel his limbs to stir, those eyes to open. But they do not. *Oh Emmitt, feel how cold his body is. If he doesn't survive I'll kill myself. Monster! Where did you hide my pills? Keep that scratchy beard away from me. I boiled you a nice egg. Well, I did. That may have been another day. Where did our nice blue sky get to?*

Thus are mistakes made. Tallis Haley, stricken by coma, is not dead. He most certainly lives. Very soon you are apt to see him dancing and singing. Being every inch his usual fool self. Who is responsible for these erroneous reports? They ignite our fear and hourly torture us.

Is that you, Ryabovitch?

It's me.

Good day?

Not bad.

Have you been listening to them? That pair by my bed?

Your parents, I believe.

They talk a lot of nonsense, don't they?

I don't know. I used to talk to my favourite horse the same way. Your day?

Busy (do you see my fluttering hand) out there. I smelled pizza. Saw X. Divine star in a black sky.

Ryabovitch: Stuffy in here. Up for a walk?

Haley: Okay.

Ryabovitch: That dog appears to be following us.

Haley: What dog?

Ryabovitch: Not that Pomeranian bitch, I'm happy to say.

Ryabovitch: Is that her house?

Haley: Whose house?

Ryabovitch: You know whose house.

Haley: Zan's? She's likely asleep.

Ryabovitch: No. She's out back, up in the treehouse.

Haley: She must be cold. I surely am.

Ryabovitch: Dress more warmly next time. Don't want you catching cold.

Haley: Okay.

Ryabovitch: Would you look at that!

Haley: What?

Ryabovitch: That man on the dark porch. Kissing the woman. She's practically undressed.

Haley: Is it your pal? Lob…? What's his name?

Ryabovitch: Not him. I bet that's the famous lover Turner P. Blindstone.

Haley: Never heard of him.

Ryabovitch: You ought to broaden your reading. He's a Sheila Shott guy.

Haley: Never heard of her.

Ryabovitch: Friend of your parents.

Haley: News to me.

Ryabovitch: Romance novelist. Anna can't put her books down.

Haley: Who's Anna?

Ryabovitch: Not your business. Shall we go back?

Haley: Okay.

Haley: Is she still up in the treehouse?

Ryabovitch: Yes.

Haley: She's too old to be messing about in a treehouse.

Ryabovitch: She's studying the stars.

Haley: In this snow? Who was that crazy woman screaming at our door?

Ryabovitch: Not your business.

Haley: You got out fast.

Ryabovitch: Quit prying.

Haley: Okay.

Ryabovitch: Anna isn't crazy. Merely high-strung. Who wouldn't be, after Chekhov got done with her? That dog continues to follow us.

Haley: Probably lost.

Ryabovitch: I dislike dogs.

Haley: Why?

Ryabovitch: Never know what they are going to do.

Haley: Like people, huh.

Ryabovitch: Lick you one minute, bite you the next.

Haley: She came at me like a bullet. Headfirst. I dodged too late.

Ryabovitch: Who? That X girl?

Haley: Ended up wrapped in my arms. Entangled, you might say. That's significant, I think. I would have been content with a mere kiss.

Ryabovitch: Ha! Kisses! Don't remind me. Well, I'll be smacked. That pair is still rooted by your bedside.

Haley: Who?

Ryabovitch: The parental tribe. Look, they are bathing you. Perhaps another bed change.

Haley: They must love me.

Ryabovitch: You're not looking good. The phrase coming to mind is *wasting away*. You may not make it.

Haley: You made it.

Ryabovitch: Different category, art. So they say. Peculiar by-laws. As I understand the matter. On top one day, disappeared the next.

Emmitt, you are a darling man, though I must say you from time to time mislay your civility. You treated that Anna woman abysmally.

I did not. What Anna woman? Who are you talking about?

There are days when I hardly know you. This appears to be one of them. I suppose you will now tell me I have just provided you with a description of one defining facet of marital life.

I will say no such thing. I will not have you putting words into my mouth.

How strange. Haven't I always? You're my puppy dog, won over by a simple caress.

Not lately, God knows.

# PULLED FROM LAKE ONTARIO

The Toronto Police Marine Unit announced today that an unnamed boatwoman on Sunday afternoon rescued a possibly drowning man from the turbulent waves of Lake Ontario. The man, thought to be in his late twenties, was taken to the home of his rescuer, on Toronto Island. Police surmise he either jumped or was pushed from the island ferry *Ongiara*.

In a brief but far-ranging discussion with authorities, the woman described the man as 'disoriented, water-logged, and appallingly handsome. He has certainly not lost the will to live,' she told police. 'The gentleman is now in my loving care, making a speedy recovery after being hurled from the *Ongiara* by a callous, scheming, dopey woman.' She gave his name as Turner P. Blindstone.

A Marine Unit spokeswoman said charges likely will not be forthcoming.

Numerous *Ongiara* passengers have claimed they saw a 'smartly attired woman wearing a red hat' violently pitch the man over the railing, just after kissing him. As many others swear he was in flight from the 'hotly attired' woman in the red hat, and 'definitely jumped'. In a revised statement to the press, the island boatwoman said, 'It would be a month of Sundays before I'd welcome an unknown male onto my property.'

'Laid-back though we are out here in our own private Lotusland conundrum,' she further added.

Speculation that the incident is a concoction of a local publishing house is rife. Turner P. Blindstone is a character in the work of popular romance novelist Sheila Shott. Ms Shott's publicist, Sneaky Deap, denied any role in the unfolding events. Ms Shott, she said, is currently touring East Asia with her latest jewel.

Police records reveal that the red-hatted woman aboard the *Ongiara* is one Rebecca Whitehall, address unknown. The dramatic on-again off-again love ordeal of Rebecca Whitehall and Turner P. Blindstone has been recounted in numerous Sheila Shott books. 'Every time a single human being draws a breath another Sheila Shott masterwork is sold,' the publicist told reporters. 'For idiot journalists who can't do the math, that's nearly one thousand Sheila Shotts sold every hour. Whereas us publicists make peanuts.'

Humongous posters arise at subway stations, on buses, streetcars, billboards:

# GET YOUR SHEILA SHOTT. YOU'RE NOT YOURSELF WITHOUT YOUR SHOT OF SHEILA SHOTT.

## FRANCHISES SOON AVAILABLE.

Everyone is asking:

*Who* is Sheila Shott?

*What* is Sheila Shott?

*Why* must my Sheila be shot?

Emmitt: Daisy. Telephone.

Daisy: Who is it?

Emmitt: Sheila Shott.

Daisy: Hello, Sheila. I hope you're not calling from East Asia.

Sheila: I am in town. That Sneaky Deap publicist speaks utter rubbish. I sell twice the number of books she mentions. So the calculating bitch makes peanuts. What has that to do with anything? I've asked the company to fire her butt. How's our boy?

Daisy: Tallis? I've laid carpet sound monitors around his bed. If he gets up, I'll know it.

Sheila: Oh Daisy, I worry about you.

Daisy: I combed my hair. All the comb's teeth broke off. Flimsy metal. I sent Emmitt to the Hardware to buy me another.

Sheila: Hardware sells combs?

Daisy: Did Rebecca really pitch Turner into Lake Ontario?

Sheila: How would I know? The hot-tempered lamebrain goes rogue from time to time. Hard to know what she will get up to. The other day I had her in a scene on a boat through Nairobi and she complained to me about the height I'd given her. All because a few other women on the boat were taller or more busty.

Daisy: It's natural for all of us, sometimes, to feel dissatisfied with ourselves. To wish we were something other. This extends all the way back to the cradle, I suppose.

Sheila: It isn't natural to me. They take such liberties. That pipsqueak Sneaky Deap tells me Richard Ford regards his characters as his slaves. I'm with Richard.

Daisy: Ridiculous.

Sheila: Love to the boy. You should spray a dash of perfume over those dirt rings around your neck. On the trolley today I was fit to be tied. Two, I assume students, females, were reading books, not a rarity in these parts. I overheard one of them say such-and-such short story writer was the best ever. Better than any novelist, she said. I was astounded. I blew my top. I'm afraid I raised my voice in calling them idiots. A story and a novel, I told this pair, is the difference between a dime and a dollar. A nickel and a loonie. One remark led to another. They were swatting their flimsy paperbacks at me. Screaming I was the loonie. Somehow the panic button got punched. Fortunately the trolley was coming into Spadina station. I saw security guards waiting. The idiots were still swatting. Pages flying. I had made the mistake of informing them I was an author. Eh! Eh! they said. What trash do you write? Carloads of onlookers shouting. Eh? Eh? I fled. Those girls and a handful of guards chased me down the long tunnel into the St George stop where at last I lost them. I split my skirt, running. I'm suing the city. Kiss Emmitt for me. Bye.

---

TO: The Editor

*The New York Times Book Review*

Dear Editor: For a biography unique to the human race and essential to the immediate cause, I am researching the life of the obscure, scrupulously upright, pimply, polite (mawkish, brainy, a hothead fatso) schoolboy Tallis Haley, who sadly passed away this winter at his Toronto habitat. I urgently seek anecdotes, correspondence, memorabilia.

Help!

Sincerely, Fyodor Ryabovitch (for T. Haley)

2 x 8 Major, Toronto

---

Go, little letter: split the Great Rock of Silence into millions of iridescent pebbles. Fly out like cinders from a blazing pyre. Soothe a layabout, comatose boy's truculent spirit. Liberate the exhausted citizenry.

Tallis Haley, lately deceased, his bones interred at ...

Anyone knowing the whereabouts of Tallis Haley, formerly of this city, and noted teenage lit-snit, please advise.

Let it be known that all parties holding debt against the estate of Tallis Ryabovitch Haley, recently deceased, must apply in writing or call in person at the departed's lifelong address, 2 x 8 Major, during reasonable (daylight) hours.

---

To Whom It May Concern:

The bereaved family of sixteen-year-old Tallis Haley is distressed to announce at this late date that their only and beloved son went to his early demise earlier this year as a consequence of an untimely mishap on his front steps (2 x 8 Major). Early morning, a snowy rain-splattered wreck of a Sunday.

His Sony headset, midway Miles Davis's *Kind of Blue* at the time, unfortunately failed to materialize after the accident, doubtlessly owing to ...

Mention of tunes said earlier to be playing on said headset is hereby withdrawn.

A confidant of the distressed boy stated that, quote, Tallis had been sinking fast, and for some time prior to the OCCURRENCE, had been aiming to take his own life. This allegation has been vehemently denied by ...

The strung-out family of Tallis Haley, popular figure about town ...

Funeral services for ...

---

Daisy, at her dressing table, gloomily aware of her face in the mirror, has these thoughts. It is how her brain works. These are pathetic journeys through endless graveyards. Horrible, but there it is. She can read the news in the mirror. Such a drawn face, get a load of those wet eyes, those sagging cheeks, those withered lips. How dare my good friend Sheila Shott speak of dirt rings circling my neck.

I must stop this. Tend to my *maquillage.*

Allow me please to compute the word's origin as I apply this lipstick.

I cannot now, for sure, say hell transpired on a Sunday.

Or that the day was snowy.

I believe I was watching eggs boil in a pan on the stove. No, that was another time.

I dislike this lipstick.

Why am I painting my lips anyway?

*Maquillage*: French, obviously. Middle Dutch *makem*, to make. To dress the face. Also a typesetting process. Eric Ambler employed the word in *The Mask of Dimitrios*. Kingsley Amis hasn't. Isadora Duncan, frequently. Virginia Woolf, rarely. The Williams girl, Joy, I mean, never. Sontag, possibly. Don't mind me, I expect I'll go through the balance of my life giving utterance to unbalanced stray thoughts. This will not go down nicely at High Table at Massey College where I am a Senior Fellow, you know.

---

Dear Daisy, I believe the honour has been withdrawn, pending investigation of that embarrassing business involving—

---

Don't you dare mention that *Finnegans* book. Kindly go look in on Tallis, please. He's an old-fashioned boy who gets fidgety seeing paint on his mother's face.

The carpet sound monitors, picked up from the Hardware at no mean expense, bear investigation. The Hardware staff vociferously assured Emmitt these supremely ugly carpets represented a technological breakthrough equal to man's first walk on the moon or Columbus's discovery of the Americas. Drop a feather on these carpets, and they will squawk. Breathe on them and the attentive ear will hear mind-numbing phobophonic bleeps, the Hardware said. The more cosmopolitan among us will swear they are hearing Maria Callas performing Puccini's *Tosca*. Specifically, the end part where the poor girl leaps to her death. Alternately, you can program these treasures to render Monteverdi's 1607 *L'Orfeo* and get Euridice's death by snakebite. Or you can do gunshots, runaway horses, sirens, grunting pigs.

*And you here, Emmitt, arguing over a few measly bucks. If an eyelash of that boy twitches your Daisy will know it.*

Daisy, awake and listening through the night, has heard three wispy beeps, like the faint tinkle of a bell around a cat's neck. She wants these carpets returned. The Hardware is proving difficult. You must not have followed the directions properly.

What directions? They're carpets. All I was advised to do was to punch O for opera, if opera was desired, and spread them over the floor.

You're acting like a dickhead, said the Hardware. Smarten up.

---

THE DICKHEADS' LEAGUE OF NORTH AMERICA,
TORONTO CHAPTER, CONVENES TONIGHT AT 2 X 8 MAJOR.
WAY TO GO, DICKHEADS!

---

When a certain Miss Ten Ants is seen advancing along the sidewalk, Emmitt Haley is heard muttering the words seen above. Such is how he and Daisy refer to Mrs Tennants, from down the street. She's a big headache. A pill. Hard to take. All in the neighbourhood so regard her. She drops in, it never occurs to her to go home. She sits in your kitchen, knees together, scratching herself endlessly. A habit, that eternal scratching. Is it some kind of disease she suffers,

Miss Ten Ants Calls at 2 x 8

I'll huff and I'll puff

that eternal requirement that she scratch? A powerful influence, that habit. Those trapped in her company develop also an itch encompassing the entire body. Suddenly you're like a trio of dogs under sufferance of an invasion of fleas. There you sit, knees together, digging nails into your flesh. And here today, again, she comes: her bent shape scurrying your way on her flat, black busy shoes, the pokey hat and coat, the elbow gloves, all prepared to hurl at you the dreaded yoo-hoo. Hasten to lock every door. Windows also. Flick off every light. Miss Ten Ants spots a light, she'll forever rattle the doorknob, the panes. Kick the door. Yodel. *Let me in!*

Is she lonely? No lonelier than those in her presence are made to feel. Emmitt and Daisy allow themselves to discuss Miss Ten Ants only in a generally simple way. Was she a bad child, starting out, who got worse, or a good child whose irregular intersections drove her to be the pest she'd become? Oddly enough, before the Public Menace, that Zan creature, turned Tallis into a heap of bloody bones and guts, he had proclaimed Miss Ten Ants to be 'a party of steadfast civility chained by the mediocrity of the availability of her ways and means.' Which view Daisy and Emmitt regarded—once they had got past swooning at the weighty extravagance of his sentence—as haughty elitism unworthy of a son bearing their name—proof once more of disorder in the universe and the decline of civilization. Obversely, he had a kinder, more gentle spirit than they.


Daisy, by her son's bedside: she's turned him, salved him, checked the tubes, the vials, the drip-drip. Clucked over his rash, the pussy sores, his dry scalp, the boogers up his nose. Pinched free a wrinkle in the catheter tube between his legs. Gone over this bod from A to Zed.

You'll pass, Haley, she says. But you can still afford to lose more than a few fatso pounds.

The way you gorged yourself on escargot, olden days.

Just kidding please.

Answer me, you pudgy blimp.

She laughs at herself. If he were in his prime she wouldn't be this brave. Pudgy blimp, she says again, fully expecting those beautiful eyes to blink.

He's hardly a butterball. Ten pounds over, if that much.

Often, in this room, she has the curious feeling she's being watched. She goes to the window, finds the street silent. A new occupant has taken up residence in the upper-storey room across the way. Nice lean-looking boy, well-groomed (lovely black hair), most certainly a student, possibly Korean. He's at his own window, back turned to her. Behind him she vaguely discerns a second figure, surely female. The new resident has a girlfriend, then. How nice.

Sorry. What did you say?

She's once more at her son's bedside, evaluating the evidence. It's very possible Tallis and the boy across the street are best of friends. Tallis will invite him over, saying, Wait 'til you have a run at my mother's escargot.

Tomorrow, fresh sheets, Haley. I promise you.

How did that sick rhododendron get in here?

The boy's father—Emmitt! For God's sake, have pity on a lost man!—fears for his wife's health. Fears mental collapse. It has snapped up—zapped and sent spinning—others in his family. Maybe it is catching. Maybe she has caught it from him.

He halts by the window in the front room. For some minutes scrutinizes a girl on the sidewalk across the street. Tented under a black coat, wind swirling. Red beret. Eating an orange, as she scans the windows at 2 x 8 Major.

He recognizes that girl. Why is she watching our house?

In these gales.

A big headache, that X girl. Is her name Zan?

He would like to extend sympathy, but cannot. May not. Daisy will not have it. 'I'd have choked her while in her coma,' Daisy has said.

Old Mrs Poindexter—he thinks that is the name though she has been known to claim otherwise—is picking up sticks in her yard. In days past the sticks, covered by snow, locked within a bed of ice, stood suspiciously erect, resembling a train of black-headed children preparing to march off to school. 'Hardened arteries prevent me from singing,' she said to him following his offer to assist. This northside neighbour suffers crippling arthritis, her figure rounded as a half wheel. She has white fly-away hair and hands small as those of the Red Witch. Someone must soon make a grocery run for her. The son surely won't. She's fond of Weetabix. Jell-O boxes by the crate. She's adept at making that, cherry a favourite. I draw the line at dog food, she's said. Fruit-cake is too rich for me. Can you reach to clip your toenails? I can't. Mine, I mean. Asleep, I dream I'm still a child. It's extremely pleasant. If not that, then I am the woman at the well, the one Jesus chats up. The Samaritan. It is such a hot day I am wearing practically nothing. I am weak, I can hardly draw water from the well. How surprised I am that he stops to speak to me. Men didn't, you know, women were mere chattel during that worrisome period. He pours cool water over his head. Pours water over mine. We are both slick with sweat. 'Such a hot day,' he says. 'All of our time's affairs trouble me, but today it is heat prostrating us all. I ask myself, Why am I walking this road? Where does it lead? In this heat, I even ask myself, Where was I yesterday?' Then, with heavy sighs, he trudges on. As do I. I have been pitched out of Samaria. I have no home. My life is defined by this daily journey, in the heat of high noon, to the well. Tomorrow I must, I shall, return. Day in and day out, here I come, there I go. Like Godot, Jesus may or he may not appear. He has the raising of Lazarus from the grave to think about. A big headache, that. Many, I am sure, believe sex was involved in my well episode. I can affirm to one and all that it was not. It did not enter our minds. Do you think this is explained by the heat?'

A young woman, passing, walking three dogs, waves.

Daisy has left rags and a bottle of Pledge on the corner table. For Emmitt to consider when he has a leisure moment. Yesterday's leisure involved a mop and pail.

'Knock, knock,' he sings now, through the heating vent. 'Anybody home?'

Headline in today's *Sun*:

# SUNSHINE GIRL

(PAGE 3)

# LOVES COMATOSE BOY

Ailandi Rosai-Maiqui, who kicks up her heels in the city's Danforth area, enjoys sunshine, cross-country ski trails, late-nite clubbing with groovy friends. Fantasizes backpacking through wilderness with sky-diving beau. But—*Eat your heart out, guys!*—the love of her life is...

## FROM THE SUN SPORTS DESK:

Our skilled odds-makers on events unfolding at 2 x 8 Major:

RUDY, jubilant hockey pro: Five gets you ten this fatso prig won't emerge from the coma-static haze.

SAM, the Blue Jays diamond man: Zero chance. The fucker's fucked.

JIMBO CURLY, all-around jock expert: A long draggy winter for the 2 x 8 folks. Flag at half-mast.

GAYLE, the girlie beat: Pluck my heartstrings, why not?

WURTHINGTUNE, resident guru: What a guy! I gauge him a 50-50, more if he dumps that ghoul Ryabovitch. Lapdogs suck.

SUN'S SUNNY PSYCHIC: I have picked him up a few times. A deep struggle is afoot between Tallis—he's extraordinarily nice, by the way, but wacky, you know, and worried about his weight—and a weirdo illegal-immigrant guy calls himself Ryabovitch. A real whiner, this Ryabovitch. Gives me a bellyache. But others on the fringe futz up the boy's visits with me.

# HEADLINE

## *Freak Accident Maims Popular Teen*

Tallis Haley was minding his own business—doing what boys do—the day his life took a decided turn ...

# STACKED, THE WOMEN'S DAILY:

*It wasn't Zan's fault!*

Do you want something to eat now?

No.

To drink?

No.

Do you have a headache?

No.

Pain anywhere?

No.

Can you move?

No.

May I take off your shoes?

No.

Shall I go?

No.

Stay?

No.

Do you hear a word I am saying?

No.

All is no this day at 2x8 Major. Daisy has fallen under the spell of the word no. She regards this as one of her more agreeable days. She asks nothing of anyone. Why should this discomfort the man said to be her husband, who paces the floorboards like a man trying out the fit of new shoes. If God dropped down through the ceiling and asked if she wanted to live she might or might not say no. To see God dropping down through the ceiling or making entry by more prudent means would necessitate the opening of her eyes. She has no intention of doing this. Not even one eye.

One block west of 2x8 Major, on Bloor's humming thoroughfare, a man called Chig, this very girl's selfsame father, is coming up for air. He is emerging from the doors of the Brunswick House, an unfavoured drinking spot, and hoping no one has seen him either enter or exit the dive.

His pockets are stuffed with Sheila Shott books. Jokey gifts for distant friends: *Love's Last Lament, Love's Explosion, Racked by Love, Last-Ditch Love, Passion at the Diamond X Ranch*—and he hopes the tavern's clientele will have had in mind Camus, Aristotle, Ishiguro's *Remains of the Day* (it is playing down the street at the Bloor Cinema) should their besotted eyes have perused his form in the ripped chair.

He hopes his lovely daughter, Zan, has given up moping over that luck-less Haley character and is hanging out with the purple hairs in one of the downtown malls.

He hopes his sphinx-inspired wife, Laura, is not biting her nails, nor reliving the horror of witnessing him vomiting over the kitchen sink. Weeks ago, but still vivid. Apparently. How she's treating him.

He fishes out a realtor card from a pocket stuffed with the same: *Stuck in a Rut? Long to Move Up! To Move Down? Buy! Sell! Rent!* CHIG'S YOUR MAN!

It feels good to be out here loose in the world, facing up to the give-and-go.

No one can say he hasn't got the world by the tail. He has seized the day. If he had a silk scarf flying in the wind, diamond stick pinned to the tie, elevator shoes! —he'd be the spitting image of Turner P. Blindstone.

Pulled from the lake? By cracky, it doesn't take a genius to know the randy galoot was pitched overboard. That Whitehall babe has flair.

### TALK ON THE TTC

Did he die yet?

How's anyone to know?

Happened to me I wouldn't know what to think.

### TALK ON WAY TO PUB

You saw the *Sun*?

I don't look at right-wing crapola.

Fa' fuck's sake! Those Sunshine Girls are aces, in my book.

### TALK AT PAUPER'S PUB

The man I was talkin' to … minute ago … the TTC … is a victim of circumstances. All racist xenophobes are.

Yeah? Well, we may be nut jobs. But unlike you, we have goals. We know our petunias.

Screw it. Let's hit another place.

### THE OTHER PLACE

Some people don't rinse dishes before putting them in the dishwasher. Then they complain. Ya know?

So whatta you sayin'?

They just don't. What I'm sayin'. Who knows why.

Makes sense to me.

You either subscribe to the necessity, or ya don't. Result? Crud.

Yeah yeah yeah.

Take a guy's parents. They didn't, you don't.

What are ya sayin'?

Result. Crud. Expensive ones now, ya don't git that problem. I mean, it never arises.

That wildcat rescued the guy from the drink, what was her name?

Ya got me. Sneaky Deap?

No, the other one. The island wildcat.

Rescued who? What are you sayin'?

Question is, she pulls the guy in from the lake, what does she do with him? People livin' on that island are funny, ya know. I bet you she never once thinks to rinse a dish.

Maybe she don't have to. *He* does the rinsin'. Some guys are like that.

I know what you're sayin'. Leave a clean sink. Rinse. Stamp out grime. Parents didn't, you will. That's progress. Evolution. Like one day we won't need toes.

Damn so.

Still need water. No gittin' around that.

And sleep.

Damn so.

And somebody to sleep with.

True. It's a maze, I'm tellin' you.

You see someone you like to have in the sack with you, my advice is don't whoop and holler. That's my advice.

You're tellin' me. Save your whoops and hollers for some other party.

❖❖❖❖❖❖❖❖❖❖❖❖❖❖❖❖❖❖❖❖❖❖❖❖❖❖

One morning into the first month of the boy's coma, Daisy awakens, scoots from the bed. Sees on the bathroom tiles a trail of wet feet. Up the stairs still more feet. Splayed toes. His size.

Tallis, you rat!

The trail leads straight up to Tallis Haley's bed. He's walking only on his heels now, but telltale water spots are visible even in here.

Sneaky brat. I knew it. Knew it all the time.

But he's under his wraps. Medical paraphernalia undisturbed.

I'm onto you, baby. I know your tricks.

She roots a hand under the covers, feels his feet. Not wet but cool. Coldish, certainly. Definitely on the cool side. Possibly moist.

Sweat?

She holds her own face over his, expecting to see a twitch in the eyelids. A blink. Smelling him. He smells fresh. The tricky bastard has got up from his coma, got up with the birds—had himself a secret wash.

She doesn't trust anyone. Not now. Never again. Especially not this boy. Silent night, holy night. Oh, come all ye faithful. Thou art as thou must, and warm am I with my Comforter, thickest wool.

Though I'm a wee trifle down in the dumps. Sick at heart, heavy of heart. Grave, grim, dreary, a sourpuss, a corpse at the feast, in a black mood, long in the face, miserable, discouraged, defeated, down in the mouth— Woman, you are a fucking mess!

Wake up, angel.

Her voice so frail, so tenuous, she must mouth this endearment a second time. Or how will he hear?

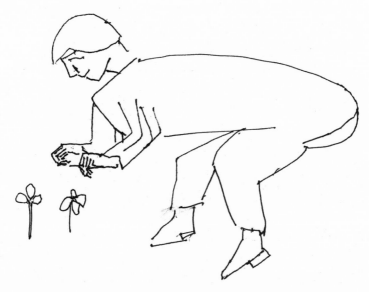

Wake up, my bright star.

She weeps. As relief from the soaps, she has been dipping into a book dealing with Nosenko (*Case Closed*, Posner, Random House, $29.50), thought by some CIA goon to be a spy, a double agent, and locked up in a broom closet, naked except for his grubby underpants, for the whole of one year. Then another, then two more. Food minimal, toilet facilities non-existent, baths never. Not even a toothbrush to clean his teeth for a full four years.

Her mouth feels like that. Laundry. Yes, today, she must do the laundry. Shameful, a crime, how she has let this house go to the dogs. Room to room, dragging herself, writing her son's name in the dust.

So, hang me. String me up.

Nosenko's toenails, when finally he is granted freedom, are two inches long.

He's a ship in a bottle, going nowhere, through four years. Tallis, too, is in the bottle.

There were no footprints; it was all in her mind. He smells like a rug.

Exchange places with me, Tallis. Here, honey, you take this chair.

She waits. No takers. The clever snit resisting the bait.

Honey, pardon me. I need to wipe my nose.

She wipes. Dries her face on the hem of her gown. No, she can't have her son waking up to see her like this. Woebegone, tearful, a hag. Gloom, go climb the chimney, she says. Go take a hike, Despair.

Though I will let Dejection sit awhile with me.

She sits primed, watching her son's face, waiting to flash him her misty-eyed, most dazzling smile the minute he …

As of this minute, this hour, Tallis Haley, 2 x 8 Major, has been locked in his coma weeks on end.

You might think he'd shed a few pounds, but just look at the little snit. Sure, she's fixated on weight. His, no less than her own. Maybe his because in her youth she … but maybe best not to reengage those trying times.

> My darling! But how different
> You appear today.

True, dear mother.

I confess I ate the whole pie.

Now, now, dear mother,

Don't cry.

Drag yourself through the day, attempt sleep, wallow forth to a bogus waking, drag yourself through another day. In relief of the maudlin drivel occupying her brain, Daisy pitifully swallows a Xanax, telling Emmitt to shove off, she has work to do. She will write a new essay. Here goes:

*If it is true, for most of us, our lives are characterized by the mind at war with itself, our options from the start are minimized. What is the mind anyway but a mire of the logical and illogical, haunted by one thing or another, on which light for the fleeting moment shines and is revelatory, and the next minute darkness obliterates the …*

Wouldn't you say?

No, Daisy, I wouldn't. If I did, I wouldn't own up to it.

Another essay biting the dust. Her brain's a dogsled pulled by bleating goats.

Daisy, hurry! Sheila Shott's on the radio.

From East Asia?

No. *Your Morning Jackpot* with Suzie Sweetwater.

Suzie: I'd like to welcome to the air one of the world's leading romance writers. Hi!

Sheila Shott: Well hello there!

Suzie: I want to say right off that some of your male readers regard Turner P. Blindstone as a stuck-up prick.

Sheila Shott: Only arrogant pricks think so. Turner is everything these men are not.

Suzie: Sounds to me like you're a little bit in love with the guy yourself.

Sheila Shott: Turner is a fictitious character. I'm not a big enough fool to be in love with a guy I've made up.

Suzie: Doesn't every woman do that? Make of their guy something he isn't?

Sheila Shott: No comment.

Suzie: You have a big Turner honcho loverboy in your own life, Sheila?

Sheila Schott: Not at the moment.

Suzie: A beautiful ultra-successful hotsie like you!

Sheila Schott: Not this very minute.

Suzie: Why not?

Sheila Shott: Do you?

Suzie: Us Sweetwater girls have done all right. We tend to marry too soon and too often, which is just how we like it. Fast boys in fast cars get one through the slippery night.

Sheila Shott: Such a sour face, though.

# C H I N G C H A N G B O N G B O N G !

Sheila: What is that awful racket?

Suzie: Jackpot! Jackpot! Some lucky caller has hit the jackpot! Hello. Hello. Your name, please.

Caller: I just want to say how much I enjoy your show. I'm so sorry that woman you're talking to lacks a honcho loverboy in her life. I couldn't live without mine. What's my jackpot?

Suzie: Complimentary cut, wash, and dye at Terri's Finest Salon.

Caller: Wow!

Suzie: You said it. Now back to Sheila Shott. Uh-oh. She's cut out. We give you now a musical interlude.

Honey? Sheila on the phone for you.

Sheila Shott?

The one and only.

Hi, Sheila.

Daisy, I'm telling you, CBC is in steep decline.

But you were not on CBC.

Because those rats refused to book me.

Oh dear.

Have you ever heard such a catty person as that Suzie Sweetbreath. Imagine. Wanting to know who I am sleeping with!

Who are you sleeping with?

Oh, Daisy. Not you too.

I never! Sheila hung up on me.

Time is slow here. Inside the coma: Black light. Picture a snail with a fifty-pound steel ball hooked to the leg. And it is all uphill. Picture a tortoise, anvils attached to each leg.

You picture it. I'd rather not.

Ryabovitch has the idea he has the mental edge. He's got the goods, his is the better claim, if only he can wrangle another invitation to the General's house. A kiss can loop you for a loop, Ryabovitch tells the boy. A kiss can knock you flat. One kiss! Think what twenty will do. Your author didn't even have the decency to have the woman kiss me on the mouth.

I've never been kissed by a single girl. Still, I got knocked flat that day I saw her sitting on the bench in Sally Bird Park—

There are not enough hours in the day for all the kisses I want, Ryabovitch confesses. Laid to waste by a quick kiss on the cheek, voluptuous aroma filling the nostrils, then denied the elusive follow-up. Women in lilac, pearls of distant laughter, the clink of glasses. War stories in the billiards room.

The door opens, he hears the soft rustle of a woman's dress, detects a faint sprinkle of perfume. She's coming. In a second her arms will encircle him.

'At last!' she will say.

But does she? No. She can't flee fast enough. Insipid girl. And now? Now, the General's house is closed for the season, the women at sail through other kingdoms. Glasses tinkle, songs are sung, dances danced, women in lilac glide on other officers' arms.

The whole business smacks of autobiography to Ryabovitch. That wretch author got kissed in a thousand rooms. Talented actresses, pretty wives dropping at his feet. Clinging to his legs: *Love me, Anton!*

◉ ◉ ◉ ◉ ◉ ◉ ◉ ◉ ◉ ◉ ◉ ◉ ◉ ◉ ◉ ◉ ◉ ◉ ◉ ◉ ◉ ◉ ◉ ◉ ◉ ◉

No, I would not call him an obsessive boy. Not obsessive in any way. Although it's true he'd lately taken an extraordinary interest in literature—in Chekhov, most strikingly. Which interests me, given that many children take an adversarial position to the parental professions. We are not lawyers who tend to produce lawyerly offspring. As I've constructed it, one of his lame teachers at school, you see, had been going on and on about the failure of families, family life, and quoting alarming statistics. Divorce, declining marriage, a bogus society—the social rot. His wife had just left him, you see. And he mentioned numerous works he saw as promoting this rot. *Madame Bovary*, all of D.H. Lawrence, *anything* authored by a woman—*all* of literature, generally. With special venom reserved for 'Lady with a Lapdog', which he read as an exact portrait of his errant wife. A sick man, obviously. Soon bundled off to an institution. This so-called rot, naturally, stoked my son's interest.

Otherwise...

Otherwise, he's a perfectly ordinary, normal boy. Never mind it sometimes has taken a hammer and chisel to get a word out of him. Oh, gifted, yes, he's something of a protegé, that's true. Smart. He won an All-City essay contest back in ... What year was that, Emmitt? He'd just earlier received in the mail, that very day, the stories of Chekhov, ten volumes, Ecco Press, I believe, and that's what he was doing out on the steps. Reading, I mean. Books scattered everywhere, wet, from the snow, trampled—the pages?—blown away by...

I can't say about *Kind of Blue*. Jazz, isn't it? Tallis was often wired to those headphones.... No matter what else he was doing, is my point.

Today, a line, the final line from a Mavis Gallant story, chews at her like waves spilling over a shore: When you return *will you still know me? I was your mother.*

No, no, I've not left the house yet, not since it happened, we have pizza delivered to the door and …

He was neat. The sweetest boy. Except that his hair was always worn too long. He is not one who defers to current fashion. You are aware, I'm sure, that we mothers study a newborn baby as trenchantly as Galileo studied the vapours of Venus. Beauty reigns, though defects do not go unseen. Unremarked upon, perhaps, but not unseen. I recall fearing my little new baby's ears were a trifle abundant in relation to his head, which head I could not kiss often enough.

I'm sure Tallis bears no ill will—well, he couldn't, could he?—against the poor girl who plastered him. X, Zan, Zen? Something like that.

She came sailing over the hedge and creamed him. Creamed my little scholar. Sixteen, but he's still a baby in my mind, you see. I was talking about that the other day, to a friend, about when I had him. But don't think you're going to get any of that out of me. Yes. Just creamed his ass. Is Irene—oh, the name is Zan, you say?—still in the hospital? She's out? Was in a coma herself, you say? Was? My goodness. No, I had no idea. I haven't inquired. The truth is, while I feel sympathy for her parents—Laura and Chig, is it?—her fate is beyond the realm of anything I want to consider. It isn't that I am without interest. But her fate and the despair of her family are not something I can contend with in my current depleted state. I'm sorry, but that's the case. I wish you hadn't mentioned her name. Our hedge is still a wreck. From her bike plowing through, I suppose. You just see a misshapen mass, but what I see is the front wheel still poking through, the back wheel flung up into the tree, the two of them one nasty, frightful puddle on the steps. Her helmet came off and crashed through our front window. A broken strap, they say. Frayed, I gather, where a family dog had chewed on it. Glass all the way back to the kitchen, slivers in my feet this minute. Sue? Good God. Isn't one ordeal enough? Do we all hate everybody that much? Tallis is murdered and we're to ask what's in it for us? Excuse me, but I don't think I ...

Yes, you see this?—Excuse me, but do you know what I think? But what I (and his father) was about to say: I had the maddest idea. Truly mad. I believe he is feigning the coma. In part, feigning it. I know how insane this sounds. Or he's in there examining the rot in family life a lunatic teacher preached about. I know for a fact he waked one morning, got out of bed, and took a shower. A fact, yes. An established, verified truth. Was there any hot water left when Emmitt took his? Not a lick. And a wet towel on the floor where Tallis always threw his. His wet toothbrush by the sink. I went in later to ... and what do you know! Yes, yes, yes, his closet a tangle, he's searched for something nice to wear. Emmitt swears he ... but I'll not mention that. You read what that professional medium said. The lady whose office door is smack-dab there on Bloor, across from the SuperSave. Well it was, I don't know where it is now. That woman's track record is the very very very best. She predicted Margaret Thatcher's fall, you'll recall. She knew the very day, the precise minute, the Pope—November 11, 1993—would fall down the stairs and break his leg. Or was pushed, as some claim. She had the exact vote on that free trade bill. Sheila Shott, she tells me, lives by what that woman says. Sheila selects her pub dates only after consultation with this renowned psychic extraordinaire. So it makes you think, about the popish incident, to be sure, during that audience with the UN people when he broke his bones. Our media naming in the nation's press precisely which bones and what oaths would issue from his mouth, and that other time when she said on *Night Beat* that Bush would puke all over that—well, whatever they call the top dog over in Japan.

So much for his infallibility, the Pope's, I mean, since *our* mystic has a far better record for infallibility than …

Emmitt, would you like to add something? Emmitt? My goodness, I think he's asleep! Poor fellow, he works so hard to declaw me. People have to be saved from themselves is a firm belief of his. His life's goal has been just that. *No matter who they are,* he says. You can see, I hope, how debilitating it can be for a woman of delicate composition to be living with a man holding such globalist humanitarian views. I'm not suggesting he isn't a prince, but it does wear on one. Why else do you think I chew my nails ragged? Though, now I think of it, I've over the years forked out thirty dollars monthly to have the prettiest painted fingernails in the whole of this city. At that cute lily pad of a Korean establishment down the street. Half-price pedicure every second Wednesday. Strongly recommended.

Emmitt believes this whole business has had a disastrous effect on our sex life. Oh, yes, that features in his complaint considerably more than my refusal to leave the house. But what I say to him is, Emmitt, nothing, nothing! ever! affects my sex life, and if you think it … I mean, you wouldn't think it to look at Emmitt, exhausted and undernourished as he is, but he might have a dozen mistresses, for all I know. His life, what Emmitt calls his life, is as secret to me as my son's is to him. Peas in the pod, I sometimes think. Which is a sad commentary on contemporary family life, wouldn't you say?

Emmitt? Glad to have you with us, dear.

That talcum you saw on the floor beside my son's bed, I sprinkled that talcum there. I wanted to … snare the little shit. So convinced was I that he was faking the thing. That coma is not what it was. Or is. Or that his case is like that famous case of a few years back, where the man got off for killing his family because it turned out that the defence proved—or made the jury think it had—proved that the man was sleepwalking at the time.

That he'd got up, dressed, driven miles to his parents' house, and shot them dead, all while in the sleepwalker's state. Plus, had driven back home, got back in bed, slept, and never knew fuck-all about what had happened until the police … Fantastic, yes? Yet exists a few matters science simply cannot explain. Which leaves our politics, our justice system, not to mention ourselves, in perennial disarray. Then come along distraught, normally angelic citizens, my own precious Other, telling me I've left an unfathomably holy copy of a certain book out to decompose in rain and snow. Out for rats, squirrels, skunks, raccoons to chew upon at their leisure. Me, for whom books are a veritable life. No future without literature, the Great Swami of Major Street said.

So it could very well be that Tallis is in a coma, or rut, of this very same fantastic type. As the sleepwalking maniacal killer. Don't you see?

Emmitt? Emmitt, would you please, for the love of God, go and freshen up this drink. Thank you, dearest. And bring me that onyx pill box by the sink.

But you don't want to hear about that. I'm sure you don't want to know what I think, but while Emmitt is out of the room—while he is, I don't know what I think about why it is I have refused, since my son's accident, to go out of that door. What I think is I am not alone. What I think on that subject is this: I think fully ninety percent of our population is afraid to do much of anything. Afraid to move beyond anything but what might be their common, relatively safe and secure orbit or home environment. They dare not venture beyond the secure and true. They fear for their lives. The only place they feel even a modicum of safety is when they are inside their own homes. Doors bolted. After they are out of their shower, or bath, you know, and realize they haven't slipped on a bar of soap and killed themselves. They sit in front of their TV sets and watch it happen to other people. Otherwise, they don't care one blue blaze about what's happening on the prime time. They are safe. Nothing can get at them. Oh, they tremble when the phone rings. They're scared shitless it will be bad news. They sit and stare at the ... box. Yes, because 'box' reminds them of 'coffin' and that gives a special edge to their viewing. Like they are participants, see? Maybe they even laugh once or twice. Why not? They're safe. They've survived another minute.

The thing about the door is that the door is so big. The space, Daisy means, beyond that door. It is such a big space, and all that air beyond. Say you are a little girl and what mostly this little girl considers is what she's doing now, an hour from now, with a concern or two about what tomorrow holds. The days multiply and now you are a little girl a tiny bit older and it is less now the present concerning you so much as it is what yesterday wrought and tomorrow portends. Some days you cry like a baby, though these cries must be held inside, these tears must be unseen because you are not a little girl any more. My goodness, you are all grown-up now. You have come of age. My goodness, how did that happen? Boys are wanting to kiss me. No more than a few minutes ago I was a little girl holding on to mother's hand. Jelly smeared my mouth. Globs flung from the high chair evidenced glee.

No way, Daisy says. No way you are going to get me out there. And nails her heels to the floor. Go out that door your own self. You bum. You're so smart. You do it. Show me. Emmitt Haley is outside, he has gone through that door and is standing there, perfectly upright, perfectly safe. No brick has yet sailed through the air to knock him flat. No car has jumped the curb. No bicycle with flying girls. No one has yet fired a bullet through his head. No rocks have fallen from the sky.

'Nothing to it, Daze. Give it a try.'


You can't fool Daisy Haley when it comes to that door. Tallis went out and look what happened to him.

◙ ◙ ◙ ◙ ◙ ◙ ◙ ◙ ◙ ◙ ◙ ◙ ◙ ◙ ◙ ◙ ◙ ◙ ◙ ◙ ◙ ◙ ◙ ◙ ◙


'The Yapochee, a three-legged animal smaller than the deer they resemble, have longer ears, are of innocent disposition, and are swift runners. Fur is a thinned-out blue, what he calls rainbow blue. A rainbow as seen through mist. He isn't very precise.'

'Thanks, Daisy. He, who? Why are you telling me this?'

'In removing those absurd *sound* carpets your friendly *Hardware* refuses to take back, I discovered a loose floorboard. In the recessed area beneath that board *your* son has hidden things. I suspect he's got loose boards all over the house.'

'The mangy cuss! Things hidden like what?'

'For one thing, photos clearly taken in secret, of that girl who tried turning him into sawdust. For another, an apparently self-published fictional work about these beings he calls the Yapochee.'

'Isn't that good?'

'It isn't good. He's stolen the colophon of a very respected press.'

'What press?'

'Coach House. He wants the world to believe they did it. Limited edition, twelve numbered copies, six *hors commerce.*'

'Signed?'

'In green ink.'

'My own son. I'm impressed.'

'Stapled, atrociously typed, crudely written. Misspellings, rampantly ill grammar. Coach House should sue.'

'Keep mum. Zip the lip.'

'The green ink intrigues me. What, I wonder, was his model?'

'I wish not to hear this.'

'He liked rooting among my shelves.'

'*You* consigned *Finnegan* to the elements.'

'A suspicion is raised. I am suggesting nothing more.'

'Fine. Let's look at the bugger's masterpiece.'

---

**FATE OF THE YAPOCHEE**

---

by T. Haley

*CHAPTER ONE*

Three Yapochee were running. The last three. All others gone. Didn't take God The Almighty to know something was after them. What the Yapochee are saying is, WHERE DID WE

ALL GO? Haven't seen any in months, except you guys. And you guys are a pain.

Another Yapochee says, I smell water.

Me too, ponders the third. Let's have a drink.

They wet the whistle alongside a rumbling stream.

The last three. All others gone. Extinck. One day a long walloping cry will rise up from eroding hills. *Where did our gallant Yapochee go?* Will the unkempt hinterlands sing their demise?

These Yapochee are like deer. Ever sniffing the breeze. Fur and flesh rippling. Puffy tails twitching. Fur coloured rainbow blue like rainbow blue in misty horizon.

Something in the air.

Something that a fourth sense—all those vanished Yapochee—is trying to tell these three solitary creatures, something important to their welfare.

But the tail of ONE continues to twitch. *Twitch twitch* twitches her tail. She continues to drink. Look at the sky, drink. Twitch the tail, drink.

You can see the giant shadow of the hungry beast menacing them. Seconds from now it will lunge.

Fate showcases its cruel hand.

Two left.

*(Chapter Two continues the tale.)*

—————————

'That bicycle—'

'Yes, Daisy?'

'As for that bicycle, some people should be disallowed. They should have licensing, and lessons, and if you can't pass the lesson and remain on the seat like a civilized person, then you should walk.'

'It says here in the *Star*, a councilman says here, last year alone, fourteen thousand bikes were stolen in this city.'

'They cannot steal enough of them often enough to suit me. You go out the door, slip on ice, and it's goodbye Clementine. That's the kind of place you've brought us to live. And that's only the half of it.'

'You've had a go at those pills.'

'Absolutely. The absolute stinking truth, absolutely. Are my knees red? I dropped a handful on the floor. Miles and miles they rolled.'

Some light on Daisy's refusal to leave the house, as reported in *SMILE*, weekend magazine for people with disabilities:

Lax, loose, slipshod, negligent, ungoverned, unruly, intolerant, deranged, uncivil, unbridled, riotous, gas fumy, heavy-handed, impolite, bullying, dour, bigoted, lecherous, fanatical, indecent, terrifying, naughty, delinquent, seditious, overpriced, revolting, ranting, rowdy, brawling, deviationist, restive, homicidal, zoned-out lone wolves, purse-snatcher gangs, delinquents, popinjays, derring-doers, cyclists, dopers, backstabbers, bricks, falling bricks, fallen angels, dictators, insolent freaks, beggars, streetwalkers, freaks, bloodsuckers, predators, purse snatchers, hanging judges, skinheads, extortioners, fanatics, traffic, traffic lights, nudists, black marketers, birds, birdpoo, lampooners, blasphemers, horses, dogs, cats, rats, cattle, spies, vandals, sadists, murderers—*and people who say they love me want me out there!* I am not yet double-pump crazy.

Daisy's *Statement of Principle.*

I will not be a party to this nonsense. I will not. Do you hear me? I will not be one jot or parcel a part of such unmitigated, demeaning nonsense. I will not.

That's fine, Daisy. Though it would help matters if we knew to what you are alluding.

I am alluding, as you contemptuously put it, to that ruffian, Ormsby by name. I rise nicely salted down from my morning face-wipe, to find that self-same man encamped by my son's bedside. He has around his neck a crudely tied necktie borrowed, he says, from those you have left hanging on a doorknob. He is in conference with Tallis, he tells me. *Private* conference, he tells me. Kindly exit and close the door, he tells me. He has papers of incorporation the boy must sign. Papers! I ask you. I won't have it. That frightful phrase *putting my foot down* occurs to me. I am putting both feet down.


In lieu of a tangible audience, in the absence of one at whom she would throw the dishes, throw brickbats, umbrage and strip raw, strip to the very core of being, Daisy Haley addresses her bile at the loosened wallpaper on the unrenovated, downscale walls at 2 x 8 Major. Mad utterance day and night and where's a woman's relief? Where's tranquility, a measure of happiness, a dollop of grace, in the face of eternity's blind eye, and chaos every minute rambling by like a runaway exploding ball of fire. The entire planet has gone amuck.

'*Amuck!* I tell you. *Amuck!*'

—And it's all the fault of that girl whose name I will not repeat in this house. I will not.


Daisy is enraged that she has been found at fault for abandoning *Finnegans Wake* to rain and snow. Does the idiot not know copies of this rare work of exhaustive unparalleled genius, of which a mere 425 were published, are routinely gobbled up by collectors at five and six figures? She and Emmitt, and anyone else troubling themselves to answer the phone, have received urgent calls from Bauman of New York, Philadelphia and Las Vegas. 'Bauman, ha!' cried local rare book dealers Steven Temple and David Mason—arriving all but simultaneously at the 2 x 8 door. Vastly dishevelled, both of them. Thomas Fisher Library footsoldiers already on the scene. Richard Landon hovering.

Dear God, Daisy, was this by chance the 1939 Faber and Faber London numbered octavo edition? ...

... in original red buckram?

... Morocco clamshell box.

... Signed by the master in green ink. Likely bearing his thumbprint.

Shoosh. How you are coming at me.

Answer, please.

It might very well have been boxed, now you mention it.

... I couldn't very well read it in the box, could I?

... I do seem to recall there was a box. If so, it would be around somewhere.

... Red binding, oh my. Yes.

... Signature? In green? Though it won't be green anymore. Will it? I can't say I gave much attention to the signage. Authors signing books say such rubbishy things.

Where is this item now, Daisy?

How would I know?

Think.

Possibly it was put on a shelf to dry. I recall doing that with some book. The pages had swollen thick as my waist. Wet, I'll tell you. Dripping. But that might have been *David Copperfield*. Or *Pride and Prejudice*. Did you move a soggy volume off my shelves, Emmitt? I do recall a little note inside the *Finnegans*, signed S. Beckett. Which I believe I discarded. Well, I must have been in a rush. Or Emmitt was shouting something at me. People, perfect strangers, so often are. It simply did not occur to me this could be our famous Beckett. Literature is my business, as you know. I'm well aware of the Joyce-Beckett relationship. No, no, I believe it was a Virginia Woolf I left out to cope with the elements. Some might think that appropriate, I suppose. *Jacob's Room*, 1922. Note inside from Tom. Tom being Mr Eliot, I presume. No no no, heavens to Betsy, what am I thinking? *Jacob* I gave to my sister on her thirtieth birthday. Not that I expected she ever would read it. Mickey Spillane, Zane Grey, the rubbishy lot, are more to her liking. Old Hopalong Cassidy movies. Early spaceship features. Buster Crabbe and such. The equivalent in their time to what so many of my students today prefer. You agree?

Daisy, Daisy, please clamp your mouth shut.

You gentlemen have put me into such a fiddle. I cannot believe you would address your wives in like manner.

Daisy Daisy Daisy. Answer the question. How, and where, did you acquire this item *Finnegans Wake*?

Stop harping at me. Three magpies chirping away. I haven't been myself lately. Someone lend me a tissue. My eyes are wet.

Where?

In London, years ago. That market area where all the hippies hung out. Tallis couldn't have been more than two. We dressed him in a splendid gentleman's suit. Velvet, it was. You've never seen such a dapper boy. The necktie hung to his knees. I still have the scissors employed to ... What's that area called, Emmitt?

Portobello Road.

It was in a bin on the sidewalk. Tallis was attracted by the gilt spine. Brightness appeals to him. I once thought it was my personality compelling him to race up and down. To flutter so.

About that *Jacob's Room*. 1922, you say? Hogarth Press, perhaps? Does it remain in your sister's keeping? Forgive us, is this sister zany as you are? Emmitt, are we not your brothers who come in peace? Help us out here.

## EMMITT'S BROTHER PASSES THROUGH TOWN

Arthur is Emmitt's younger brother. He's dropped in on his way to Sioux Falls where his firm, an electronics emporium, is establishing new quarters. Sheila Shott, romance novelist extraordinaire, is leaving as he arrives.

'Who are you?' he asks.

'Sheila Shott,' she says. 'Romance novelist extraordinaire.'

'I write poems,' he tells her. 'Somewhat in the manner of James Tate. My mentor. I studied under Jim at UMass.'

'Amherst. I am widely admired on that august campus.'

It's clear she's taken with this younger image of aging Emmitt, who is standing by, holding Sheila's luggage. A taxi by the curb awaits her. She's off to East Asia in scant hours. She wishes now she didn't have to go. Emmitt is bemused. He never before has witnessed Sheila in flirtatious mode. Her high heels catapult her inches from Arthur's face. Is it his lips she's now kissing, or is she about to bury her face into his neck? Her hips wrench right and left. It's possible to make the claim that his also move.

Arthur is single, likes women, is on the market. What's the harm? But must they smooch, demonstrate such amazing dexterity—footwork, hands, lips—the moment they meet?

Finally, she goes.

Toodle. Another time.

She's gone. 'It could very well be,' Arthur says to Daisy, 'that I should read that woman's books. Now may I pay my respects to my stricken nephew?'

*I was on my daily walkabout when I saw this party I thought I knew, sitting on a bench eating lunch. I was invited to join her but the minute I sat she said she had changed her mind and wanted quickly to get home. It had started to rain, which was why she said that. I could come or not come, she said, it wasn't far. Home wasn't as close by as had been my hope, not that I mentioned this. We arrived and tea was served. She was forty-eight years old, she said, and lived a good life, but, sorry, she hardly remembered me. By this time, which was getting late, I realized she wasn't the party I thought I had come upon. I told her this. She said it hardly mattered, since we were friends now. Rain still poured and I said what a typhoon, I may never get home. She said she'd drive me, she had a roadworthy heap, but had first to pick up her oldest child who was getting off work about now. We did that, and the boy said, Who are you? in a voice that might have been unfriendly, or jokey, or I didn't know what. He mellowed out on the long drive to my place. He told me of his girlfriend, of his workload, of his minimum wage, of his aspirations in life. He confessed he deeply regretted the loss of a friend whose legs had cramped in the gravel-pit pond and was no longer of this earth. His mother kept saying I never knew that, you never told me that, such is news to me. The heap we were in rattled a good bit. It was not easy hearing what anyone was saying.*

*Finally—it was a dark night, the rain drumming—we arrived at my place. The wife said, There you are. There you are. There you are. She said this three times. I found this remarkable. She hardly seemed herself.*

Arthur wrote that. He left it on the mantel for Daisy and Emmitt to find. He said it was a James Tate–type poem, a present for Tallis when he woke.

Maybe the poem will strengthen with age, Daisy hoped. In her present state, self-defined as zombie caretaker to the stubbornly inert form disguised as beloved son, she hoped she could be forgiven for displaying zero enthusiasm for anything other than the son's continuing breath. It used to be that words strung in proper sequence, like clothes flapping on a taut clothesline on a stormy day, made her scalp itch, her heart flip over, her flesh quiver, her spine jitter, her feet tingle. All in the past now. *Oh, do not ask, 'What is it?' Let us go and make our visit.* Indeed. Oh, indeed. *In the room the women come and go Talking of Michelangelo.* Indeed they did. And she went with them. Indeed she did. Her heart singing. The pulsing heart in overdrive. The very equivalent of Tina Turner exalting a field containing multitudes. Uncanny, since in reality there split-toed Daisy was, her own puny solitary self, under a lamp's pale blue light, eyes glued to the page. Exalted! Roaring silent approval! What a difference between the Then and the Now! What a cataclysmic fall! Now, indeed, Mr Eliot's yellow fog had developed into a monstrous shape darkening every window. The hot black tongue licking and lingering. *Shameful. Dear sir. I plead insanity. I plead mitigating circumstances. I blame all the sorrow inhabiting this household on the action of a careless girl. All the same, I'm a reasonable woman worried senseless and confess to having dropped three lovely capsules in the past hour.*

Allow me to speak softly to you, Tallis, dear boy, of my condition, or what I perceive my condition to be, a condition drawing perilously close to what I perceive yours to be. It's like I have, through days and days, been sitting shivering with cold by a fire that flashed its last flame weeks ago. Was it Clytemnestra who slammed her way into the palace and murdered the bathing Agamemnon? Don't ask me. My mind is at rot. Mould grows on me. My brain is a pile of peat moss. Tangled seaweed. I'm a thick stump through which worms churn. I could not this minute tell you what an isosceles triangle is or what utility it serves. Of what am I thinking this minute? Of the time a woman stood on my foot on a streetcar when I was on my way somewhere. I'm ten years old. The woman will not get off my foot. Isn't it odd the peculiarities lodging in the brain of someone who this minute can't tell you what form an isosceles triangle may take? That woman was old, thick waisted, with white hair, a beaded necklace, drooping chins. She had dark eyes, wore white stockings, carried a black shoulder bag. My shoe was a flat-heeled Capezio, coloured sky blue. I was afraid if I shifted my foot the leather would scratch. It cracks me up to consider that my memory of that incident is, among sundry other thousands, clearer than my memory of the pain experienced at your birth. Isn't that riotous? Well, pain recedes. It does us the courtesy of accomplishing that.

Sometimes.

Thank God it does, as relates to giving birth, or I'm sure we'd have, worldwide, a declining birth rate.

I don't believe pain would diminish if the worst happened to you. It is altogether possible I'd crawl out like a demented crab and do to that girl what Clytemnestra did to Agamemnon. We'd have the full Greek tragedy all over again. Your father would go bananas. He wouldn't like that one bit.

Allow me to put it this way: the *worst* could happen to you. You can lie there in your smiling innocence and heavy eyelids, but it could.

Not that I for a second believe it will. Or I wouldn't think it could, if I believed in my heart you were a boy who could be counted on. Warn you not to do something, didn't you always do it?

One thing you can forget about, Mr Haley, is you can forget about those photographs you so smartly hid beneath the floorboard. I'm not sure I can forgive that trick. Your father says you went at that board with his adored power drill, removing screws cleverly camouflaged by wood putty. Then hid away your treasure, replaced the board, applying as final gesture your own dastardly devised putty. I would not have thought you so well-versed in woodwork. I have ever seen you as a somewhat awkward child given to excess body weight thanks perhaps to the swim of mischievous genes.

Emmitt, please be quiet. Surely you can see I am conversing with your son.

In the meantime, I sit here in my heartbreak, recalling the numerous nursing occasions when you, the baby, purposely eluded the nipple I tried inserting into your mouth. Then you to suck deliriously there like a fiend never meaning to let go. Eh? Eh? The sword of Damocles required to move you over to the other breast. Eh? Were you proud of yourself? Eh? You hear me, don't you?

Don't you?

————————

Daisy did not perceive merit in Arthur's gift found on the mantel, though her weight of sorrow lifted somewhat. It had lost an ounce or two the previous day when a hawk had swooped into the rear garden. The hawk had given a pensive stare to the bird feeder on the ground, half buried under dirty snow. The hawk seemed to agree with her that matters did not stand in good accord at the 2 x 8 house. It knew that feeder, of old. In weather-friendly times thousands of sparrows assembled by that feeder. Squirrels dining on its seed had moved from infancy into old age, despite the heavy lacing of red pepper flakes and doses of cayenne.

Arthur, on the point of leaving, had said, This house could stand a bit of cheer. He said: I suggest we mount a stage play. For Tallis. Please retire to his room.

Daisy and Emmitt did so. After some delay, Arthur entered, a mop riding his head. My name is Mary, he said. I am the maid.

He proceeded to clean.

Daisy and Emmitt gave him a blank look. They were in the dark. They did not know this play. They were not in the mood. Arthur was not at his best acting the fool.

Arthur said: I, Mary, have spent a very pleasant afternoon. I've been to the cinema with a man, and to drink some brandy and milk and read the newspaper.

Emmitt's face lit. He leapt up. He dashed from the room.

This interested Daisy. Emmitt did not normally move so fast.

Now he was back. He was carrying a valise. He approached Daisy without fanfare. 'Was it by chance that I glimpsed you at Manchester station, madam?' he said. How uncanny! How bizarre. Inasmuch as I engaged that very train myself.

Daisy pinched herself. Memory would not divulge this play. Emmitt's forehead was tight against her own. It struck her that he desperately needed a shave.

He said: And is it possible, dear lady, you possibly reside on Bromfield Road? How bizarre. How uncanny and revelatory. How unnatural! As I most positively reside in that very No. 8 domain.*

Daisy managed a small squeak.

Emmitt exclaimed: Elizabeth! My very own wife! We are united again!

It was all perfectly dreadful. Such terrible actors. That she had failed to recognize Ionesco's *Bald Soprano* was mortifying. In penance she will from this day forward ever say to anyone calling at the door, *My name is Mary. I am the maid.* Tallis will like that. He loves saying to strangers, 'My name is Tallis. I am the son.'

———————————

She had much the same edifying remarks to make about another James Tate–type piece arriving in the mail a few days later. Arthur had written this one, he said, on the train to Sioux Falls. 'While thinking of you in your quandary.' Also in the envelope was a bottled product, fancifully labelled *Body Engine Oil.* They were to employ this oil in massage of the boy's feet; Arthur had observed dis-colouration there. 'The oil carries the endorsement of a doctor-friend out in California,' he wrote. 'It's devilishly thick. Mix with beaten, organic egg. Apply.'

'Is your brother a prankster?' Daisy asked. 'This looks to me like the stuff mechanics pour into autos, to make gizmos under the hood work.'

They massaged the boy's feet, in any event. The treatment was successful. 'Goodness! Look how pink! While here, I'll clip his toenails.'

———————————

* With thanks, *Bald Soprano* (Eugene Ionesco), for words and inspiration.

# Another James Tate–Type Piece

PLANS

We had plans and no one to tell them to. The boy wanted to go back to sleep and the girl said she wanted to go out. We thought of going out with her, but she told us she had other plans, we had to stay home. We stayed home, home not a footnote in our carefully wrought plans. The boy waked in a snit, we didn't know why. The girl came in and went out. She was changing clothes, one clingy thing then another, and I said She's like a lizard, how she is, without really meaning she reminded me of a lizard or of much of anything else other than a girl wanting to get somewhere fast and look sexy. These were clearly stated plans, since she often said, Git out of my way. We had no objection, it being clear by this hour that we couldn't tag along. The boy got up, in his usual snit, telling us to our face, If you have plans for me you can forgit them, I've got other things to do. We all have these other things to do and sometimes they fit in and other times not. I don't believe anyone heard me say that. I was left alone, with nothing to do. I immediately made plans to combat the inevitable.


Daisy said the piece wasn't Yeats. She couldn't see why reputable people called such things poetry. In the night, wiping down her son, she recalled her father, all his life, out of pure stubbornness, pronouncing the name Yeats to rhyme with feets. Each time he said it that way tears would come into her eyes. Then her father would punch her shoulder and laugh. He said it to vex her and she each time fell into the trap. You take this literature business too seriously, he'd say. Me, I'm sticking with Ogden Nash.

Dear old dad.

Upon his death, to find among his papers, ream after ream of his own secret scribbling:

> If once upon the loom
> We failed to thrive
> Then next upon the loom
> May we strive.

One of Daisy's doctors, meeting Emmitt in the Hardware, says to him: It is a grievous undertaking, and a gross humiliation, to attempt an understanding of the marital life.

What's the trouble, Doc?

Eleanor complains she never sees me. Claims I'm wedded to the hospital. Said she sighted, the other day, a portly grey-haired gent in the distance, and only when we were face to face did she know it was me. Shocked, she was. Asked when it was my hair went grey.

In marriage, I've noticed myself, a paw full of drooping flowers on the birthday don't do the job.

No?

No.

What does?

Utter male sacrifice. Absolute dedication to the task of keeping the woman entertained and happily composed, secure in the belief you'd be nothing without her.

All that?

The claim may be made that such is how they transport themselves.

You don't say.

The chief ingredient of a long marriage is romance.

With whom?

Now stop that.

Every day is an education. My wife, a skinny woman, sits on my lap and we debate abstractions.

Your wife is not what I call skinny.

I'd sit on hers but for my girth. A brief period after our marriage we found we had little to say to each other.

The honeymoon was over?

We, apart from the other, devised a list containing topics for discussion. Just yourselves at dinner, what to talk about? Many of our topics were downright ridiculous.

The precipice awaited.

Over time it developed that we both wanted, demanded, the floor. We were wrung out, emptied and refilled by the sheer cascade of the other's view. Terrain stretching before us had no end. How's the kid?

Same. Slumbering like a saint.

Daisy still strung out?

More than ever.

Sorry to hear that.

What brings you to the Hardware?

Tools. Eleanor likes tools. Likes building things. She buys wrecks, you know. Reconstructs them. Art. Backstreet Gallery today, MOMA tomorrow. Hope reigns. Good to see you. Bye and so long.

One will do.


The doctor was a Chinese man of polite companionable disposition, taller than Emmitt. It seemed to Emmitt the Chinese often were. Maybe he was himself shrinking. He liked thinking he was the one riding tall in the saddle. Maybe he'd lost his saddle or now carried it elsewhere. Maybe old age waited around the corner, grinning. So nice to see you, Old Age would say.


How's the boy? people on the street were asking.

The record shop was piping music into the street. Jazz, Blues. A sign in the window announced: *Day-long broadcast. The 100 & 1 known recordings of 'Little Girl Blue.' Rodgers & Hart, 1935.* This minute, George Shearing (piano), Joe Williams (vocals), going strong.

Go home. Come back with a chair.

*How's the boy, how's the boy?*

Up there, at the intersection, waiting for the crossing sign, that girl, X. Zan. Whatever name she has. Is that a blue tint in her hair? Or a blue cap? Giant bag on her shoulder. Too heavy for her, obviously. What is it? Salt? Cat litter? Concrete? He hums along with 'Little Girl Blue'.

Zan takes a second look at that figure down the block, rooted to the sidewalk. Baggy trousers, slumping shoulders. Is that T's father? Giving her the fish eye? Where's that music coming from?

What a nice song.

There's Nancy Cee dining at Chicken-A-Go-Go, laughing at something her table companion is saying. Time to scoot.

Fuck. Wouldn't you know it? Here comes snow.

Nighttime. Somehow it does always fall. And here are those rabid rare-book creatures scouring 2x8 for the lost *Finnegans*. If the copy exists it must be salvaged. They refer to it now as the Portobello Road copy. Mason calls it the Piccadilly copy and is soundly chastised by Landon and Temple. Piccadilly. Ho-ho. Call yourself an expert. Of the trio, Landon gets the most abuse. That rogue Landon, they say. The Fisher despot. The Fisher King. Fisher has deep pockets. You've got to be on your toes to beat Landon. His wife, too. Avoid going up against that pair near the time the new budget comes in. Institutional pull. U of T. What chance does a pocketless independent have? Adroitness. They have that. Skullduggery. They have that. Maneuverability. Strike first. A good mercenary goes in fast.

*Where is the book? What did the insane woman do with the book?*

Once found, pages will be unstuck. Let's hope the woman has not scribbled senseless remarks onto every page. These academics! The Portobello Road copy: Even a stitch of green in the Joyce signature might fetch dollars. But if Portobello exists, which they doubt, and *if* it retains the number, which is unlikely, and *even if the red cover is warped like a rainbow*, which it will be, then they will know which idiot it was let rain and snow besmirch the prized elements. What was the item's number? Was it numbered? Don't bother putting the question to Daisy. She hems and haws. *I do vaguely recall noticing a number.* Everything about Daisy is vague. You want vague? Go talk to that woman. *I vaguely recall folding a recipe inside the pages. A curry dish. Spicy. I had been flipping through* Bon Appetit *at the time. Thinking about dinner.*

Now the be-crazed woman throws in a bomb. Tallis has these secret coves. Under the floorboards. Hiding spots. *Are we to rip up every floorboard in the house? Do we have your permission? We are willing. Eager. Back tomorrow with our crowbars.*

'Tear up the house? Certainly not. No book is worth that.'

The pain these dealers bear, hearing those scandalous words.

*Finnegans* is not found. The dealers exit 2x8, swearing and swatting at each other. We are all imbeciles. Such is what they say. They will not sleep easy tonight.

Daisy has located a peculiar folded note in a rarely used sewing basket. The note bears a name much lately heard: Beckett. Samuel Beckett here has written, GONE FOR DRINK. *Didn't they always!* —so she has asked herself. Joyce and Beckett, she means. At heart, all authors are sots. Female tribe excluded (some doubt here, about friend Sheila Shott. No doubt whatsoever when it comes to E. Bishop. D. Parker, J. Rhys, M. Duras, A. Sexton, J. Bowles. *Slurs on the divine in our nature*, Duras said. Rest assured Brontë, Austen, Emily, Wharton, Fanny Burney, historical others, not so calumniously enshrined).

Daisy suffers the alarming suspicion that said note once nested in the *Finnegans* about which these raucous dealers are being so outlandishly fussy. She has made no mention of this find, nor intends to. She thinks she may very well set fire to this note. Gone for drink, indeed.

The sewing kit resides nastily in her lap. It overflows with tangled spools of thread, countless needles, scissors too small for a human hand. Useless scraps of one thing and another. The wretched top refuses to fit.

Nothing has gone right in this house since Comet Girl struck. She hears herself saying this aloud, and wonders why her voice is so scratchy. Is it time for a drink?

I don't leave books in the rain, she hears herself saying. Another idiot did it.

Shall we concede Daisy may be under the influence? Scores of runaway pills pinch her bare feet.

*Tonight we breathe new life upon the glass*, B's note further said. *Adrienne to pay.*

---

It happens—it just happens to happen—that the Zan (of Major Street, next block down, where she has lived the how many years of her life) … it happens that Zan, recently of a comate status, let us recall … on this night of numbing cold, snow in churning fall, high wind in rake of objects not thoroughly secured ... is taking a slow walk under deep shade of troubled mood, sombre but thoughtful at heart ... when she finds herself yet again pausing for breath. Where is she? Squarely in front of the beloved's house: 2 x 8.

Scene of the crime.

Her question to herself, as ever it now is—Will she dare? Will courage fail her once more, resolve slop away. Guilt leave her puddled by the curb. She longs to knock on the door. *It's me. I must see him.*

Let's see, she tells herself. Let's stand here, toes freezing into crumbs, and see what resolve decides this time.

Her superbly devised plan is not working out. She has made friends with an extremely nice Korean boy. Seong is an older star student science major at U of T—is it science? Of this Zan is uncertain since the field Seong passingly mentioned is science of a kind she did not know existed. Seong is tall, lean, and shatteringly handsome. How she met him, he was a cool guy, sitting, ears wired, on a bench in nearby Gwen MacEwen Park. She passed. Hey, he said, a long legs like you, you know grunge? She stopped. Thinking he meant a shared reality, she said, Who doesn't? He pressed his ear jacks upon her. Mother Love Bone, he said. The guy you hear is grunge maestro Andy Wood. Recently self-parachuting into drug heaven. You're not a druggie, are you?

The important factor concerning Seong is not his handsome façade, his personable nature, his questionable musical taste; it is that he rents a third-floor apartment in the house directly across from Tallis Haley. Almost directly. From Seong's high street-side aperture she has a straight beeline into the beloved's chamber. Almost straight. She must edgewise herself a trifle. Bend the backside, crimp the knees. Seong's view on the world is restricted; his is possibly the smallest window in the city.

Where her plan has gone kaput is Seong is not home. Seong is likely off learning finer details in the science she never heard of. A promised key has yet to find her hand.

Bravo, however. For once there is movement—signs of life—inside the boy's house.

*A coma, you know. The boy. Dire straits ...*

*Like a mausoleum in there…*

*All but see the wreath on the door…*

Tonight, thanks be, her beloved's room is lit. She sees a man at the window. He's striding back and forth. He appears angry about something. He's dressed in a blue suit, has a military-style cap on his head. The cap is of loopy, foreign design, like you might see in an old movie. He carries a book in one hand. Now that's interesting. He's flinging out his arms. Now and then he laughs, but she can tell it isn't a happy laugh. Often he pauses, which means to her that another party occupying the room is saying something back to him. And she well knows who this other party must be. Her beloved is having a frightful argument with this unknown man. Golly, now that man is ripping a page from the book. He's crunching up the page. He's tossing that ball at …

'*His Excellency Lieutenant-General von Rabbek invites the gentlemen to drink tea with him.…* That's how my troubles began,' Ryabovitch has been telling the boy. 'From the beginning, your author was arranging matters so I could be played the fool. The proof is here in this book.'

'He gave you life. Without him you wouldn't exist.'

'Nonsense. I was born, wasn't I? I had parents, didn't I? I wasn't hanging around waiting for an author to find me.'

'I wish I could have attended the general's party.'

'You're one hundred degrees unconscious. A comatose boy would not have been welcome.'

'The girls would have fussed over me. They would have felt sad for me. I might have got a kiss or two.'

'You dream. I'm not talking adolescents here. I'm talking full-blown womanhood. Were we to drag you in on a litter? Install you on the general's bed? The chatter, politics, would have bored you. A general's party is no place for children. Note this. If your author had sent Anna Sergeyevna to the general's party rather than to Yalta she'd have been spared decades of misery.'

'Anna again. Who's she?'

'Someone behaving most severely to me. She's changed since your bud Chekhov's time. She's becoming—in the lingo I'm now hearing—a tough old broad. Still beautiful, no change there. But embittered, yes. With the least justification she will suddenly lash out. And why not, given the history that rogue author laid on her? By nature a good, sweet-natured, loving woman placidly constituted. Like me. Now she may at any moment strike with the deadly viciousness of a snake. One careless word, one thoughtless act, and venom fires from her mouth. Last night she was cold, refusing my touch. Attempt a kiss and she spins away. One minute she's in full surrender to the throes of love, next second she's smacking your face. Last night she said I had never once put my arms around the waist of a decent woman. How offensive was that?'

'Don't ask me. I'm an innocent boy. Never been kissed. Never likely to be.'

'Oh, quit your complaining. I'm the injured party here. What do you have to do except lie around mostly unconscious all day? On your back, eyes shut tight, night and day in aimless float through impenetrable time. Where's the stress in that? Me? I'm daily out in the fray wearing out shoe leather dodging throngs of shoppers who excel at not seeing me. In a new city, a new country, in an actual love affair with an honest-to-God actual woman. Frightful, let me tell you. Did Mr Chekhov prepare me for these hurdles? *He* gave himself the luxury of vacations in Yalta, the company of gay curvaceous actresses, but what did he give me other than an inferiority complex? From which I will never have relief. Do you imagine lovely Anna does not see that? Does she not ask herself, Why am I spending time with this nincompoop? They don't pronounce my name correctly in this town. What's the matter with people in this country? Did they never go to school? Why couldn't it have been me, and not Dmitri Gurov, meeting Anna at Yalta? Made to live duplicitous lives, both miserable. Don't tell me Gurov's wife and children didn't notice his hangdog face. Or Anna's lackey didn't observe hers. Whereas. Whereas had I been the party idling away my time in *dusty, boring Yalta*—criminal, your author painting beautiful Yalta that way—my presence could have saved each from decades of heartbreak. *Pathetic* Anna would have been happy. I would have been. Why didn't your revered master think of that? Because he's an imbecile, that's why. *He's* happy, running around bedding his actresses, looking after hapless relatives. He's a physician, I've learned. Personally, I expect more from one of that profession. Us, his characters? From him, a constant flow of our faults, our failures, our deadly compromises, frustrations, delusions, lack of fulfillment in a swiftly altering universe. Fine and good. Satire does not repulse me. I can take humour as well as you can. But what he gives me is the rustle of silk, the scent of lilac, a kiss meant for another party. Probably meant for that jackass Lobytko. Life isn't fair. Literature isn't. Nothing is. I mean, look at you. In a coma, for God's sake. Hardly the most sparkling company. See this? I'm tearing up his pages. Following your mother's example, I'm mutilating the book.'

'Leave my mother out of this. Stop ranting, you make me tired. You'll live forever, thanks to Anton. Where did you get that suit? You seem to me to be doing okay. You seem to have this Anna.'

'I've done that my own self. Shown my mettle. Taken control of my affairs. Authors be damned. What do you say to that?'

Nothing. Tallis Haley can say nothing to that. Love, he believes, ought to bring improvement to one's character. Thinking about the wondergirl Zan makes his head run cleaner. A rippling stream that head is. On this love business, he'd like to confer with the Yapochee, ask how they behold the matter.

Too bad, now he can barely remember who the Yapochee are.

Was one of them little Zan Yapochee? Something sweet and sentimental like that. How he views his friend Anton: loads of sentiment. Empathize with the frivolity, no less than the ache. *Be* them.

The Yapochee are in a predicament of some kind. He remembers that. They are vanishing from the earth.

---

Dear girl. Your name Zan? You are hurt? Teeth chatter. Hands blue. Why you out here? In dark. This freeze. Put blanket over. Why so unhappy? I walk you home. Which house yours? Don't cry.

*Elderly Portuguese man walking Zan home.*

Nothing to say to that. Tallis is in a deep sleep. He does not hear his mother at the bedside, complaining about confounded rare book dealers. About a book she did not, *did not!* — leave out in snow and rain. For squirrels and raccoons to chew apart. Something about a note finding its way into a sewing kit. Nor does he hear Ryabovitch still mouthing off.

Ryabovitch's difficulty with the lady with the lapdog has as cause a robust passion infused with a strong dose of jealousy. The banker who stole her heart in Yalta has tracked her down. *To such a distant city you fled? Immigration to Canada! What time and expense I've endured, tracking you!* True, in Yalta he'd taken advantage of her. Just another pretty woman to be trifled with. Dalliance without meaning or significance. Bed her and forget her —such was the tune! Ah. How stupid. Love's volcano erupts. *I plead, I beg for love's mercy. I grovel at the feet of powerful love. I can't go on, I must go on. My children are grown, my wife dead. Society indifferent. Marry me.*

'I might,' replies Anna. 'I might very well should. Yours are the words for decades I prayed to hear.'

*Stop babbling. Say yes.*

'Too late. There's another man in the picture, you see. An officer gentleman named Ryabovitch.'

Gurov can't refrain from thinking the obscene: *Ah! Still the pathetic slut she was in Yalta.*

Does he say this to her face? No. Shame silences him. Love rebukes him. Chekhov, so many eons ago, doomed him.

———————

Daisy Haley has this minute found herself inside a romance novel by Sheila Shott. Sheila is a friend. Friends have obligations to each other. She will dip. *Nights Beneath the Elm* this one is. Is Sheila borrowing from Eugene O'Neill? O'Neill, Daisy dimly recollects, was not a happy father. He did not sire children happy with him, daughter Oona perhaps most spectacularly. Lovely Oona briefly went out with young J. D. Salinger. Heavens to Betsy, was there a clashing of personalities on the dates? In her teens she marries the most famous man in the world, Mr Chaplin. Decades her senior. Gives him eight children, some to achieve acclaim. All I remember of the alcoholic playwright and his tribe. *The Iceman Cometh* my personal favourite, should you want to

know. I could waltz into an *Iceman* production, this minute, playing to perfection the role of Hugo Kalmar since he's blind drunk or passed out almost the whole of the play. Fantastic, the lives many people live.

She dips.


The heroine, Rebecca Whitehall, was panting hard. The hand of Prince Mansfed of Morocco was inside her bodice, caressing her breasts. His groin pressed hers. Rebecca Whitehall was hanging on for dear life. Her breathing came hard and fast. She was in a tizzy. How—*when!*—had his hand got there? Her mind was spinning, and she could not stand up. Fortunately, this was not a necessity. Prince Mansfed was kissing her, his tongue looping inside her mouth, the loops igniting sparks inside her brain. Somehow, he had got her to the bed, or she had got him there, and she felt a surge of gratitude. It would have been so embarrassing, such a strike against womanhood—*a slur on woman's divine nature* (yipes! Sheila—or Rebecca—has read Marguerite Duras?)— had she slumped to the floor in a wild faint. It was in her mind to tell him, 'Do it,' although this would have been silly, for wasn't he already?—well, no, he wasn't, as it happened. He was drawing back; he was rearranging his clothing. Prince Mansfed, noble man, had come to his senses. He was, after all, a prince. 'We may not, my darling. My troth is to Seymour, as you know. I cannot imagine what wild horses came over me. You are so breathtakingly beautiful. Yes, that is the explanation. Your beauty unravels me. My very spleen is at shudder.'

It was at this moment that Daisy flipped forward a page. Flipped back. Closed her eyes. Did her best to step into Sheila Shott's revelatory book. She, Daisy, was on the bed. Rumpled, kissed all but to the death, Armani skirt up over her hips, legs open. Panting and flushed, pumps kicked to the carpet. Champagne bottle on its side, dribbling, dribbling.

No hope.

Well. Not truly. Her foot had cramped.

She flipped forward again. Rebecca Whitehall watched the prince fit the scarlet cummerbund back around his waist, stoop to give a quick polish to his shoes—with her curtain!—her curtains! The beast! How atrocious. This prince fellow was cleaning very black shoes with the lacy white window curtain. What luck that she had escaped the clutches of this abysmal, shallow creature!

How far she had fallen since Turner P. Blindstone had forsaken her to tend a failing sister's ten-thousand-acre Kenyan coffee plantation said once to have been the property of Nobel Prize contender Karen Blixen.

'So beautiful,' Prince Mansfed said at the door. 'Of course, we shall say nothing of this. We shall not let it cross our minds. Incomparable though you are, inspiring though you be, my faithful heart belongs to Seymour.'

Who in heaven's name is Seymour? Daisy dared ask. Would Seymour, man or woman, ever show up in the book? Daisy had doubts. Had Sheila extracted the name Seymour from Mr Salinger? Likely not.

Rebecca Whitehall leaps—in the flesh, just *leaps!*—from the page. Which so startles Daisy she drops the book. 'How do you do that?' she wants to know. 'Almost gave me a heart attack!'

'That prince almost gave me one,' Rebecca says. She's furious. 'Fucking Sheila just threw me at him. All this crap she puts in my mouth, I don't know whether I'm coming or going. Don't you have a bottle of something we can drink? The book heats up later. I go to Kenya, help Turner save the estate, we make love during a hurricane, and through harrowing torment triumph. Sheila truly knows how to give the reader goosebumps.'

Daisy stays on inside Sheila Shott's book. Rebecca Whitehall rises from the pages now and then, joining Daisy in a drink. Daisy feels a developing kinship coming on. Rebecca, it turns out, is no one's fool. She's a thousand times smarter than anyone, including Daisy, would have thought.

'You should go easy on the lithium,' Rebecca tells her. 'Cut back on the meds. I see you clenching Xanax bottles in both hands.'

'One is empty.'

'For a while there I thought you were going to fall asleep before you got to my best scenes. Who knows what is going on inside your son's mind? Maybe something is. And maybe it is not the hell you think. Why should it be? He's a nice boy. The inquiring mind exists in sleep. Why not when comatose? No foul injury has been diagnosed in the brain. Doctors may induce comas. Surely they may therefore be self-induced. It could be that he is looking after himself. I mean, that his mind is. I am so happy I dropped in. I've been wanting to talk to you. As for those pills, I don't know about you, but I have seen entirely too much bourgeois hysteria in my day. They pick me up in the drugstore, the bookshop, and I think to myself, uh-oh, here we go again. I can't tell you the number of housewives, girls after prolonged despair, who have dropped in. All suffering the same malaise, all running from—or to—the same thing. I'm their sweet sanctuary. Meanwhile, Sheila Shott's running over the countryside in her Mercedes. She's gay as the blades, not a brain in her head. I supply all her best lines.

'I resent it, to tell you the truth. Yet she's such a pro. She can set a lovely scene. She always tells the reader what we are wearing. What we are thinking, making up our face. A line from Faulkner's, she says, Nobel speech, on the wall by her desk, where he says the heart in conflict with itself is the only thing worth writing about. Well, she certainly conflicts me. Do I wear a size-six shoe or a size-eight? She never can remember. Sometimes I've got what she calls a straight Roman nose, other times a small bump from when I was a child falling out of my high chair. That part is true. I remember falling out of my high chair. I remember because I was reaching for a banana my father was dangling over my head. He was trying to catch me and the chair and his hand smacked my nose. *Crack*, there went my one noble Roman feature. I don't recall any other childhood accidents. Sheila claims I was trampled by a pony's hooves when I was eight, but that is total fabrication. Okay, not totally, and not a real pony. It was at this fair, on a hobby-horse roundabout, when this obnoxious kid pushed me. Naturally, I had been pushing him. We both fell off. There went my last chance of retaining a good Roman nose.

'Look, Daisy. Do I have a good nose? It isn't bent, is it? Too bumpy?'

'Oh, honey, yours is a perfectly fine nose. I don't see any bumps. I'd say you have a Sophia Loren nose.'

'Thank you, thank you! My goodness! Sophia Loren.'

'You have her chest, also.'

'I do? Goodness gracious, aren't you nice! Actually, I'm quite a bit smaller than she. Such is my understanding. I love chatting with you this way. May we have more wine? …

'… Are you falling asleep on me, Daisy? Please don't. Although I've noticed people often do. I'm so mouthy, I guess. I'm so happy you approve of my nose. Sometimes I've thought I might have a small, attractive nose ripple, like, say, Julia Roberts, but you—do you think it's possible that people, when looking into a mirror, can see themselves as they truly are? I believe not. And a good thing too, as Sheila would say. I do wish she didn't have the habit of putting unimaginably uncouth words in my mouth. Granted, it seems to work. Everyone likes me. And she has given me the most incredibly divine wardrobe. I'm so refined I gleam. I tried one day to talk her into giving me a PhD in something like Theatrical Performance—I yearn to play the role of one of the prostitutes in that *Iceman* show you were talking about a while ago—but she said her fans wouldn't go for it. No, she said, I'll give you pep and personality, together with a grinding need for love. And adventure. These will serve you well, she said. And it's true: I do have this *grinding, aching, crucifying need* for love! It eats at me, the need!

'… I haven't sorted through the whole issue yet. That aside, now my entire motivation is simply to prove myself in a man's world. Love, sex and capital gains. I can all but smell the yacht scene; in the Caribbean, in my bikini, where I charm the daylights out of everyone. I just wish Sheila would let me talk deep philosophy occasionally. I do have a bachelor's degree in the stuff, you know. I had Jungian interests, in my teens. I won a national competition in higher mathematics, though Sheila won't tell you this. Or she won it. Sometimes I get confused about what is mine and what is hers. Given that it's this love business that activates her plots. These pricks she shoves into my life, until I can inveigle the one killer guy who will set my heart reeling. Turner P. Blindstone, I'm afraid. Truth is, sometimes I can't wait. To find out what Sheila has planned for me. Like it's just like real life, you see, and what does the future hold? I get caught up in the stuff. In the meantime, that Turner, though, he is such an everlasting eternal prick. Sheila is perfectly aware he's not my type. That I loathe his guts and want to throw up when he touches me. Still, she insists on putting me through my paces. I've got to fail, you see, before I succeed. Otherwise, my success doesn't mean anything. Plus, he's right-wing as a one-legged rooster. Sheila's done research. After thrillers, romance is the top seller. About three sold, worldwide, every second. Median buyer age, forty, and falling. Mostly what I feel are perfumed, bejewelled hands picking me up. Sweaty, putting me down. One, or two at most, torrid sex scenes are sufficient, in her view. I can handle that. She's so far held off having Turner suck my toes. We are off to the Caribbean in the next book. It might happen there. I keep asking which foot. But she goes mum.'

Daisy hears Rebecca Whitehall saying: 'I could help you find the lost *Finnegans*. One thing I've learned from Sheila is that we all have powers not plumbed. I'm not just a pretty girl. I have unemployed mental assets. I require a higher-class citizenry than the international set accords me. Do you find I too often speak of myself? Often in glowing terms? A shade narcissistic, do you think? It's because I'm lonely. But you don't need to keep reminding us you are a literary scholar involved in the writing life, possessing knowledge of the less-than-glamorous details of every known writer since Cro-Magnon Man first shook a stick. I could name names also, modesty preventing this. For your information, I may drop in and join Mr O'Neill in a drink anytime I wish. Those attractive book gentlemen interest me. I wink at them when passing, only to be rewarded by a show of studied indifference. They possibly believe I can't read. That Ormsby chap likes me. Boozy men do.'

Dark night, the weather atrocious, snow biting his face, Ormsby moves cautiously along the Major Street alley. He's toked up with confederates; while it lasted the rum was heaven. Somewhere in one pocket or another is the heaven-sent key. He'd prefer not to go to his death tonight. The day hasn't been kind to him. The cops have confiscated his mattress. Five dollars at Salvation Army, not too potholed. He was minding his own business, pushing the mattress along Bathurst in a filched wheelbarrow. Causing no one the least headache. When, on the long downhill stretch above Dupont, somewhere in there, an icy patch pounces up and socks him in the jaw. There goes the runaway mattress and wheelbarrow hurtling along, car tires screeching, horns blasting away. The wheelbarrow flips, the mattress goes airborne. And wouldn't you know it, always in the wrong place at the wrong time, along comes Johnnie Law. Wasn't Ormsby lucky, though? Never let it be said, excusing the Nixon time, luck doesn't come Ormsby's way. Because right there next to him is scrubland, a handsome wooded area. A bitch to climb, dead branches hiding under snow to snare a running man's feet. But that's good too. No way those cops are going to dirty the uniform, chasing him. The cops have got a busy thoroughfare to clear. They've got a mattress and wheelbarrow to deal with, traffic to get roaring along, somebody else to throw in jail.

He has the key in hand. His pockets have holes but thanks to foresight the key is safely looped to a belt. A man can't get anywhere without foresight, he can thank Dook for teaching him that. Yes, excusing Nixon's presence on the scene, he can lay no blame on Dook for what's happened to him. Duke U, for the feeble-minded. Trouble is now the cold has frozen his eyes. Fingers won't bend. A shoe, he now notices, was lost somewhere in scrubland up beyond Dupont. But worse is he can't figure which is the Haley garage. Month ago, the boy, giving him the key, said look for a small blue catty-corner type door hanging by one hinge, you can't miss it. But maybe he has. Wait, here 'tis. The lock frozen. Will the key go in? No. Well, blow on it, fool.

He's inside. Hundred degrees warmer in here.

Look! Bedding. A plug-in heater.

There you go. Soon be the South Pole.

Food, though a good many weeks past prime.

Car taking up space, but you can't say cramped.

All missing, a spot of rum to christen the new residence.

What's in that bag?

Whoops! Behold!

No flies on that Haley boy.

Pity about that girl Zan. A walking ruin. Must straighten people out on that accident.

In late November, on the seventh day of her daughter's comate status at what her mother, Laura, called the Hospital for Wounded Angels—after an artist's book discovered lying open on the girl's desk at home—on this day at the Hospital for Wounded Angels, it bathed in deathly silence, long empty corridors under wash of strong light, nursing stations dimmed, here and there the soft *whish* of a closing door, the rumble of a distant elevator, the muted ring of phones—on this day Zan, last seen in the future hiding under, spying from, a bush—on this incredible day, Zan batted open her lovely eyes. 'I smell oranges,' she said. And all at once, in the view of her mother, sitting there half-asleep, a five-year-old copy of *People* magazine forgotten on her lap, pursuing a haze of dream that carried her all the way back to her own unafflicted happy childhood, and mixing with this upsetting, unsummoned dream a plethora of mind-numbing irritations at her absent, wilfully unpredictable, maddening husband, Chig—all at once, to Laura, seated in sad half-doze beside her only child…

… all at once the ceiling lifted, the skies rained a blaze of radiant light, music erupted from the very walls, tubas blared, the drooping poinsettia on the windowsill shot up ten feet high, racing footsteps came and went, and a thousand cheers echoed throughout the Hospital for Wounded Angels. Laura bolted in shocked disbelief, exaltation, wonderment, from her hard-board chair, all at once the veil lifted and the mean, ugly world vanished even as a new one formed before Laura the mother's eyes. Suddenly, magnificently, all was right again.

The lovely eyes opened once. Next, an exhausting passage of time to be endured. The halls again retreated into silence, doors *whished* open and shut as if in one's dream. Ringing phones were so muted the sound was unheard, deathly shadows danced upon the shining floors.

Whence, the lovely eyes opened a second time.

'I smell oranges,' the girl named Zan, sometimes calling herself X, maniacal cyclist, renowned individualist, a stubborn reed, Free School's *difficult customer*, Major Street's *problem child*, a parent's nightmare, Zan the String Bean, through dry lips, haltingly said.

I smell oranges. Why are you looking at me like that? What have you done to my room?

How many hours, days ago, was it in advance of this declaration, that the tired father, too weary, too unsettled—wrung out!— to make the cafeteria journey, had sat in the chair the mother this moment occupies—had sat there messily peeling then eating an orange.

'Days ago. But you, my darling, you smell his orange.'

A doctor is running. Nurses are piling in. A miracle has occurred. The unconscious girl is awake. Tragedy is avoided. This was not portended. The patient seems deeply irritated by the activity around her bed. She wants to know why this foul gown encloses her flesh. Why is she hooked to all these gadgets?

This is not your room, my darling. You are in the Hospital for Wounded Angels. My own angel!

The day Zan revived fell on Sheila Shott's birthday. None but one in the Hospital for Wounded Angels—the staff now employed that nomenclature— had known the day was Sheila Shott's birthday. Or even who Sheila Shott was. A friendly, gabby, radiantly attractive nurse named Nancy Cee had stressed the fact. Nancy pointed out that fabulous events of this kind often transpired in Sheila's many books. Nancy was amazed none had heard of the fabulously beautiful authoress, winner of multiple Nubile Awards from the Chapters bookstore chain. Her character Turner P. Blindstone was more famous than Moby Dick. And tempestuous Rebecca Whitehall was a whiz ball.

Nancy had loads of Sheila Shotts in the locker here, should anyone be in the market for a loan.

---

Emmitt encountered Dr Ying while canvassing the menu board outside the Bloor corner's Chicken On The Run.

You eat here? the doctor asked.

Not often.

While ago, wasn't this place Chicken-A-Go-Go?

Bustling city. Who can keep up?

Everything copacetic on the home front?

Knee-deep in morass.

Daisy ever find the Portobello *Finnegans*?

Not yet.

Your floorboards remain intact? Rare breed, rare-book dealers. Never knew Daisy was a *Finnegans* devotee? Thought she was in the feminists' kaboodle. Oldies. *Middlemarch, Pride and Prejudice*. Henry James. That lot. *Heart of Darkness*. That lot. *Handmaid's Tale*. Read Daisy's *Globe* take, rushed out to Book City to buy it. Wife did, I mean. Read it, wouldn't talk to me for three days. Me, I'm a non-fiction enthusiast. Bit of Sheila Shott on the sly. That woman can *write!*


By Robarts Library, Emmitt is greeted by another professor acquaintance. In philosophy, Emmitt thinks. He's a scruffy elderly man, on the eve of retirement, scattering bread crumbs to a flock of pigeons.

'So, how's our popsy?' the professor asked.

'Pardon?'

'The good woman. How is she?'

'Daisy plugs along. It is our son who is bedridden.'

'You don't say! Lots of nasty germs floating about. Had a sniffle myself only—'

'He is unconscious. Comatose.'

'Oh, is he, is he, well, my word. That's rather going to extremes, isn't it? My goodness, what next?'

'Pardon?'

'Oh, I see. I see, yes. I do see what you mean. Heidegger's influence, I would think.'

'Pardon? Heidegger?'

'Umm. Yes, Heidegger's influence shades most things. A very long shadow, *Sein und Zeit*, I'd venture to guess. In your wife's case. Time and being. Forgetfulness of being, most certainly, although Heidegger argues the condition exists at a mass level. The People, you see. Foremost crisis of civilization, he maintained. Would you go that far? Me, I sneeze up to it. No closer than that, in my case. But your wife has jumped in fully clothed, has she? How daring of her. Taking Heidegger by the horns, is that a fair surmise? Sums up her position, you'd say?'

'Sir?'

'He is! He is! How extraordinary. Jumped right in with her, did he? Amazing. Still, I have heard he was a bright boy. Dallas? That his name?'

'Tallis. Yes.'

'Of course, we have a bit of the Hegelian entering this scenario as well. His foot into most matters, as I adduce the issue. Thesis generating antithesis to create synthesis, no mean thing that, as it gives rise to the new triad. Oh, it's all very Hegelian, difficult waters, and I'm not surprised Daisy would lose herself. Flounder a bit. But the boy, too, you say? Both in a coma? How extraordinary indeed! Or 'fantastic' as my wife said last night of that movie we saw at the Bloor Cinema. *Not a Day Remains*? Something like that. Strongly recommended! Strongly! Daisy will love it! The boy, too, take my word. Come for supper sometime, bring the pair. Be a pleasure to pursue the subject. Tonight? You think tonight?'

Professor Riegle, philosophy department chair, is still pumping Emmitt's hand. The old man seems lonely, seems not to want to quit Emmitt's company, or take leave of Heidegger, Hegel and other giants residing within him.

'Your class, sir?'

'What's that? You are in my class? How perfectly amazing.'

'No. I'm asking if you don't have to get off to your class, sir?'

The professor swats a hand against his brow. Black spectacles dislodge and clatter to earth.

'My word! Yes. A half hour ago. Do you imagine they've waited?'

'I expect so, sir.'

Emmitt meant it. Riegle was up there with Northrop Frye.

A final pumping of hands. Glasses secured. Tuck of briefcase under the arm.

'Give the young scholars my encouragement. Funny, and here I had been thinking zoology, botany, horticulture, the sciences were Daisy's baili-wick. Not that *Finnegans* chap. Hard-rowing, the *Finnegans* chap. In the rain, I'm told. Pettifogger edition, they say. Stomped on it, I hear. Pulped *Finnegans* in the Cuisinart. Valuable, my word. Not to worry, those book people will sort it out. But it's Heidegger, you're telling me? Not the Irishman. Good. One could do worse. Poor fellow never got over not getting an invite to the French congress. Turned Nazi as a result. Turned out every Jew on the faculty. Fine university. Top dogs. Sent Husserl, father of phenomenology, his mentor—every Jew—global saints—scurrying. The rector, you see. Hannah? You know Hannah? Arendt. That Hannah. Loyal, I'll say. Never got over him. Recall the night I had dinner with her. First love, she said. Powerful influence, the first love. Forgive anything. Banal, yes. Prisoner of love. Shackled. So she said. To my face. Rather adamant. My wife in shivers beside me. Fingers digging. Into my thighs. Nails like razor blades. Dear Riegle, Hannah said. Pleading. "What else may I have done? No exit. Anguish. All our friends betrayed. What do I, Jew beloved of virulent Nazi, tell Nuremburg?" Judges. The trial. Everlasting trial. Important decisions warranted. History watching. Hannah's tears pouring. Wife's nails pinching. "Tell Hannah what to propose." My wife saying that to me. Good. I can do it. "Stop his teaching," said I. To Hannah. Such sobbing. "Five-year sabbatical," said I. "Send the brute home." Havoc in the dining room. Fine evening, even thus. The best. Adieu, then. Sorry, what was your name?'

Emmitt.

'Emmitt! Yes, Emmitt! Emmitt and Daisy! A good ring, that!'


It often confounds Emmitt to appear in these halls and have the huge canvas of Daisy's knowledge spread before his amazed eyes and lolling tongue. He will come upon her within an assembly of colleagues, shooting her mouth off on any variety of subjects he would have wagered she knew nothing about. Economics, pathology, history, the new physics, space technology, astronomy, art, politics, sports, the affairs of industry and government, global warming, the lifestyle of the Aztecs, the Inuit, the Gozanza tribe of Borneo. In discussion of more esoteric subjects, such as bone-throwing practices in medieval northern Europe, the design, course and consequence of phantom ships sailing off the Cape of Good Hope, Africa; the Erinyes of Greek mythology, flood levels in Venice, funeral customs of the Jinju people in New Guinea in contrast to that of the Hutee, the Weejee, the Howsaus of what is now southern Belgium.

All completely elusive to his repertoire and never once referred to in his presence. Similarly so with items and individuals peculiar to popular culture: rock stars, movie stars, bungee jumpers, new dance crazes, TV personalities, radio talk show hosts, marital practices in eastern provinces—any potpourri of trenchant trinkets.

These colleagues hanging on to her every pronouncement, waiting, sometimes not very politely, to cut in. He, too, at such times, shuffling his feet as he waited, to slide a word in edgewise.

—Honey? Were we to have lunch?

It grates on him that with all this she's so much low-woman-on-the-totem here at her own college. Used and abused and so often—like so many others— hung up to dry. Impossible teaching load, frightfully inept committees, endless academic absorptions designed to keep the wheels turning. Well. Until the Tallis accident, when she suddenly stopped showing up.

Emmitt stands well to the back of the elevator, head down. Students, faculty, arrive and depart in hordes, jostling him, stepping on his toes, briefcases swatting his knees. The ancient machine rumbles, hisses, hiccups, ascends with spurts and groans.

He alights, and all but runs down the empty hall, wanting to escape visibility, ensconce himself behind the protection of Daisy's office door. This negotiating the public domain is killing him: the endless greetings, explanations, mock and/or felt sympathy one must endure.

He makes it into Daisy's office, a broom closet affair, and slumps in relief, sweating, against the door. No bullets in the chest this time, thank God. He staggers, collapses into Daisy's desk chair. Books, papers, files, umbrellas, countless departmental memos, computer disks. Shoes, scarves, handbags, together with scads of paper clips, pens, pencils, computerized grade cards, postcards, letters (many, it seems, still sealed), makeup utensils, snack cartons, foam cups containing congealed liquids. The debris surrounds his feet, all but ascends to his knees, his elbows. How can she work among this chaos? A dead potted plant tilts onto the computer keyboard. The window a sheet of grime. The chair he sits in is wedged within its spot; he can't lean back without striking his head on filing cabinets, on bookcases spilling over with texts, reports, dying plants. Laundry. There is his best shirt in a plastic bag. Pinned to the one free wall; pinned to the door-back, ageing doodles Tallis created when a child. And she claims a kinship with order. Proof of distress.

The boy grins at him from a cracked frame on the window ledge.

Cobwebs grab at his face each time he moves.

*'A good omen, gentlemen!' cried a young officer. 'Our setter runs in advance. There is game ahead.'*

His eyes slide with the type, land elsewhere.

*'You are too many to introduce singly, gentlemen!' said the general loudly, with affected joviality. 'Make one another's acquaintance, please—without formalities!'*

Emmitt snorts, flips a page. Why is he wasting time when he has errands to run, matters to see about. One of these days he must at least make a stab at his own work, or fool everyone into thinking he means to. Any second of any day impulse demands he halt whatever he's doing: race home, race into his son's room, look his son in the face. He is always having these twin feelings, this anxiety that ever fluctuates between wild joy and intense fear: the boy is no longer breathing, you must race home. The boy has emerged from his coma, hurry. Visions swing with the ease of a clock's pendulum.

He's dead: that one always knocks him flat.

Pneumonia, encephalitis, Grob syndrome, needle poisoning, contaminated fluids, chronic vibricocis. Endless, the evils waiting to pounce.

Surely in all this rubbish of Daisy's there is something on which he can blow his nose. Dry his eyes.

Here, under the scuffed blotter, Daisy in list-making mode:

*wash hair*
*dry cleaners w/ slinky dress*
*confirm meet w/ Lin. & Mike, Dionne, George and Martha*
*John & Rosie arr. Wed.*
*stop off at bake*
*ask Em stitch hem*

And these urgent notices wherever he looks: *We sympathize with your current sorrows and regret your absence. We must request, however, that you immediately vacate your office of all personal effects.*

Screw that. Not today.

Exit Emmitt, slamming the door.

Takes a few long strides. Halts. He's steaming. Bless my hide: his old haunt, the Grad Students' Pub. Not today, he thinks. Today I'm being good.


Arriving home, who does Emmitt find sitting alone at the kitchen table but Miss Ten Ants. Her long coat loops a chair. One hand straddles a teacup; the other holds a cookie at her mouth. Emmitt watches her small teeth nibble. Watches her scratch: the cookie, the knees, the top of her head. The teakettle whistles on the stove. 'Daisy is upstairs with the bed-ridden,' Miss Ten Ants explains. 'Refuses to come down. Raised her voice at me. Some people simply do not know how to behave.'

'Why are you here?'

'Your back door was unlocked. Dilatory of you, I must say. A thief or a murderer could have strode in. By the way, I've used your last tea bag. Time to restock.'

A tread is heard on the back steps. Ormsby's shape looms. His knuckles rattle the glass. Where did he come from? Why is he here? Ormsby bashfully exhibits a tin cup. He wants change? He's the kind neighbour begging a cup of sugar?

Miss Ten Ants has leapt from her chair. 'That man frightens me,' she asserts. 'Some people ought to be put away.'

Emmitt withdraws, shaking his head. He leaves the house to its dementia. It is either that or remain and assault the pair with the vigour of a psychopath. Daisy's addled. She must contend with the chaos as best a doped-up wife can.

A few minutes later he is shambling along Spadina, by the university gym, muttering intemperately to himself, his planned good intentions reduced to rubble. 'Explicate, repudiate, behind the eight ball … no way out, the end begins.' Such is the nonsense escaping his lips.

'Pardon, sir!'

He has grabbed the arm of a neat young man attempting to pass.

'You are a student in this universe of the damned? What is your name?'

'Seong, sir. How may I assist?'

'I seek a haunt of ancient familiarity. Known in my day as the GS Pub. It does not appear to be where it was ten minutes ago.'

This Seong gives Emmitt a chastising look. He does not himself drink. He's too often, among classmates, witnessed the result. This dishevelled gentleman in assault of him he's seen before, though he can't recall where.

'Where is it?'

'There, sir.'

'There, where?'

'There.'

'There?'

'Yes, there.'

'That's a parking lot.'

'See the door?'

'Where?'

'There.'

———————

Hours pass. A blue moon rises.

———————

Comin' up!

Comin' up!

Oh Lord,

Oh Lord,

I'm comin' up!

Comin' up!

For air!

Help! Help! Some drunk on our street is singing in the rain!

## ITEM ON THE EIGHT O'CLOCK NEWS CIUT-FM 89.5 ON YOUR RADIO DIAL

Residents of a multi-block area near the university were alarmed this hour when a voice was repeatedly heard calling for assistance. It seems an older gentleman, raucously singing and much under the influence of strong drink, could not find his way home. 'One thing for sure,' a local said, 'the man ain't Gene Kelly. He can't sing.'

———————

Would you like your lips moistened, Tallis? I have this new dry stuff said to clean hair. May I? Your father came home drunk, singing an insipid song. Do you hear me, Tallis? I know you do. You're not fooling me.

———————

The day the hospital was letting Zan go home, Chig was bowled over when Nancy Cee, swinging a urinal pan, inquired if he would like to join the Sheila Shott Fan Club. The fee was modest, she said, and by way of being a good deed. All the applying member had to do was show a stub from the post office, proving the applicant had dispatched a Sheila Shott romance, used or new, to an emerging African nation. Her precise words.

I'm pretty certain, he said, they'd prefer their own stuff. Bongo drums?

You're not very politically correct, are you? Nancy said.

Laura happened along. Here, push this, Laura said. Zan was wrapped in blankets, riding a wheelchair. I turn my back one second, Laura said, and there you are, flirting with another nurse.

Nancy Cee had told Chig of next week. The fan club. When that week rolled around, Chig was among the earliest arrivals and the last to depart. Certainly not again to meet up with Cee. My God, no.

He had rarely been in a room—munching on cookies, sipping on deathly wine—with so many talkative women. He liked talkative women, and most particularly, today, when they were talking about Sheila Shott. The author was to put in an appearance, but where was she?

What did it say about men that the romance field, the romance novel, romantic movies—romance in general—was perceived to be the women's gruelling niche? That was Cee's question. Grab a crotch, and be done with us?

Cee was bouncy one minute, hands-on-the-hips watchful the next. He flirted back, if that's what Nancy was doing. She was dressed in an off-the-shoulder puce-type thing. Easy on the eye, certainly. Looking quite different free of nursing attire.

'I have my car. Happy to drive you home.' Chig said that to Cee.

Such a good, thoughtful guy.

She said: 'What are you up to, Mister?' And laughed.

---

Night. And Ryabovitch is feverish. He is dreaming. Dream dream dream, Ryabovitch is dreaming. Of what is Ryabovitch dreaming?

'I was laid out. Hands laced over my chest. A mourner by the graveside was saying, "Poor Ryabovitch ... A princely fellow, was our Ryabovitch." Now I'm melancholy. I'm lost.'

'Me too. Where are we?'

'Lost.'

'Quiet!'

'I am quiet.'

'Someone came in.'

'Who.'

'I don't know.'

'I smelled alcohol.'

'That wretch, Lebozts or some such, back from the general's party.'

'Quiet.'

'I am quiet.'

'Someone is mopping my brow. Do you feel it?'

'How could I?'

———————

'Funny thing was ...' Chig was saying this—few hours ago—to the guys at the Hardware. 'Funny thing was, the minute Nancy said. "What are you up to, Mister," laughing, I laughed too, and both of us in that second knew flirting was a thing of the past and we were going to be good friends. Fact is, she's dropping by the house tonight. Wants to see how the patient is doing.'

'How is old X doing?'

'Sleeping. In resurrection mode. Getting her strength back.'

'She back on her bike yet?'

'Not yet. How much are your rotary beaters? What I come in for.'

'Rotary beaters?'

'Yeah. I was thinking I'd bake a cake.'

'You?'

———————

Chig? the man said. That's your name?

Yeah. Anything wrong with that?

The man told him his preference would be for the plural. Chigs. 'Chigs, now, that implies a deeper guy. A guy with certain layers. Depths. Yeats, for instance. Keats. You ever think of that? The plural name. You get it. You ever hear of a Charle? No, it's Charles. You get it? Charles. Like, you got the plural. Yeah, Chigs, I think. Implies the deeper realm. Oates, Otis, Adams, Jorge Luis Borges, Cat Stevens, Elvis, you take my point? You're more than one, an infinity of selves. Me, I'm Sims. I'm Sim, who would I be? No one. My advice? Change your name. How much can it cost you?'

## DAISY DEMANDS AIRTIME

'Hello, my name is Mary. I'm the maid.' I like saying that line. Although it has been a while since I've applied the Pledge. Anytime I answer the phone, I say, 'My name is Mary. I'm the maid.' I derive some pleasure from that. At times I think I'd like to be Mary, without Mary's line of work. It may very well be I have, as the saying goes, let myself go. Of the twin continents to which I have been dispatched, I prefer languor. Lassitude seems so final. I expect any day now I'll be calling in at the Port of Desuetude. From which there is no return. When Napoleon arrived on St. Helena such is how he referred to it. Tallis, I'm sure, has noticed. Not that he would ever mention it. Tallis is the tolerant member of the family. Sight of Miss Ten Ants makes me gag, but him? He can ride with it when a person has bumps on the face or bristles on the chin. On the Danforth that time a one-armed man dropped his packages, and Tallis picked them up and walked along with him. He was like a dog the way he would sniff people and follow them. After they got where they were going, Tallis shook the man's only hand, without even thinking. His father could never have done that without a show of embarrassment.

Since I've been holed up here in the house, Emmitt has been bringing home stories. Our situation is now totally reversed; before the disaster I'd ask him how his day went, and he might say all his kids at school had been little shits, though usually he'd shrug and say nothing. But he came home yesterday with a wild story about a professor friend who wants us tonight to come to dinner. We've had to pass on that invitation. I could have worn these ratty slippers I have on now, and this smelly housecoat. I suppose I could have managed to wash my face. Emmitt stopped in at the Grad Students' Pub. Obviously he had stopped in somewhere, if by 'stopped in' one understands he spent untold hours there drinking like Godzilla.

These winter sunrises, the arrivals of dawn, even though grim, give me a certain pleasure. I like how slowly the light comes. It's like when I'm watching Emmitt and I see him trying to flag down some idea. How slowly he gets it. Count to ten, to a hundred, and the dawn is still coming up, in his brain.

Emmitt comes in today, stomps his boots free of snow, shakes ice pellets from his hair, and even as he's taking off his coat he's regaling me with what he saw out in the footloose world. His cheer is so false you want to puke, but I have to admit I'm interested.

Three little girls were playing hopscotch in the snow, around the corner. A bird flew straight at a window. Melons at the Bloor SuperSave are only forty-nine cents. The Hardware laughs at a guy buying an egg beater. Some guy telling him where the Grad Students' Pub had relocated. The girls at the checkout send greetings, he says. This I do not believe. Then he pins me down, he makes me unfurl my hands, looking for capsules. He gets a washcloth and expects me to allow him to run it over my face. But no, the washcloth is for Tallis. Still, he's not done with me. He pantomimes drawing a white line over the floor. He says, 'Let me see you walk this line.' He's so intense in his manner I am wondering who he thinks he is. Men. Surely the day will come when they no longer interest us. Heaven, I say. He gets serious. Clearly, something is bugging him. 'Now,' he says, 'tell me how you came to have knowledge of bone-throwing practices in the middle ages. Tell me, goddammit. And I want to hear about Rufus the dancing dog,' he says, 'and where you learned about a dance craze called the Mukluk, and what's hot this month on *Prime Time* and when the bejesus you ever had time to study up on the dialectical practices of the Foofoo, how you have come to know so much about desalinization processes from antiquity to the present, desinence in early Egyptian stone carvings, the Ook religions of Inner and Outer Ook! All that shit! And why in living hell you left the Portobello *Finnegans* out in the rain? Out with it! How! Why!'

I can't help my reply. I look this man I love in the eye. I stand up from where I've been wallowing in misery on the couch. I plant my feet. I poke a stiff finger into his chest.

I say, 'Emmitt, you married an educated woman. An educated woman bones up. She digs. She roots the information out. She is not a weepy ignorant prig sleeping on your doorstep.'

I tell him that.

I go on poking his chest.

'I have been improving myself,' I say. 'We all could.'

———————

Emmitt Haley is smitten anew. He feels the way he felt when he fell in love for the first time. The first time, my God! Like riding in a Loop-O-Plane. Like being smacked in the noggin by a willow branch. Never mind what it's like. Daisy is back. She's waded through oceans of lithium, whatever else she swallows on the sneak. Never mind her wading. Hope dribbling away drop by drop. Bend the head and a swamp awaits. Dead leaves rustle underfoot where the bad snake slithers. Poised to strike. Never mind the snake. Daisy is back. She has the old fire, the crusader's punch. If only briefly. Briefly is good enough. He'll accept briefly. Tangle with Daisy at your own peril. Things are looking up. Daisy today, the kid tomorrow. Hot dog! Hot diggity dog!

———————

Down along Bloor's Varsity Stadium Sheila Shott hits her stride. Her heart beats faster. Her arms swing wide as a parading cavalier.

Hurry up, now. She's looking for Major. Where in hell did they put the street? She knows this neighbourhood from her old days at U of T. What heights it was she had scaled back in those days, before the beginning of time. God, to be a student now, with so many hot-dog he-men out on snowy turf pitching footballs—in T-shirts, shorts, in barely anything. There! There's the place where years ago she'd washed dishes over a Mother Hubbard sink. Fifty cents an hour, if that. Now selling, what, falafel? What in glory's name is a falafel? She needs more researchers, why should she be doing all the dirty work herself? Ah. She was zinged in now. Up there across from the Bloor SuperSave, a bunch of beggars, pranksters—spare-change guys—assembled in friendly confab. Fork over a dollar, will they purchase food or shoot up? Who knows? Why does their grunginess cause my heart to leap in fear? I know why. They bring to mind both the sorry in nature and the downtrodden—the hapless poor, the spiritless and helpless, those going nowhere and knowing it—who in wake of the misplaced word, may smack a wife, the wife smack a child. Have a fit. Listen to yourself, lady, you sound like a socialist. Sorry, lads, I'm strictly out of small change today. So I house a bias. The parental influence, possibly. Socially affirmed, that much a certainty.

But. A good place, this. Her town. Everything a little girl from the sticks ever wanted.

The rough and tumble. All right, sweet lips. Turn your butt here.

Sheila Shott strides on, wary for dog poo. Ought to be a law. Whatever gave dogs such a hot reputation?

Uh-huh.

Trouble was all over, running wild, to include her publisher. A rotten advance. Who are they kidding? Hack writers raking in the dough. Illiterates. All right, not illiterate, Socrates, for all I know. But hacks, all the same. High-prestige bums. Me with my puny little Nubile Awards.

*Cede thyself no sorrow, cede thyself no pain.*

Not the time to be thinking *From Here to* (Fucking) *Eternity.*

Wow, am I in a stew! I've stormed right past Daisy's 2 x 8. Here I am at College. Fuck's sake. Oh, my aching feet!

I'm not myself today.

———————————

Hey, Ryab?

You're talking to me?

You have Yapochee in your country? Deer-like creatures? Delicate of nature? Three legs. About so high?

Never heard of them. Why are you asking?

They're in deep trouble. Something sneaking up on them. Can't we shout a warning?

What are you going on about?

The filly has a face pretty as Zan's. I think I'm going to scream now.

———————

Daisy: Did you hear a scream?

Emmitt: Wasn't me.

Daisy: Maybe it was Sheila. She's at the front door.

———————

The cold, when a singing Chig stepped out his alley, almost knocked him down. But no, it wasn't the cold. It wasn't that bolt of frigid, scalp-numbing whistling air. Turned out it was none other than the Ormsby bum. Wild Bill, whom Chig had seen around. Gnawing on a pizza slice, forever thrusting a paper cup under his nose. Change. You got change? The Nixon nut.

Although, as it developed, today it wasn't the same old deadbeat, one-hundred-proof Ormsby, but a new incarnation altogether. Behold. A man could faint. Sighting a cleaned-up, spiffy, Bay Street–type Ormsby incarnation, and one not trying to shake him down.

Suit and tie, my gosh.

But whose suit? Hadn't he seen that suit on another guy. Going to and fro the Hardware, the drugstore. Parent of the stricken boy. That Haley guy. Looking horse-whipped these days and who can blame him?

'What gives, Ormsby? What brings you to my alley?'

'Common thoroughfare, I believe.'

'True.'

'Taken up residence. Live here now.'

'In the alley?'

'Garage. Up there.'

'Garage? Whose? You have permission?'

'None of your business whose. On the QT, please. I know you. You put five dollars in my cup a week ago. Thursday, it was. Hope I said thanks.'

'You did. You look good in the suit. Coat a little tight?'

'Tight is good. I like tight. Been meaning to talk to you.'

'To me?'

'Who else? I saw that bike thing. Fried his butt good. Hers too, I hear. Wasn't her fault. That's what I'm saying. Somebody ought to tell your girl that. It was the streaking cat. Nobody wants to run over a streaking cat. The guy in the car didn't—guy coming up behind her?—didn't manage that well. Driver brakes, car goes angular, sliding, mere millimetres from your girl. Streaking cat, speeding car, dipshit weather. Slip and slide. Bust a nut. Not her fault. Not remotely. What I'm saying. Car shoots away. Hit and run, could be. Yeah, it's tight. This suit. Nixon didn't know how to wear a suit. Couldn't do a Windsor knot. Had to have his pinched knot in the wrap. Repubs go for the little dimple. Pre-tied tie. Woolworth's tie, those days. Red tie, pinched knot. Awful fellow.'

'Nixon, the crook?'

'He's the one. Dook. Duke, to you. Bastard gets a state funeral I'll shoot myself. Did. One time.'

'Shot yourself?'

'At Dook. People out to establish the Nixon Presidential Library. Museum. In woods behind the law school. No way I'd tolerate that. You tell your X. Not her fault.'


Back home again, Chig hears a babble of voices. In the kid's room. He's had to run out for milk, how he chanced to run into Ormsby. Nancy Cee takes milk in her coffee. Nancy Cee is saying, excitedly, Who made this wonderful cake? *He* did! I can't believe a man made this! From scratch? Are you certain he did not buy this cake from Harbord Bakery? Sneak it past you?

It's his first cake, Laura says. Who is going to clean the kitchen is what I want to know.

Zan is propped up in bed. Her eyes are closed. She isn't having cake. Her memory today is cloudy. Some days it is. I was in the hospital? When? How long? Why? These are not questions she has asked of anyone. Fact is, she's had very little to say. Which is disturbing to the parental unit. Normally, you can't shut her up. When she does speak her voice is not her own. It is not a voice the parental unit recognizes. So soft they can barely hear. Sorry, darling. What did you say?

The party has left the girl's room. They now stand in the hallway. Chig is helping Nancy Cee get into her coat. It's a monstrous coat, narrow sleeved. She must get into her boots also. Narrow-toed. For this, she would like to sit. There is no chair in the vicinity. She must therefore employ Laura's shoulder as a brace. The two are exactly the same height. Not a splinter's difference. Their eyes share the identical deep colour so mesmerizing to any viewer. Identical skin tone. Hair style the same. Same high cheeks. Chig does not know why he finds these details tantalizingly remarkable.

All eyes jump about. Nancy Cee has asked, Where did I deposit my cake? I am not leaving without my cake. She means the take-away gifted cake in the bagged box by the door.

You have received entirely too much praise for that cake, Laura tells him once the visitor has gone. Once he returns from escorting Miss Cee halfway up the block. I hope this does not mean you'll be impossible to live with through the coming weeks.

I've heard TV cooking shows have got big. I may audition.

You're smitten.

Am not. The beautiful form compels admiration.

You watch yourself, Jack.


Nancy Cee carries away with her an important secret. She and scores of others at the Hospital for Wounded Angels have signed a non-disclosure agreement specifically related to the girl just visited. In the hospital the girl is now spoken of, always in hushed tones, as The Patient Who Disappeared. Unknown is how this happened. The time she is known to have occupied this status is estimated to have been eleven hours. Shortly after 7 a.m. on a Tuesday morning, an apprentice nurse noticed the girl's bed was empty. Out of curiosity, she took this news to a superior to whom she asked two innocent questions: What happened to the girl in 814? She didn't die, did she?

What are you talking about?

Minutes later the superior saw with her own eyes the empty bed.

No one tells me anything, was her response. How can I be expected to run this ship? Am I surrounded by dunderheads?

She assumed the girl had been removed to another unit for tests of one kind or another. Such was the usual practice. At times she would be made aware, or make herself aware, of the details. If not, it was no big deal. Patients were a small cog in a big wheel, the wheel endlessly turning,

In early afternoon a tired, hurrying Dr Ying opened the 814 door. For several seconds he studied the patient's chart, only observing the oddity of the bed's emptiness when he glanced up. Where is Zan? he asked. It was at this juncture that the Hospital for Wounded Angels became concerned that one of their newest angels had disappeared.

During the day a number of employees, visitors, the odd dignitary, had observed the appearance of the body on a gurney shoved against the eighth-floor corridor wall. To witness a gurney along the corridor was not unheard of. One thoughtful nurse did think to herself, surely that person is cold. She returned seconds later with warm blankets. This marked Nancy Cee's first sighting of the girl. She was busy, gave the matter little importance, and a moment later had forgotten it.

Over the course of hours, by one means or another, the gurney's position altered. Staff, pausing to chat, exchange information, pass the time of day, gave the gurney a small push, thoughtlessly moved it a few feet along. The gurney, and the figure upon it, ended up close by the elevator. Here it received even less attention. It was assumed the patient was being directed to another floor, the movers had been charged with a more urgent assignment, very soon someone would direct the patient to the designated chamber.

Thus did the girl reside by the elevator through the hours. Until at last someone thought to look at the ID band encircling the purple wrist, and connect the name seen there to that of the missing angel.

Eleven hours. Unforgivable. What peculiar explanation, outright lies, must have droned into the ears of the hovering parents.

Dr Ying's deep concern was over what had transpired to get his Zan off her own bed onto another. He could not concede that an alien force, by which he meant a second party, had conducted this treason. The most logical explanation, was that the girl had surfaced. She regained consciousness, got up from the bed, left the room. She found this extremely tiring. Another bed was seen. Likely she perceived no difference between it and the one just left. Or knew whereof she stood. She climbed onto the new bed, and fell again unconscious.

Do you honestly think so?

Nothing else makes any sense.

Walked a few feet, you say. Of her own free will.

I couldn't claim free will had much to do with it. Will, perhaps. Free? No.

She did it herself. We are not culpable.

She was on a gurney thirty feet removed from her room through eleven hours. We are not culpable?

Some blamed Nurse Cee. Nurse Cee comes along, sees a young girl with legs exposed, hustles away to get a warm blanket.

They laughed about it, but some thought that.

One way or another us nurses will catch the blame. Why not we say an orderly did it?

Not us. Blame it on the cleaning crew.

Since when did we have a cleaning crew?

No jokes. Please.


Wild Bill Ormsby, in from the cold, will not let the Hardware people go. He is, he tells a gathering crowd, in the grips of, experiencing the bounty of, a gloriously fantastic personal transformation. He isn't the same person anymore. He's born-again—born-again, thank you—though hardly in that sappy, constricted, one-eyed, bigoted, delirious way of your usual run-of-the-mill nuthouse religious fanatic. No, he's seen the light.

A water puddle forms around his boots. He's been yammering away for some while; he's spaced out on the New Life that has so surprisingly come his way. He is without regard for the flow of Hardware shoppers trying to edge around him; he's oblivious of the happy Hardware staff yelling polite insults at him. He doesn't every day come. They were falling asleep before he came in.

How many times must you tell a customer where to find the nails, where the paintbrushes are? Today he's welcome.

He might (Wild Bill is saying) take up the law again, can he reclaim his licence, can he obtain a favourable rendering from the association. Scrum with that toasty bunch, he says. Those sapheads. The Law Society, the legal watchdogs whose job it is to police the ethics of his excruciatingly immoral tribe. But why not? Why not go into the thing thinking success? The Board is sure to see he's a different man now. Notice, he tells his audience, the shave. Notice the new Reeboks pinched an hour ago off the rack. Down there. Honest Ed's. No trouble at all. First criminal act of my career, and appropriate, I think, that I do it just as I'm making re-entry into the noble profession. No question, I'm done with old ways. All that persecution crap. I was sick, see, but now am well. Take up thy bed and walk. It is like that. Although someone ought to re-write that bull, because, like in the modern world, global interchange, Saddam invading Kuwait, the Berlin Wall coming down, Mandela set free, it ought to have occurred to someone that in today's modern climate the homeless have got no goddamn bed. That advice has gone by the boards and is offensive to a thinking person's ears. So I'm still running on some of my old juices, you see. Certain beliefs, like the brotherhood of man and woman, I am not about to renounce. But my more extreme obsessions, I have shed. Zip! Gone! One, no more Nixon bashing. Man was a crook, couldn't tie a decent knot, greasy hair, a wife wouldn't talk to him. Steal your very toothbrush. Harangued us about evil China throughout his life, then gets credit from Repub chiefs for opening the China door. Not so you'll hear me expounding those truths anymore. I don't mean to downgrade the terrible impact those hours with Nixon had on my life. Root of all my troubles, you want to know. No Nixon those sunny southern afternoons under Dook's Gothic bells—Duke, you know, the fabu-lous U—Blue Devils, indeed—I never would have sunk to vile drink, run out on the loving family, lost my internship with the moral majority.

You don't mind me saying to some of you, your widget eyes inform me you got a little problem developing yourself. In that regard. Avoid drink. Drink, and the demon's tongue licks, licks at you. Calls you sweetheart in the soft voice of a lover.

Now you'll excuse me, I got to make a house call.

Where you going, Ormsby?

Going to commune with the Haley boy. Got to know is he coma-struck or pulling my leg.


About the same time Ormsby was alighting from the Hardware the phone was ringing at 2 x 8 Major. Daisy, nearby, belting her gown, answered.

'Mary the maid,' Daisy said.

She heard Sheila Shott saying, Since ages ago I been on my way to visit you, but I got sidetracked by East Asian spices in Kensington Market, where my shoes by mere chance happened to land. Then by a friend of yours, Mrs Tennants.

Miss Ten Ants, Daisy said. Ten Ants is no friend of mine.

Sheila was not listening.

Yes. Turns out Mrs Tennants, charming woman, is a great fan of my work. I dropped in to sign a few books, and we've now enjoyed endless teas together. Mrs Tennants has proposed we both drop in on you. Is Emmitt home? It appears an enmity exists between the two.

We do not willingly allow that woman into our home. No sensible person does.

Goodness, aren't you querulous today! Very well. I shall arrive *in my solitude*, as they say.

———————

An odd sort of hush hovers over Major Street. It is a golden sunny-bright day of melting snow and soft wind. The air, what Daisy can surmise of it through the grime of the front window, has the look of spring. A bit brazen of spring, she thinks, to so falsely announce its arrival. In Victoria they'd be sprucing up the city in celebration of Flower Day. Among the rank of parked cars, she sights their ancient Mini, windshield heralding a brace of ... flyers, not tickets, she hopes. Now why on earth is the Mini parked out there, rather than in the garage?

In the spring, if shoes can be found, she means to go through the door. To venture out. If only for a minute. If only in remembrance of better times. She's got a bead on black tumbledown vines, a lone hedge smitten by winter, treasured perennials wrecked by you-know-who. A dog over there is looking at her.

Here comes Sheila, layered under a fussy hat, a short, ridiculous Siberian coat. Clattering brightly along on heels higher than Daisy's arms are long. Give the woman credit: she's a lengthy stick of dynamite. Looks fresh from the hairdresser. Fritzed today like my heroine author Colette. What that dear French woman put up with from that plague-of-a-husband, Willy, does not bear contemplation. Oh, the horrors a good woman must suffer.

Ten Ants? No Miss Ten Ants, thank God.

That woman! Sheila exclaims, whooshing inside. Your friend Mrs Tennants suffers Delayed Brain Syndrome. I feared I'd never find release from her endless chatter, her unnerving smile, the rock-hard cookies she insists one eat. Here, she sends you a bag. Drop that bag on your foot, it's goodbye toes. Why does she scratch so incessantly? Is it catching, do you suppose? Hello, Daisy. I'd kiss you, but my lips are numb. Shall we close the door. A godawful breeze just flew past us.

True. Ryabovitch has come in by the same door. He hastily mounts the stairs.

You're looking pleased with yourself, the boy observes.

Sightseeing, the Russian replies. The red, two-decker bus. Most informative. In an idle moment, stopped at a building called the Metropolitan Library.

Have fun?

Research.

Researched what?

Your man Chekhov. Here's what Sofia Tolstoya—

Tolstoy?

—thinks of your man Chekhov's work. Erudite woman, Sofia. Quote: We have just read some Chekhov, which was very pleasant.

Dipping into your story, perhaps?

Quote: … Then read some more stories by Chekhov. I can never laugh, so I took little pleasure in them.

Perhaps that day Leo had refused her warmth. Intolerable man, Daisy decreed.

Another day. Quote: Today I painted a view of the grove and read some Chekhov—very clever, but he sneers a lot and I don't like that.

He sneers?

Quote: We tried to read some Chekhov this evening, but I find him so tedious. End quote. Tedious. I could not have said it better myself. In addition I have here further evidence: a photograph, Gaspra, Crimea, 1901. Seated, right to left, daughter Maria, Count Tolstoya, Sofia Tolstoya and your unhappy spectacled gent about to put on his hat. You will note all parties, faces solemn, have their backs to him. Conclusion: He was reading to them his new story, 'The Kiss.' All said please don't. No more, please. A verbatim, factual report. The Tolstoyas panned his work. Anna and I were in the clouds. We couldn't stop kissing.

———————

Daisy instantly feels old friend Sheila Shott's magnetic force. Lesley Stahl had similar oomph. God in heaven, women with oomph bring such joy. Most women do. Whereas, men, mostly cast in stone … Oh, let's not go there. She wants to run barefoot through busy streets, crying out, *Where went my oomph? Who dared tread on my oomph? Thief! Return me my oomph!*

Here in her charwoman duds, hair a hamster's cage, swept up by the author's gale, apology for the state of the house flows from her mouth, a duelling gale. Nowhere to sit, dust everywhere—pizza boxes, milk cartons, yellowing newspapers, nose tissues, discarded wear, books, spiders wary in spidery webs. Emmitt had fallen down on the job. Under every cushion, another hidden medical vial: Zaxan, EZSleep, pretty Nervous Nellie hallucinatory pills meant to enable the drab housewife to speed through walls. Stave off hysteria until the next time.

No oomph.

House a pig's walk.

'Never mind, darling,' says lightning-bolt Sheila Shott. 'Let us hang like bats from the ceiling, if need be.' *And that electrifying poet-brother of your husband? Have you spoken to him? Did he mention me? Oh, good! No debonair man in my life, I run short on oomph!* They clasp hands, they embrace, they talk. They set sail into near and distant kingdoms, they ride the wide sky, swooping here, thrusting there; together they are like pecking hens, introspective, inquisitive, gossipy, rapacious to their very core: a raft of material to assess, problems to unearth, experiences to detail and explore. Emblazoned on today's menu are a thousand subjects misty and divine, of and not of this earth.

Sheila Shott, too, is today riding high. What magic elixir has found its way into her system?

Horrors they've seen, horrors read about, gravy trains, the radical chic, the unradical chic, left hand/right hand thought, social debts, social indebtedness, cloning of one idea to its aberrant next. Miss Ten Ants, these filthy rugs. Sexual improprieties, the lack of opportunity thereof, food, where to eat, where not to eat in Bologna, Venice, Milan and Barcelona. The daughters of Daksha, the Erinyes of Greek mythology who splattered evildoers under guise of the betterment of humankind — 'Dear God, Sheila, you do recall, do you not, I hold a PhD and a professorship in English literature!' 'I do recall, darling, but what has this professorship to do with the Erinyes or the daughters of Daksha?' Persian food, Italian food, matrilineal predominance over patrilineal in a variety of cultures, brother-sister relationships in Persia, Ceylon, Wales. Joyce's line 'In ferial tone he addressed J. J. O'Molloy' erroneously dispatched by Daisy onto the pages of the lost *Finnegans*, fats and oils, the best sauce for barbecue, carpenters, carpet beetles, kinetic art, light houses, microelectronics, pig culture, seeing-eye dogs, un-seeing-eye dogs, applied dynamics, is there such a *thing*, frozen fish, fishing off Labrador, fishing limits, limitations in general. How sows interact, bird calls, mating calls, the crippling rigours likely to attack a ballet dancer's foot, feet, fetes, frost and frost warnings, the song 'Midnight at the Oasis', Mel Tormé's scat singer superiority over many another when it comes to the jazzy piece; family, family woes, crushing family woes—

*—and how is our Tallis, Daisy, that dear boy?*

At which point conversation ceased and in mutual panic up to his room they flew.

For a prolonged spell they sat in silent observation of the boy.

He's up to something, Daisy said. What?

I am gifted in probing the secret mind, Sheila said. But your son resists me.

He was always a secret devil. When little he pitched a fit every time I tried reading *Goodnight, Moon* to him. Doesn't every natural child love *Goodnight, Moon*? On the other hand, he was accepting of disaster stories such as 'Henny Penny', 'Three Little Pigs', 'The Big Bad Wolf', 'The Fork-Tongued Snake'. Any mob panic story.

You've done a good job on his hair. Is that rouge I see on his cheeks?

A smidgen.

It's most attractive.

He's an attractive boy. I considered freshening his lips.

Did you consider your own?

Don't start in on me. I like your Colette hair.

Who is Colette? I prophesy your son will break many a poor girl's heart.

He *will!* He *will!*

Back downstairs again, Daisy asked Sheila what her heroine Rebecca White-hall was up to these days. When last seen, on page 382 of my current opus, Sheila said—in draft, you understand—I rewrite till the cows come home—she up and quit what I had her doing—preparing scalloped potatoes—announcing to me she was going to get her nails done preparatory to a meeting at the Vatican with the Pope for a discussion about modernization of ecclesiastical policy. Rebecca Whitehall knows nothing whatsoever about ecclesiastical policy. Can you believe it? I'll grant she's good at swishing her hips but a brain-dead moron can do that. It was at her insistence I allowed her to kiss the Pope's hand. The blasphemous idiot wanted me to have the Pope, the Pope himself, slide a hand over her ass. That's how vain she is. Thinks herself irresistible! Now and then I do like to throw a wrinkle into the routine formula, but here I had to put my foot down. In the Sistine Chapel she wanted this, no less. The first time the Pope does this, she tells me, she thinks it could be an accidental brushing. But then she's admiring Leonardo's ceiling work, and the Pope does it again. Slides that hand directly onto her crotch. The Pope! Under Leonardo's masterpiece! I tell you! Rebecca's too ignorant even to know who did the Chapel. For all she knows, someone named Sistine did it. Or Picasso, the sole artist she's ever heard of. Then the little hermaphrodite gets truly bitchy. She tells me I'm always shortchanging her possibilities. If I don't move with the times, impart a bit of intelligence, lay on some significance—if I can't write better sentences, demonstrate a touch of the poetic into my narrative, she'll *muse herself out*—her imbecilic words—to a serious author. 'Who?' I said. 'What serious author have you ever heard of? "Three Little Pigs" the most your brain may digest.' Can you beat it? Just imagine. What an extraordinary backstabber she is. I truly hit the roof. 'You think it's poetic,' I said, 'for the Pope to feel you up? That's poetry!' A real slugfest, we have. My editors, they'd go nuts. They are already hinting she's an ill fit for the customary mode. She's irrepressible, they say. No sane romance reader can identify with her. It's true, too. I'm thinking I'll kill Rebecca off in the next book. I'll have Turner P. Blindstone hold a pillow over her face.

Oh, Sheila, *don't!* Daisy says. *I* identify with her. Emmitt does. I'm sure

Tallis would. She's our lifeline to a better time. She promises us hope of relief from the terrible status quo. She has *oomph*.

An avalanche in the Alps, mayhaps. She's skiing with loverboy and a whole mountain piles down on them. The stroppy twat's eyes go into mean spitballs. She knows exactly what I'm thinking. Kill me off? she says. You'd be nothing without me. You living your dull writer's existence, you're jealous of me. Confined to your desk while I'm out in the world living the heroic life, having a gay time. You're a jealous twerp! Twerp, she calls me. Her creator! Helluva thing, when characters think they are writing the book. Before you know it they'll be wanting the royalty cheques in their names.

Departing, Sheila Shott hangs in the open doorway, in mounting rage. Snow is again falling, the author taking no notice. 'I created that bitch. I can un-create her in the twinkle of an eye. That priss can prance her twat back to Rome and do what I tell her or I'll have her eating hominy grits out of a greasy bucket. I'll revise her ass into a hooker, have her snorting coke while scrubbing the floor in a flea-bag brothel. The pedestrian crone. Opens her mouth another cliché flies out. She can be content with the lofty estates in which I place her or I'll have her become a toothless hag trembling for hooch in a cardboard box under a railroad track, choking on vomit.'

*In trail and track of acrimony*
*the beating heart doth not cease:* Daisy's thought, closing the door.

Daisy goes upstairs, to find the bum Ormsby and none other than Rebecca Whitehall in chairs drawn up by her son's bed.

How did you two get in?

You were busy with your dishrag friend. Entered by the back door.

Did you hear what Sheila was saying?

I insert earplugs each time that woman speaks. Cliché City, that woman.

Is Ormsby asleep?

So that's his name? I thought it very rude of him not to tell me his name. Oh, look. Are you aware you have a bird's nest in the eaves above your back door?

It's still there?

Sort of. It's in disrepair. These tiny scraps of paper appear to have fallen out. Look.

Goodness me. These scraps look a lot like *Finnegans*.

Where has Zan got to? Jiminy Cricket, where has that sweetheart got to? She ran away, that much we know. Surely, people have seen her, that we may assume. Possibly she's feeling sorry for herself, is licking her wounds, wants nothing to do with us. Let's not bother her. But why not? She's not some precious princess whose wishes must not be violated. Okay, let's bother her. Let's intrude.

Hello Zan, what are you doing, Zan, hiding away from us? You're not Brer Rabbit in the briar patch. Come out, come out.

Leave me alone.

Let's coax her. Soft words must be used. Please, Zan, precious angel, reveal yourself.

I'm in here reading. Don't bother me.

In where? Reading what?

None your beezwax.

Zan is flying through air. She is flying, flying. Why is it that she may not reach where it is she is going? Why is it that she cannot touch down? She was on her bike, bound for the Bloor SuperSave, three folded dollars bunched in one hand. Cat litter. We are out of cat litter, darling, and would you be so kind? So, yes, her hands, one with its crunched-up cash, are on the handlebars, and she is zipping along. Boy oh boy, is that girl ever flying. Wind on her face, that dumb blue safety helmet pinching her neck. She looks a freak in that piece, she's such a skinny slice, toothpick thin, say the boys. Take a look at that lean rump, take a look at those limbs. Parents ought to feed that girl. Out of the way, Ormsby, she'll run you down. Now swerve past these parked cars, so many cars. One coming up behind me, I see it. Hop that curb, zip up here onto the sidewalk, what's the big deal? Shoosh, so much dirty ice, snow, snow piles, people too lazy to shovel the muck. Oh, look, a kitty, a kitty prancing into the street, is that my kitty? Casey, you fat butterball, are you following me? You want your litter that much? But no, it is not her cat. So let's shift our gears, let's truly get this sweet mummy flying. She goes to throw up a friendly hand to that porch boy, I know that boy, there goes my three dollars, hit the brakes. Watch out, cat! ... and all at once, *woops*, Zan is

# F L Y I N G

---

Two Yapochee have crossed over into another country. They are flying. That is what Father Yapochee is thinking, in his dream. Another country. Your tongue laps at berries on a bush, and the taste is not one known before. Sometimes you spit it out. Too bitter, well Jiminy Cricket, we can't eat that! The same-wise with the bush: you've never seen it before. That's how he knows it is another country. Other-wise, the terrain is similar: uphill, downhill, water, no water, everything dense and leafy. Or a long, virtually lifeless plain. Occasionally, a village, but we'd best avoid those. Stay out of sight, daughter, please. Hunker down. Know what I mean? Keep a low profile. Wait a minute. What's that nice feeling I am feeling around my ankles? Is that you, Mother? Yes, it is Mother Yapochee entering his dream. How nice of you to visit. She is licking his left ankle. Oh, does that ever feel terrific. Mother Yapochee goes on licking. Now and then her tongue caresses this thing of his that is not quite a hoof, and both quiver in excitement. Father Yapochee wants to lick her ankles, too, but ...

But he's awake now. Mother Yapochee is no more. She may arrive only in dreams. Death has carried Mother Yapochee over the rainbow into a better world. Better? Oh, who knows?

Certainly not a Yapochee. His worry now is reserved solely for Little Sissy Yapochee. Little Sissy Yapochee will likely never experience the divine harmonies. Because all the other little Yapochee have disappeared. It is going to be a bleak future for this last Yapochee child. But, again, who knows?

These leaves are sweet. Grass tastes good. Try these, Little Sissy. Mind the thorns. Step around the bad snake.

(Chapter Three continues the tale.)

The last Yapochee?
I think Not."

Like when I looked at Tallis tucked away inside his coma, what I truly saw was me in a mirror. Laid out like on a slab. I was ashamed. I felt shame at how I looked, of what the boy would think of me. I wasn't worthy to sit in the same room with him. He had unloaded on me the garage key, hauled in the heat. *Mini key on hook by back door. Git sober person can drive, move Mini to street. Folks rarely use Mini. Probably not notice. Remember change Mini street position each too weeks.*

Boy an awful typist.

Now spiffy as the Ritz, the garage. Nice reading lamp the boy pulled in. Read 'Lap,' read 'Kiss,' the boy writes.

Emmitt's shoes mighty good fit. No socks?

True, that Rebecca person paid me dispiriting insult.

This dashing woman saw me at the garage door, she said, Heavens to Betsy, my name is Rebecca Whitehall, not the maid, who are you? She talks like that, highfalutin like you hear from the rich at Dook. I followed her tail in by the back door, saying stuff she paid no attention to. Her interest being in what the women in the front room were talking about. Don't mind me, she says, I'm putting cotton in my ears. You should see the ache poor Sheila endures, writing her drivel, she says. Sheila suffers such pain you might think she was an old crone living in a box in a ditch beside a railroad track, trembling from hooch and vomiting on her knees. She tucks a woollen blanket around her ankles when writing. For good luck, she says. And because her feet get cold. She pinches a nipple, if the right word doesn't immediately come. She must first douse herself in Joy. Joy is a ritzy *eau de parfum*, sir, which employment, if you don't mind me saying, you could make use of. I don't want your reek carrying to my dress. Sheila's been ages between sweethearts, she says. Now has a yen for a poet-type fella, James Agee. Nope, sorry, she says. Tate, Tate, James Tate.

On she goes. Writers are strange birds, if you ask me. I'm sure Van Cliburn performing Tchaikovsky, Gould doing Bach, didn't find it necessary to practise such rot. Yes, it is a splendid dress, isn't it? Sheila Shott's sole virtue is how she attires me. You could buy a Lamborghini for what these shoes and purse cost.

On and on she goes. Swell woman, can't shut up. Reminds me of me.

I then doze off. It's like I'm in the boy's head, where I see these deer-like creatures running like to high hell. Terrain vibrating, volleys of dust. Turn on a dime, jumpers like their ears are wings. Faces pretty as my grandmother at eighteen. Night was coming on and it is night when I see them. Daylight hours, other things are busy frying the brain. In my experience. I'm not speaking for anyone else. A harmless garter snake, no need to worry your head over Little Sissy. Three legs. Man, can they zoom.

I'm somewhat assured, the boy asked me how I was as I sat down by his bed. I'm certain he said he was doing okay. Nothing to complain about. Said he hoped I was finding the garage quarters to my liking. Somebody else I couldn't see said something sounded like *Here come those damned Yapochee.* By then, I'm falling asleep. The Whitehall woman's chatter has worn me out. Everything has. Isn't easy, being me. My disbarment from the practise of law was weighing. I hadn't yet got around to drawing up my letter to the law society. What to say in my appeal.

Secretary, please to take this down:

---

RE: ORMSBY

This office hereby serves notice of...

Like so, and so on.

Secretary, you please to complete the letter. Then courier it over to the city's foremost attorney for signature. I'm sure Mr Ruby will be happy to sign.

Wait. Say this:

AT A TIME WHEN A GOODLY NUMBER OF THIS NATION'S JUDGES, POLITICIANS, COPS, PRIESTS, FELLOW LAWYERS AND SUNDRY KNAVES ARE BEING INVESTIGATED FOR AND FREQUENTLY CHARGED WITH AND CONVICTED OF CRIMES HORRENDOUS IN SCOPE AND DEBILITATING TO THE HUMAN CONDITION, MOST PARTICULARLY CRIMES AGAINST OUR INDIGENOUS PEOPLES, OUR

WOMEN, OUR CHILDREN, OUR ANY MINORITY, OUR DUMPED-ON
POOR, IT IS ALTOGETHER FITTING THAT MR ORMSBY'S RECORD BE
SET STRAIGHT THAT HE MAY AGAIN BE FREE TO FIGHT FOR THE
NOBLE CAUSES HERE AND WORLDWIDE.

In CAPS, please.

---

What I saw, outside the boy's window this snowy day, was sixteen women, teen girls, I mean, flimsily attired, dancing in fluffy snow. Me and Tallis and this third fellow at the boy's window clapping our hands. Dancing, it seemed to me, a kind of ritual pagan dance, like a dance a choreographer would design to be done in pure, empty air, if the choreographer could figure out a way to keep his dancers up so high heels never touch earth. At Dook one time I saw in a gallery five women painted red circling like these were. True, my eyes were blurry. By Matisse, I'm told. Idea got from Collioure. Nothing erotic about it. Nothing smutty, or a come-on, or would lead you so much as to think dick. What it was, was a Forgiveness Dance. These sprites, angels, doing a Forgiveness Dance. In forgiveness for what, well there you got me. Maybe to tell X, Zan, don't go wingy. To tell Tallis, you pups are now invincibly united. You git it?

*You hear what I'm saying?*

Sheila Shott could tell you a thing about Dook. She's invited down. Humongous fee. Elucidating romance talk in the cards. Last minute, cancelled. You're meaning to talk romance when our big racist Senate race is going on? Jesse Helms? Neck and neck? No way. You're cancelled.

Okay. Got that wrong. Before her time. Could be that it was Eleanor Roosevelt coming down. I never claimed myself attuned to the historical perspective.

Nixon? What the future pres got acquainted to, fond of, down at Dook was fatback. Fatback bubbling in a frypan. What the constitutionally circumvented poor people eat down there. Season your cabbage with fatback. Pure fat—from the back of a pig. You don't have butter, oleo, lard, then fry up, bake, broil—whatever—the cornbread in the silt of fatback. Eggs. Eggs and fatback. Punch a hole in the biscuit with your finger, poke in your fatback. Eat. Salty, yes. Bad for you, yes. What Susan Sarandon, Kevin Costner ate in 1988 hi-jinx baseball movie *Bull Durham.* So I'm informed. Not saying you'll like it. Fatback, I mean.

I might have been proved wrong, regards to that snake. Little Sissy is weeping. She's hobbling. That bad snake got her in the ankle.

---

Daisy, in bed, has her eyes closed tight. She has hopes of keeping them that way until something good happens in this house. In her youth she'd played softball now and again. At bat, she'd swung at the ball with eyes tightly shut. This had been the coach's advice. 'The ball comes in shoulder-high, you swing at something around your knees. Try shutting your eyes.'

'What is the matter with you?' Emmitt wants to know.

'Don't trouble me. I seek the unconscious state. There, I shall communicate with our son.'

'What's that red welt on your ankle?'

'Something bit me. Go away. I feel a dream state coming on.'

# Barbara Walters Interviews Daisy Haley

**FIRST TAKE**

BW: Daisy, now that your son has been in a coma these many weeks, with no reliable assurance he will ever again recover consciousness or experience a normal life, how do you manage to maintain the brave face?

D: Noted mystics commune with me.

BW: You consider that a *normal* existence.

D: Miss Walters, Barbara, will you please tell me what 'normal' is?

BW: For one thing 'normal' is being allowed to conduct an interview during which I ask solidly researched questions, and my guests try not to be wingy. Sit still, sit erect. Remove the fingers from your mouth.

D: They warned me back in the green room you'd be tough.

CUT! CUT! CUT!

## SECOND TAKE

BW: Daisy, the cameras are running.

D: I am limp as a dishrag. Those little capsules …

## CUT!

## THIRD TAKE

BW: Our nation has taken your family's tragedy to heart, and grieves with you.

D: The People, yes!

BW: How are you coping?

D: It helps to appear on shows such as yours because I find I am in dialogue with myself all the time anyway, so I feel I am not wasting my time by walking all the way to New York City in my housecoat and slippers and drinking café au lait in ABC's downstairs bar.

BW: Daisy, I am known and respected in my profession for knowing how to probe and dissect a guest and elicit information from them that is truly earthshaking. What can you tell me that might blow the lid off these airwaves?

D: I have put powder around his bed.

BW: Powder?

D: Face powder.

BW: Any particular brand?

D: I used to like Opium, in the pretty wine-coloured box from Yves Saint Laurent, but now I will use any old thing my hands fall upon.

BW: I see you have been rather ferociously biting your nails.

D: I usually sit on my hands but the woman in Makeup said I shouldn't.

BW: Shirley?

D: Daphne, I believe she was. She kindly smoothed a cream over my ankle welt. She said she thought my maggoty old housecoat would go down really well with the viewers, since that's how many home viewers would be dressed, and that I could keep on these tatty slippers because the camera wouldn't shoot them anyway. I hope not, because Emmitt will be watching and he is fed up with this outfit, and with how I tend myself generally.

BW: Strife on the home front we all know well.

D: Our bedsheets have not been washed in three months. We lack the oomph.

BW: Where has Big Brother put you up while you're with us in the Big Apple?

D: At the Waldorf. I had a café in the lobby and it cost me twenty-four dollars.

BW: Why didn't you charge this to your room?

D: They thought I was homeless. They didn't believe I had a room.

BW: In addition to the powder, what other world-shaking revelation might I elicit from you?

D: I'd like to talk to you about that woman in Nova Scotia who in a case of mistaken identity married her son. Her case bears upon my mind.

BW: Our viewers have zippo interest in that woman.

D: I weep for both.

BW: Not here, please. Our viewers might instead like to know how you have become the recognized world authority on bone-throwing practices in certain backwoods nations.

D: I try to keep up.

BW: It takes your mind off your troubles.

D: Yes. I find I can go an entire day without once thinking I have died.

BW: Thank you for putting all this out on the cutting board where everyone can share your pain.

D: Any time.

Emmitt strides into the 2 x 8 bedroom, acknowledging the presence of his wife within an entanglement of covers. 'Wake up', he tells her. 'You must eat something.' She mutters a string of words lost to his ears. 'What did you say? Get up. Eat something.'

'I ate at the Waldorf,' she manages to say. 'Go away.'

'You at times are not worth talking to.'


*Has he gone? True, what he said. Oh, how it hurts.*


A woman, walking a road in the dead of night, New York City to Toronto's 2 x 8 Major, fell headlong into a deep divide that had opened that very evening upon the road, and with the morning light the woman sought to bestir herself, feeling enormous trepidation, because she felt a presence in the midst but that presence offered no assistance, none whatsoever, nor did it volunteer even the smallest sympathetic word.

'Who's there?' the woman shouted, and she went on shouting, and swinging her walking stick about, since the presence gave no reply.

The woman took to the road again. Farther on, she heard a beating of something like hooves, and creaking limbs, a woeful cry, and more thrashing limbs.

Whereupon, onto the woman's path hobbled a strangely beautiful creature suffering a swollen hoof, the creature saying, I was bitten on the ankle, I see yours is a kind face, is it possible you may offer aid to a wounded Yapochee?


weary with desuetude
and unable to lift a breath
in reply


Emmitt picks up a parcel from the Spadina postal station. The parcel is addressed to his son.

What is it?

Books. Chekhov. The plays, this time. He owes $146.69. We are to remit immediately.

Night, and the boy's brow is hot: *Emmitt, hurry! A cold cloth, an ice pack!*

*He's fine, Daisy. Stop worrying.*

Knock, knock. Is anybody home?

Go Away is home.

Go Away is at home in our darling boy's bed.

'Daisy, don't hover so. Let the boy breathe.'

'You're the party about to smother him. Take your panic attack elsewhere.'

'You calm down. According to this thermometer his temperature is perfectly normal.'

'Don't be silly. Feel his brow.'

'Oh Lord in your high realm, grant us surcease from pain, the cessation of despair. Thine vineyard is abloom with flowing clematis and thine starships are at sail through the heavens.'

'Stop that. Our boy is in no mood for poetry.'

'I used to hide under our house when I was a child. I hid from everyone. I'm confident I was the most shy boy ever lived. I hid under the house with the dog. It was me and the dog under the house, wondering what kind of future we would have.'

'Quiet! Tallis isn't interested. Tell him your life story another time.'

'Me and the dog. Then the dog died and I was alone.'

Daisy's sister, Flute, known for flouting her promiscuity through her teens and even now, calls three and four times a week. She calls at midnight, at four a.m.—anytime. You don't hear from her for weeks, for years, then she's suddenly at your elbow every minute. The phone doesn't even have to ring. You're walking by, cup of tea in hand, on impulse lift the receiver, and there her voice is.

'Daisy? Daisy, sit down. I've got news.' And she does indeed have news: she's the 400 Club, she's the twenty-four-hour CNN. She's your on-the-spot news dispatcher. 'You remember Auntie Stone, Daze? Our old auntie, Auntie Stone, Wonderful old Auntie. Sure you do.'

'Vaguely. Which aunt was she?'

'Dipped snuff. Snuff on a stick, dipped into the tin.'

'You dipped snuff, Flute. Ten years old. Swore it gave you orgasms.'

'I never!'

'Orgasms. Age ten.'

'Tube Rose Scotch. I still dip sometimes. Should I want an orgasm. You remember my disfigurement? The finger I lost?'

'You've always been missing something, Flute. Like a brain in your head.'

'You're the dumb one. Gracious! Can't recall your own aunt!'

'I've got to go, Flute. Tallis needs me.'

'That boy can look after himself. He always has.'

'You *dare*! You *dare* to claim I've not been a good mother!'

Squeals at the line's other end. Flute laughing. How these two sisters ever taunt each other.

'Listen, Daze. Do you need money? How are you fixed? Financially. Are things tight?'

'I'm selling my best bathrobe. I'm selling these slippers I've worn twenty-two years.'

'Shut up, Daze. Remember auntie's property? Her land? The argument that went on for a hundred years about did the land have water? All those hayseeds out there with their goofy clothes-hanger divining rods?'

'What property? What water?'

'Remember my first husband, Wagner? Wagner and his wagging rod?'

'You could you pick them. I remember that.'

'Anyway, why I'm calling, honey, is old Auntie finally kicked the bucket. She's gone up to snuff-heaven. And you know what? Around here, where I am, land of eternal sunlight, they have to pipe in water from, like, a thousand miles. But you know what? Aunt's land has about a zillion gallons. The property is worth a mint. You know what else?'

'I'm losing my patience with you. What-for-God's-sake else?'

'She left it to us. To me and you.'

'That's crazy. I barely knew her.'

'I put in a good word for you from time to time. She liked it I dipped. Unlike you, had orgasms.'

---

Ryabovitch slips into 2x8, muttering. He's wet. Rain has caught him unaware, which he partially corrected by acquiring an umbrella. He laggardly discovered, after several times smacking the instrument against the floor, it opened by pressing the thumb against a hidden button. The umbrella swished open, striking his chin. Someone also sought to remove the umbrella from his hand. These combined to sullen his mood. In a sprawling bookstore he was further assaulted by a young woman attempting to rip from his hand the book he had idly picked up. She had screeched rather impressively, attracting a crowd. He had been forced to swat his way free. He, in fact, had found it necessary to run. The shouted 'thief' word was heard. Thankfully, once on the street, little attention was given him.

The book was for the boy. The boy, it seemed to Ryabovitch, had lately been depressed. One could hardly get a word out of him. As, for instance, now.

Inspirational self-help book. *You Don't Have to Be the Almighty to Be Great as You Deserve to Be. Awesome*, the cover says. *Guaranteed to put you on Easy Street*, it says.

You're welcome, mutters Ryabovitch.

No response from the boy. A thermometer seems permanently stuffed into his mouth.

Daisy Haley regards with heavy concentration this sleeping son. Flesh of her flesh. Dead flesh of her dead flesh. Dead to the world. A dead duck. Dead as a doornail. Circa 1350, Eastern Europe, that cliché.

You must hold your head over his chest to know he breathes.

Wipe your eyes, Daisy Mae.

Where did that stupid book come from? And that umbrella dripping water on the floor?

Daisy Haley, in her chair drawn up to Tallis's bed, wipes tissues over her cheeks. Wipes her eyes. This box of tissues, how many gone through in a single day? Oh, the amount of time in any girl's lifetime devoted to tissues. Stubbed toes, parents, classmates, boyfriends, husbands. The ruin they heap on you. Blow the nose, wipe. Daily, the tender pink nose. Small wonder Mary wept. Such an ugly box, this one. Who would bring such an ugly box into her house?

Emmitt, you and I must have a chat,

Wipe your eyes, blow your nose.

This room: heartache dribbles down every wall. Pain seeps in through the cracks. Should the flooring be warped, we know why.

You're cracking up, Daze.

But Daisy Haley is done today with thinking about tissue boxes, heartache, pain. Yes, dammit. To hell, she says to herself, with it. Daisy Haley has the home sewing kit on the floor. Between two fingers of her right hand she holds the longest needle she has been able to find. You can stitch leather, murder an elephant, with this needle. She has held a match's white flame to the tip. She is going to plunge this needle into her son's flesh, and is this second choosing the precise spot.

Now, damn you. Respond.

React. Raise a stink. Kick up a fuss.

Flinch. Scream.

But she can't bring herself to prick her beautiful boy.

*Astronomers on Mauna Kea Observatory*
    *Sight Bereft Mother on Moon Blowing Her Nose.*
*Comatose Son Strokes Weeping Mother's Face.*
*Bewildered Mom Stabs Self in Chest with 10-Inch Needle.*

Emmitt, mounting the stairs, is at first curious, then mildly upset. Some mindless sap has left splotches of water all over the steps. Idiot! Has Miss Ten Ants slipped in?

———————

Zan and her father had frequent conversations, none going anywhere, and usually unpleasant for both, often concluding with one or the other bolting from the house, hurling harsh words at a lampooning sky.

'You're telling me you're jacked up in love with a boy who nearly killed you?'

'I nearly killed him.'

'You did not. You were the innocent pipsqueak out to collect kitty litter, then victimized by a near-fatal accident. I'd like to strangle that cat. Forget that boy. He had no business sitting on his stoop on a wintry day—that in my youth was called hog-killing time.'

'Get real.'

'Don't use that tone on me, young lady.'

Etcetera.

There went one or the other out the door, squealing like a slit hog.

The truth is Zan had long taken an interest in this Tallis. She attended the same Free School he did, a windswept barn below College Street, and thus had scads of leftover time to fall head over heels for anyone she wanted.

'You have totally different personalities,' Zan's mother more than once observed.

'How can you possibly know that?'

'Your personality is unique. Chances are his is, if not minimal, standard.'

'Hardly. He's both athletic and brainy. He likes Chekhov stuff.'

'Literature of that rank is not generally referred to as stuff. Please speak precisely. Be sedulous.'

'I don't know what that means.'

'He hangs out with street people. I'm not insulting those people. It's just that they never do anything except wave paper cups in my face. They don't contribute.'

'What do you contribute?'

'A sizable portion of my wages, thank you. Christ, we are like falling snow, your father and I, how much we contribute. Forget that boy. An infantile fourteen is too young even to be thinking about boys.'

'Going on fifteen, please. How old were you?'

'That is not germane to this discussion.'

'Thirteen? Twelve? I've heard all about your fanatical kissing marathons at drive-in movies.'

'I've never been to a drive-in movie in my life. We do not need a pregnant fourteen-year-old in this house.'

'You treat the one you have like she's a baby. Why not another?'

Zan by no means meant to imply that her intention was to hop into bed with Tallis Haley at the first opportunity. Or ever. Heck, she hardly had breasts yet. Certainly, some of her girlfriends had done so without turning into frenzied rabbits. Well, one or two claimed as much. Certainly, sex exceeded citizenship as a topic of discussion among these many friends. Some perused junky manuals depicting hardened rods, orgasms more powerful than an exploding Mount Vesuvius, more draining than the dredging of the Erie Canal. What Zan thought about when her own mind approached the subject was that she might very possibly submit, if … if … The ifs did seem to pile up. She just might. She just possibly would. What she couldn't quite admit to herself is that she was a straight, upright girl of the old-fashioned school. She fully expected she'd have several *flings*, odd encounters now and then, perhaps even one or two fly-by-nights, then get truly zapped by love. Like what had transpired with that lapdog woman. Herself, she'd flee to unknown parts, fling herself into the mighty ocean and perish. Such was how she saw it, and even if Tallis Haley proved to be the ultimate prince of romance, she assuredly believed it not unreasonable to suppose she might alternately wind up stoked on coke or heroin like that incredible trumpet player singer guy whose 'Little Girl Blue' made her cry her eyes out no matter how many thousand times she heard it.

The uneventful way this thing with Tallis was going, the best she could hope for was a miserable life full of parental torture, and skin defects no cream on earth could erase.

The practicality of this situation was that she'd plowed headfirst into the boy, and thus were they insolubly linked. Like by destiny. Of course, she'd admired him a long time before he got trammelled.

She was minus a fixed opinion on any of this. Nice would be if she could immediately ship herself out to ... well, let's say the West Indies. What was important was ... well, one day wouldn't she figure that out? She was too smart to be eternally stupid.

Mr Evers, counselling her group at the Free School, had said:

'It's exceeding likely, when all of you students are my age, you still won't know anything.'

*We will be, like, so stupid.*

'You will go to your graves knowing you never got anything right.'

*We will be, like, so pathetic.*

Nasty old man.


*Did you not with full intent, out of full homicidal impulse and malice afore-thought and in the fullness of youthful savoir faire, maim, cripple, and assidu-ously attempt termination of the life of the fair-haired boy known to one and all as Tallis Haley.*

Yes. I did so do.


The parental unit shrieked. One held Zan by the shoulders while the other conducted microscopic study of her arms and legs. *How did you get these cuts? By God, are you into self-mutilation now?*

*What are we to do with you?*

It happened. The cutting came when she was at a low point. It had not been planned. She didn't know why. Yes, she could see how crazy the act was.

*What do you imagine that boy would think? If he saw you like this.*

*Oh. You're right. I hadn't thought of that. I will never do it again.*

On the phone, Nancy Cee advised Chig and Laura to remain vigilant. Even a pimple on the chin can evoke suicidal depression. Among those her age. They'd immolate themselves if they didn't need matches for the next cigarette.

'Zan doesn't smoke.'

'You both do.'

---

# Police Crack Deadly Ring

Misdemeanour charges for 'crimes against society' were yesterday lodged against a 'mostly blue-haired woman' domiciled in Toronto's troubled Major Street area. A dawn raid at 2 x 8 resulted in the arrest of alleged ringleader Daisy Haley. She is charged with:

- ❶ Failure to sweep floor.
- ❷ Failure to cook.
- ❸ Failure to prettify self at local parlour.
- ❹ Failure to remit $146.69 to NYC publishing house.
- ❺ Destruction of rare book *Finnegans Wake*.

Emmitt, exasperated, said, Daisy, Daisy, it's madness. Why do you keep coming up with these absurdities?

Daisy said, 'I read it right there in the *Star*. See for yourself. Page 9.'

On page 9 Emmitt finds a full-page ad from Hudson's Bay for cashmere sweaters in six glorious Benetton colours at $39.99. '$39.99 is a good price for cashmere sweaters,' Daisy said. 'I hope you'll buy me one. Maybe the raid story was in the *Globe*. Quiet! Was that Tallis I heard calling?'

'Squeak in the floor. Oh, Daze, what am I to do with you?'

'He came out of me like seed out of shell, my brief-hanging moon, my ...'

'No more of that, please. It's maudlin.'

'Oh, Emmitt. I'm bereft. I crumple in despair.'

'Go to bed. I'll take the watch. I can't take the watch. I am the watch. I must go on. I can't go on. I'll go on. Who said that?'

'Don't mollycoddle me. I said bereft. Not stupid. Don't quote Samuel Beckett if you can't do so accurately.'


Emmitt calls and calls. He gets no response. Are you hungry? Anything you want? No reply. He knows she's by the boy's bed. Is she asleep? Waltzed away in her head to another Barbara Walters interview? She's eaten nothing today, little yesterday. In fact, when did she last sit down to a solid meal?'

There you are. Daisy, Daisy, Daisy. I see tears flooding your cheeks. This is your friend Barbara. How may I help?

Go away. It's too heart-rending. I can't tell you.

Try.

I heard that girl took a blade to her body, and it tore me up. I felt someone had hauled in a dump-load of mud, and the mud was me. A potter grabbed handfuls and pounded and slapped and punched me one way and another. I was pitched onto a wheel and went around and around. But the potter couldn't make anything of me. I fell into useless clumps. But I still could see the girl's bloody trail as she crawled the floor.

Medication may be called for.

It *is!* It *is!* I'm doing that now.


ABC's late-nite Pat Sajak show denied today that a recent guest was 'sloshed to the gills' on lithium and assorted other drugs while appearing onstage. 'ABC does not condone inane behaviour,' a spokesperson said, 'and takes every precaution.'

In a related development, critics across North America were unanimous in their praise of Ms Daisy Haley's 'comeback' performance on last night's *Larry King Live!* 'She won the debate hands down,' wrote *The New York Times* drama critic. 'An existential knockout,' said the *Denver Post.* 'Ross Perot pigged out on Mexico, Gore sucked thumb, but Daisy tossed the bombs,' reported the *Washington Post.* 'A SLAM-DUNK' opined *USA Today.*

Ms Haley also used her podium to launch a vigorous attack on the CIA for its inhumane treatment of Yuri Nosenko, the Cold War KGB officer connected with Lee Harvey Oswald, who defected to the West in 1964. She called for a United Nations Court of Justice investigation of ALL CIA activities, debunked U.S. positions on Cuba, Nicaragua, Haiti, Somalia, Chile, El Salvador and sixty-eight other countries, while finding time, often in the same breath, to reiterate what she described as a 'wholesome' stand on gun control, abortion, the criminal justice system worldwide, gender-bashing, equity employment, deficit spending, health care, funding for education, appropriation of voice, Camille Paglia and Rush Limbaugh. By the time Ms Haley's show (so critics described it) ended she had taken over Larry King's desk to deliver a resounding lecture in support of art and the artistic life and its value to 'teeming humanity without which sewers would open and slime dominate.' Seven million letters—yeas, by and large—flooded the network mailroom.

Ms Haley is said to have walked barefoot in ratty housecoat across rural Ontario and most of New York state, through snow over her head, to appear on the show. The controversial guest spent the night in a downtown coffee house, sipping café au lait, resting up and tending sore feet, she said, for the arduous journey back to her modest claptrap home at 2 x 8 Major.

BRING HER BACK! goes the resounding cry.


'There,' she told Emmitt, 'is the vain woman you married. Once upon a time, in my dreams, I merely slipped into a bikini and shipped myself off to Caribbean isles.'

'With or without me?'

'Depended on my mood. On whether you had been loving or horrid. Would you like to see another of your son's Yapochee installments?'

---

Little Sissy Yapochee has crossed over mountain and deep valley, wailing. She has lost her father, lost her mother, is now herself lost in a wooded thicket. A fox was devouring a rabbit, the rabbit ripped into a hundred pieces, and she has stepped into the blood puddle. It is what she deserves for walking with her eyes shut. But she did not want to see the fox's mutilation of the rabbit. I'll close my eyes and pretend, she told herself. And did precisely that. Now her hoof, if hoof is what it is, is ankle deep in blood, and what choice does a Yapochee have but to lick lick lick. To lick the ankle clean. She can do this with her eyes closed, thank goodness, though any minute now she will have to open them. Because things are crawling inside her fur. She will have to snort and prance and find a nice tree to rub against. There. At last, the ankle is clean. Clean enough. No one around here will be giving her a hard time about a little blood on the ankle. Though you never know.

Bitter, bitter is the taste in her mouth. Mint would be heavenly, eucalyptus divine.

*(To Be Cont'd)*

---

From Seong's window one night, the sky incredibly bright, Tallis Haley was in plain—all but illuminated—view. He lay under white sheets, head high on an abundance of white pillows, looking peacefully beautiful. A serving tray rested on his stomach. On that, in turn, arrived a small cake with dark icing, flickering candles centred.

'His birthday,' Seong said.

'Spectacular!' Zan said. If so, it meant they shared the same birth month. 'Mine is next week. I'll be sixteen.'

'Fifteen,' Seong said.

Heads side by side, they watched the candles flicker. They saw the boy's father remove them, cut the cake, and place the slice on the boy's saucer. In gloom they watched the slice remain untouched.

'They are singing, "Happy Birthday" to him now,' Seong said. 'They are wishing him many happy returns.'

Zan found she could not speak. Seong left her side, returning a moment later with a box of tissues.

They both cried.

The following day was not without interest. Zan had been snooping along Bloor Street, trying to decide if one dollar's small juice at Country Fresh would squelch her belly-rumbles, when she spotted Emmitt emerging from the Hardware. In one hand he carried, high against the chest, what Zan took to be a can of paint. Beauti-Tone: she could now decipher the label: White Exterior Enamel. Now he was stopping, examining the paint can, his expression grave. Puzzled. Out of the Hardware had come a man dressed in the usual employee uniform, red shirt, black trousers, shuffling up. She observed their exchange of brief remarks, the drooping of shoulders, the father's out-flung arms. Now the Hardware man was clapping the other's backside; with the paint, shaking his head, he was now returning to the store. Emmitt had neglected payment.

Crossing Zan's mind was the possibility that the parental unit saddled with her had suffered similar addlement.

Nah.

Patooey.

Nobody loves me.


Over coming nights, sometimes it rained and sometimes snowed, which made the watch gruelling. She dressed appropriately, only catching a mild cold, though her hands, feet, nose, ears suffered mightily.

ZAP THAT Girl ir Tree

One dark night a raccoon family decided to breach her limb, and in fright she nearly fell from her perch. A police car stopped at the curb another night. They put a spotlight on her.

'Come down from there, or we'll taser your ass.'

Mrs Poindexter had reported peeping Toms. In the tree watching her undress.

'Why are you up there, miss?'

'I don't know why. I lack good sense, I guess.'

'Your scalp is bleeding,' a second officer observed. 'Did you suffer recent injury?'

'A raccoon slashed at me,' she said. 'I was in the way of her babies, I think.'

'Go home. It better not be we see your butt again.'

Zan wasn't sorry she'd given herself the exercise. She reckoned she'd picked up vital information—along with itchy streaks on both thighs—about a great many things not entirely relevant to the boy she—with every breath—knew to be her beloved.

**Chapter 10:** For a time, Little Sissy Yapochee was subsumed by an onslaught of what she thought might be ponies, though in height they were scarcely taller than tall goats and shared a goat's dexterity in rocky terrain. They were wild, all the same, and coarse of manner, liking to think they were faster and brighter and more at ease in the world than she. They were, which sent her sailing off into sour disenchantment, a moodiness they maintained was foreign to their constitution, making them laugh. Most galling was their endless chatter about absolutely nothing, a saddening trait she had been raised to believe was the sole province of children. This provoked in Little Sissy the assurance that she was practically an adult now, another thing that induced the ponies, if such is what they were, to tumble into paroxysms of laughter. Their appetite was of wide—to her mind, disgusting—scope, in that they ate and adequately digested whatever chanced before them: dead sticks covered with greenish fur, rotted piles found in a ditch, the sawdust of beavers, nettles hosting thorns long enough to kill a ... to kill a horse. Most often, living, frantic animals squealed horribly within their potent jaws. Even rocks, gravel, sand, the wormy stumps of fallen trees. All glomped down as though in proof of their mettle. Too many times they told her to stop being so snotty, so snooty, to grow up. She was not one of them, they said, and no better, whatever airs she put on. They laughed, they chortled, they teased her mercilessly. Nobody invited you to hang in with us, they said. You don't contribute, you lack the gang mentality. You're no fun. We detest orphans like you. All you Yapochee have the brains of a mongoose otherwise you wouldn't be dying off.

Horrible. Mean one minute, gay libertines the next.

One morning she woke to a drifting so silent she initially believed a new, warped curve had altered the known horizon. They were far in the distance, a beclouded entity pausing now and then to look back at her—Are you coming?—then in the next second clattering onwards into invisibility.

She knew herself then to be still a child, because, in their absence, solitude leapt inside with such force her anguished cry echoed back—bare of bone, a shriek pared of self, akin to the final whimper of the lizard between a pony's teeth.

*No one loves me! Poppa! Mama! I am so lonely!*

(To Be Cont'd)

---

No one doubted the Hardware was overstaffed. Customarily, a minimum five were on hand, often with nothing to do. The five consisted of one skinny black man, at rare times a woman. The rest were family. It could be the woman and the black man were also family; politeness didn't favour an inquiry. After Emmitt's entry, the five assembled by the cash register by the front door. Today's assembly did not include the woman.

'Where did he go?' It was the black man asking this. He seemed to be today's boss.

'In the back.'

'Better check. Be surreptitious.'

The man addressed, went.

Today's boss said to another, 'The other day. You're convinced he was addled.'

'That would be my word for it.'

'Didn't know if he was coming or going.'

'How much was that paint?'

'With tax? Four thirty-nine.'

The fifth party returned. 'Did he come back this way?'

'Hell no. What do you mean?'

'He's not back there.'

*Back there*, riding deep into the store, were three long aisles. He wasn't in any of those. He wasn't in the rear, where paints were mixed. He wasn't in Nuts & Bolts. Nor in Light Bulbs. He wasn't anywhere. A siren would have sounded had he exited by the back door.

'He's not anywhere.' This is what was said, the five again up front.

'Did he slip by us?'

'No way!'

'Anything missing? Like a snow-blower. A refrigerator?'

'We don't sell refrigerators here. Cramped for space.'

'Space,' today's boss, the black man, said. He was thinking. 'Cramped.'

'Yeah?'

'That's where he is.'

'Yeah? Where?'

'Follow me.'

In the very back, along the east wall, was a small all-but-hidden door opening to a narrow corridor. One had to stoop, entering. Here glass was stored, though not cut. Cutting took place elsewhere. Small cuts only. Cramped for space, you know. This was an Authorized Employees Only area.

'Is he in there?'

Not all could get in. Today only today's boss could.

'Yes.'

'What's he doing?'

'Nothing.'

'Ask him. He's not allowed in there.'

'I'm asking. Keep your shirt on.'

---

**Chapter 10 1/2:** Liberty, of a sort, crept in, after a score of days stricken by hard rain and tumultuous weave of the heavens. She ventured upon a grouping of what she took to be cows—somehow without movement except for their mighty lips—grazing in a sodden, fence-enclosed field. As one, they raised limpid eyes in slow regard of her. *Who's she? What does she want? Why is that drab Yapochee pussyfooting over our estate? Can't she read the signs?*

To her puzzlement, she had seen the signs: *No Hunting. No Fishing. No Trespassing. This Means You.*

The cows dropped their heads back to stingy tufts of grass. *Well it's no business of ours. Let someone else deal with her.*

She stopped by the fence. Could she jump it? Yes, and end up with a broken leg. Why jump it anyway? Instinctively, she knew the answer to that: always matters were better on the other side.

She jumped.

The cows didn't look. They had more rewarding things to do.

Not a jump to boast of. Had skinned the left knee. Hurt, too. But nothing to cry over.

Above, the sun glowed like a massive pendant looping the all-encompassing chest of a tranquil sky. Through the hours the cows scarcely moved, such dreamy thoughts as they possessed ascending above them, as into a single empty cloud no force today dared disturb.

Without appetite, ignored by the stolid herd, she nibbled at this and that. As darkness settled she sensed a deep worry developing among the group. One by one heads were lifted, hooves shifted in the muck, bodies turned: low murmurs, inquiry, petulance, scorn. *Late, always late. Has he no sense of time?* Little Sissy had questions, too. What were they talking about? Why this sudden show of life? She turned in the direction they all were looking. And a moment later did indeed discern something approaching: an alien, two-legged figure of a species she had been warned to avoid. This one was a grungy, battered, decrepit, grizzled elder. He was opening a gate; the cows, happy now, packed tightly together, sloshed through, grunting mightily.

And here came another, running. Something went *blam blam blam*. To her side. Leaves shook over her head.

Such a pickle.

*Blam, blam. Blam.*

*Run!* She ran.

Nightly through remorseful days, Little Sissy's old ankle injury reasserted itself, emitting a sweet resin as simultaneously her father's deep voice preyed upon her mind. Heed the snake, he said, Little Sissy leaping about in the vain hope she might catch sight of the snake. Some snakes were bad, others not. She supposed it was conceivable a Yapochee could be bad, though she personally had not known of one. Her mother had laughed at the very idea.

By degrees, Little Sissy sought to cast aside to the elements the name given her. Little Sissy Yapochee was a babyfied name. She wasn't a baby. She decided to be done with that name and all the name involved, for she lived now in a world of constant threat, and was more and more feeling what Mother Yapochee had warned her about: the first stirrings of desire. These stirrings she fought—as Mother Yapochee had advised—by running in ever-widening circles until fatigue forced her to ground.

Father Yapochee had had other ideas. He had been quite emphatic about the desire thing. He said: What to do with this eruption of desire thing, how to combat it, why? Running in circles no help, no help, running in circles, ever-widening circles, is what the doctor calls for but what does the doctor know, some do, some don't, some run in circles themselves, promote fanciful ideas, nothing to be done about that, too long everyone running in circles, when it came to circles—begging your mother's pardon—the circular view of history affirms the total lunacy of the insane idea.

Which speech had impressed Little Sissy no end. Night after night she found herself saying, Excuse me I'm just experiencing this little desire thing, no big tragedy you know a minute from now the desire thing will go, I'll be myself again, no need to get excited by being overwhelmed by the desire thing, heckfire, I am still just a child.

She would say that, but a minute later she would be heeding the motherly advice, clopping headfirst into these ever-expanding circles, covering another and another, must be a thousand miles covered before she quits. Then to take a cold bath, throw herself into the freezing lake, dip her head into an iceberg.

Circles only, God help the poor confused child.

Good fortune to arrive finally in the form of invigorating sleep.

And in that sleep what does she do? She decides she will retain her name, nothing wrong with Little Sissy, it's the name loved ones gave her, it's who she is.


One pony in the gang had been kind to her. Little Doozy, he was called. He had a sore on his neck he forever fiddled with. Worried about. Stop fiddling, you're making it worse. The sore on Little Doozy's neck, his fiddling, made Little Sissy want to cry. She wouldn't. Little Doozy had a mother and father, he had playmates and beautiful legs. A neck sore was nothing to cry about. Let the father cry, the mother gush tears, Little Sissy wouldn't. A snake bit me, did I cry? Well yes if you must know. But not much because there was a haranguing father thumping her withers, *didn't I tell you to watch out for that horned adder! didn't I!*—and a hand-wringing mother—well, if she had possessed hands.

The birds take flight, Little Doozy wasn't a bad pony at all. A good pony with legs to take the breath away. The tail, too. Muscular haunches rippling like a cascading brook. They had blown wind together, running. They had touched noses. His icy cold, despite heavy sweat. Aromatic sweat, should you wish to know. Perfume, you might say.

In lieu of another, Little Sissy consents to dream that barrel-chested braggart sprout Doozy. Dreams apparently accommodate desire: Come morning, she would feel well and good. Renewed. Desire was okay. But no need to go all slatternly sluttish with it. Circles were good, too, never mind you never got anywhere. *(To Be Con't)*

PLACE
POSTAGE
STAMP
HERE

# *Postcards from Rebecca Whitehall*

**POST CARD**

It never occurred to my bitch author to provide me with a family. Whoever they are or could be they wouldn't know me if I dropped in on a parachute at their Sunday dinner. To them, Miss Hot Pants says, I'm a dead woman gone none too soon, and good riddance. I'm claiming you guys as family.

# POST CARD

The bitch keeps telling me to watch my weight. Like I need her advice. Truth is, I've been fearful of stepping onto the scales. Today summoned the courage and to my delight discovered I'd shed four pounds in the past week alone. Only two, last week. In celebration I trooped fast into Club 22. Downed three double vodka martinis and a huge dish of nothing but scalloped potatoes. Heavenly! Hurried home. Three pounds back. Smashed the scales with hammer. Now the bitch is starving me.

Daisy, you may not realize the degree to which you intimidate me. My bitch author only creates cardboard dunderheads for me to associate with. In remedy, remembering your feverish mention of same, bought used copy Finnegans Wake. Been back and forth over first page night and day. Losing beauty sleep. Up the creek, need your paddle! Lying bitch author brags she ripped through it in one sitting. 672 pages!

Dear Daisy, Emmitt, Tallis: Urbane bitch author has me off to Siena's Piazza del Campo in morn for the running of the horses! Taking Finnegans (first page)! Sheila makes me feel so slatternly sluttish I want to wring her neck. She calls it romance.

folked
by
Demon Love

Daisy, in receipt of Rebecca's missives, contemplated visualizing the dear girl among the throngs in the stands at Siena's lovely Piazza del Campo. She wanted to know what outfit Sheila Shott had dressed her in, and whose hand was on Rebecca's knee. Turner P. Blindstone, as honorary citizen and world-famous bronc-and-bull rider, would naturally be in the saddle of the mount crossing the finish line. This after stopping to save another rider from being trampled by a pile of fallen horses. Such, anyway, is how Daisy would do it. And there, through the mish-mash, sat Rebecca Whitehall, mindless of the hand probing her thigh, so thoroughly immersed was she in *Finnegans* that Siena, the whole of Italy, the noble hand cranking along her thigh, had ceased to exist. Did the hand belong to a mafia boss, or was it Berlusconi's hand? Daisy couldn't decide. So she went back to what Sheila would have wrapped Rebecca in. Sheila liked to think she promoted a feminist perspective. Likely, therefore, Rebecca would be fitted out in a knock-dead Diane von Furstenberg or Donatella Versace.

Daisy was midway through this inventory when raps vibrated the front door. Heckfire, who can that be?

There stood a sagging Emmitt in the company of a mellowed-looking fella from the Hardware. 'You need to put your husband to bed,' the Hardware man said. 'He is not himself today.'

'Few of us are,' Daisy said.

Emmitt refuses bed.

Things to do, he said.

What things?

Man stuff.

Bloody hell.

An opaque substance leaks from Tallis Haley's mouth. It has obeyed the laws of gravity by following the contour of the boy's inner lower lip, beheld an obstruction at the mouth's corner, gathered in volume, overflowed the found crevasse, and now trickles down his chin. Here some of it will dry, crust, deepen in hue, and widen as more follows the made path. The substance conveys no scent, perhaps evidence of the boy's purity.

A slow beat emanates through bed and floorboards, which one at first may take to be the pace of his heart but is the basement furnace stirred into action. Among other discomforts — he may have come down with a cold— Emmitt trembles in bed. Daisy has the thermostat set high. Trembling also, possibly feverish, suffering the runs, she has been slack in her duty. This will, shortly, be deeply regretted.

*A blind man asked his deaf wife where it was she felt the most dreaded pain. In my heart, she was about to say, when a third person, speechless since birth, came stumbling up the road, clutching in both hands that very part of her body which did not ache.*

No salt-water fish, Daisy likes to keep up with the Booker Prize nominees. The italicized paragraph, in a book on the current short list, is given by oddsmakers a minus ninety chance of winning. Grim but bold, decorative but flavourful, critics have opined. Spotty, Daisy would say. She, too frequently perhaps, looks to find herself delineated in books. Old friend Jim Munro, bookseller by trade, once said to her the books most exciting to him were those featuring a protagonist who shared his age, social status, political acumen, was married with children nearing adulthood, was in or beyond divorce proceedings, and worked in an allied profession. Characters like me, he said. Sooner or later, we all want books like that. Confirmation. Reprieve. Solace. A corona of hope in surround of the grit. Propping up.

In this Booker instance, the third person interests Daisy. Experience has taught her that in exorbitant number exist those whose function in life is to render asunder the parts of yourself not aching until they came.

Down the hall is her son, leaking from the mouth. Still she tarries. Locked within the tedium of useless thought. Intellectual dementia, she would name this. On better days.

Good God, woman. Go tend your son.

Numerous times she has heard the in-and-out slamming of the back door. Snow and rain have warped the frame. It's a door, sometimes they must be slammed. In and out, in and out, blam, blam, blam. Sometimes a wife must shout to the thoughtless other, *Stop slamming the damned door!* She does that now.

*You're giving me a headache! Stop with the damned door!*

There is a minus ninety chance Emmitt Haley will stop slamming the door.

Woman, forget the door. See to the needs of your child.

Emmitt Haley not long ago discovered a feral cat assuming tenancy beneath his back porch. An uglier, angrier cat he had never seen. The cat hissed, spat, and clawed at him. It was a deeply disabled cat, with protruding bones, pocked fur, a tail funnily bent. The frightful face reminded him of Elihu's discourse with Job of Uz: God speaks to us only through vision and the imparting of pain. Food the cat appeared not to want; what it wanted was its claws bloodying your face. That was then. Now it was almost sane. Now it was almost handsome. Morning and evenings its face appeared at the back door. Where are you? the cat seemed to say. I've missed you.

And why not? For a month now, he has fed that cat precious food costing twenty-five dollars a kilo at Bathurst Pet Bureau. He has seen it playing with the odd toy purchased there. Back and forth to the Hardware has Emmitt trooped. Back and forth through the swollen rear door has he trooped. To skid on ice. To fall and break a leg. Wrench his back. Here in this numbing freeze. He is building this cat a house. He will hide that house away beneath the porch. Already he has on hand a unit to melt ice in the cat's water bowl. Already he has a heating unit for the interior. Needed now is another blanket, a soft something for the cat to sleep upon. And paint. Must have paint.

At a distance, the feral cat goes low on its haunches. It watches. It wants to know by God what he is up to.

And, inside, there is a screaming woman. *Stop slamming the damned door!*

Must hide her pills. Stop popping them myself.

Night descends. Night goes bang.

*The entire estate of Tallis Haley, I, Tallis Haley, drooling at the mouth, leave nothing to … those in neglect of me.*

A day like so many others in the morning turns out in the afternoon and on into nightfall to be a daylong string of phone calls—*My name is Mary. I'm the maid*—all for Tallis Haley. All, it seems, panic-stricken friends of the comatose boy. 'Tell him trouble,' they say. 'Tell him our butts are covered in trouble. He's got to do something.'

'Who is this?'

'You tell him.'

'He's in a coma. He can't move!'

'He'll move. You tell him.'

But Tallis Haley cannot speak. He cannot move. For all we know Tallis Haley is dying. Possibly of inattention … *unmourned unmoored unsung undone unavenged unattractive unwooed unhinged unsated unmanful, un—…*

Ryabovitch? Are you there?

No Ryabovitch. Ryabovitch has gone AWOL; he's out scouting the general's house, pining for the touch of a woman's hand. But women, mysterious as steam, are also AWOL.

Where is everyone?

Who's there? Hello? Is that Mary?

Panhandling one day along Spadina's busy Ave, Ormsby got into a discussion with the cityboy Tallis Haley.

The reason Daisy is telling this Ormsby story over the phone to sister Flute in Arizona—year-round sun, precious little water—is that Ormsby and several of his street friends are assembled this minute in her 2x8 kitchen. Drinking whatever she has been able to find for them, and they will not leave.

'They WILL NOT, Flute. And they are scraggly, they are rude, but I cannot kick them out. I really have no time to talk to you now.'

'Daisy,' Flute says. 'You have been talking to me for hours. What have Ormsby and his people been doing all that time?'

'The same thing, Flute. Saying the same thing over and over. They must speak to Tallis. They won't leave until they do. And lots of other things. They seem to think he has a brother living here, someone called Ryabovitch. I can't convince them he isn't real. They think he's a street person, just as they are. That he's a guy with a bad problem, going through a hard spell. I can't convince them he's only a character in a story. They've come to help, they say. The boy is having a hard time, they'll do what they can. They owe it to him. All those doughnuts and what-not he's shelled out for them, including—I don't mind saying—whatever drink, apparently, he's found in our cupboards.

'Mother of God!'

'They regard Tallis as some kind of saint.'

'Saint Tallis!'

'Don't poke fun. I can see him that way! Don't you dare say he isn't.'

'Get control of yourself, Daze.'

'I've always had my doubts about you, Flute.'

'You're the oddball. You haven't been the same since you were on *Larry King Live.*'

'You saw that?'

'Of course I saw it. My own sister on *King*, you think I'm going to tune in to a *Perry Mason* rerun?'

'How'd I do?'

'Stop fishing for praise. You were okay.'

'These layabouts say he's not in a coma. He's only sleeping it off. They say that he'll come out of it soon, just as they always do. Unless they freeze, get kicked by a mule, have had at the antifreeze, overdosed. Ormsby says the head is a funny place. Like a stuffed backpack, all the trash in there. The brain? Like an old refrigerator. Rotted meat, leaky veggies. Soggy, mucky, mouldy, smelly.'

'Mother of hell!'

'Tomorrow, next week, next year, I'll come in, find him sitting up. He'll say: "I'm hungry. When is dinner? What's going on? Why am I in these stinky pajamas?" You know he doesn't wear pajamas. He's always hated pajamas. We all do.'

'Did you get the lawyer's cheque?'

'What cheque?'

'Mother of hell!'

# Psssst!

'Don't do that, Emmitt. It rattles my nerves.'

All the same, Emmitt was first to notice.

'Emmitt, for God's sake!'

'He's perspiring. Sheets are drenched.'

The washing machine hums, the dryer sneezes, shudders and clicks. The Haleys are running out of sheets. For them, any old rag, for the boy one hundred percent Egyptian cotton, thread count no less than 450. And Daisy insists these sheets match, pillowcases as well.

Today, Tallis's father is trimming the boy's nails, hands and feet. They've never seen him thrashing, never witnessed the smallest twitch, but something other than repeated washings is slitting the sheets.

'Then get more.'

'Our Visa's busted. Credit line has a flat.'

'Try theft. Try hanging out at the 24-Hour with a foam cup.'

Late last night, sleepwalking about the house, Daisy thinks she saw Ormsby, running low as a rodent along the alley, disappear like a weaving phantom into their garage. But she also hears cat feet on the roof every night. She sees snowmen with stick eyes remove the sticks and walk. She entertains and receives mail from fictional characters. She's half-convinced she's Mary the maid when answering the phone. She sees her son's criminal assailant, that X girl, everywhere. She's a devotee of powerful drugs. She'll never get back into the classroom. She sleepwalks. Emmitt, useless with tools, is building a doll house. Why? Afraid of the answer, she balks at asking. Cat food. They have no cat. She does not consider herself a reliable news vendor. Visions have struck lately. She remains silent on Ormsby. Ormsby is her son's friend.

Emmitt's brother drops in. Emmitt, Arthur recalls, spent much of his time under the house. As a boy. It was how they bonded. Going under the house after Emmitt. Taking him supper. Throwing dirt-balls at him. Poking with sticks. Emmitt. Such a great fool. 'Taught him how to tie his shoes. How to button his shirt. How to slick down spiky hair. How to read and count. This little piggy and that little piggy makes how many piggies? Try again, I'd say. This little piggy, that little piggy, at the market. How many piggies?'

'But you were youngest,' says Daisy.

'Your man Emmitt was a slow learner.'

'Still is.'

Emmitt laughs. He loves this. Arthur was ever his saviour. Supplanted, one lucky day, by Daisy. Who now says to Arthur, canny expression on her face: 'Any woman in your life these days? Seeing anyone I know?'

'I am.'

'Serious?'

'It is.'

'How serious?'

'As it gets.'

'Marriage contemplated?'

'Could be.'

'God save you,' Emmitt says.

'Shoosh.'


Daisy Haley, another day—cold but pristine, more snow in the cards—is dialling a number. Her personal physician. Dr Evelyn. Dr Evelyn has the goods. Evelyn has at her fingertips an end to Daisy's midnight patrols, this war zone where the listless and the hysterical, the trite and the true, battle for her soul.

'Doctor?'

'Doctor.'

'Evelyn?

'Hello, Daisy.'

This morning Daisy Haley felt a draft. A gale, blowing through the house. And toed herself to the upstairs landing, crouched, and saw the front door standing open. Turned, and saw, in her son's room, his window. Open. But definitely open. How to explain this? Is some loathsome ogre playing tricks on her? Are the forces of darkness stealing her mind? Is her jokester son slipping from the house on a rope ladder?

'I found him covered in goop. For a moment, I thought him a disfigured mummy.'

'He has his own doctors. Call them.'

'It was nothing. I washed his face.'

'Why are you calling?'

'Prescription renewal, please.'

'Absolutely not. The addiction peril, remember?'

'I dumped all in the garbage.'

'Because he resembled an unfurled mummy?'

Talk goes on. These women have a fondness for each other. They go way back. Daisy does not tell her doctor-friend that after dispensing medicines into the garbage she afterwards upended the receptacle over the kitchen floor, and on her knees, over endless minutes, fearful of discovery, reclaimed a sizeable portion.

'I can't sleep. That's another of my horrors.'

'I'll fax in the renewal.'

---

Weather changed drastically: first the air with a nip at dawn, thunder and lightning far off. Quickly the sky blackened so that you'd think a bucket had fallen over your head. Wind whirled; the whole world shook and clanged. Limbs snapped and spun each which way. Trees, wrested from the roots, sailed away. Lightning bolts criss-crossed the sky. Hail, boulder-sized, thick as a shield, decided to fall. It was under these challenging conditions that Fate the Trickster hurled together Little Sissy Yapochee and Little Doozy Pony.

Sissy: Do you feel as though a bucket just landed over your head?

Doozy: Something like that.

Sissy: What do you think?

Doozy: Often that bucket falls independent of weather.

Sissy: I meant what do you think about us?

Doozy: You and me?

Sissy: Yes. Do we portend?

Doozy: Portend what?

Sissy: Portend.

Doozy: As in presage? Signify?

Sissy: Something like that.

Doozy: I don't know.

Sissy: Do we portend an uncertain future? Disaster? Lots of sleepless nights crying.

Doozy: I surely hope not.

Sissy: A *Sea of Melancholy*? Love by *The Blue Lagoon*?

Doozy: Do we have to talk about this?

Sissy: I am merely curious.

Doozy: Me too. Now you bring up the issue. You and me.

Sissy: We could go to sleep now.

Doozy: We could.

Sissy: Are you sleepy?

Doozy: Desperately.

Sissy: I love sleeping with you.

Doozy: Same here.

Sissy: Because we portend.

Doozy: We do?

Sissy: We prop up the here and now.

Doozy: Are you really the last Yapochee on earth?

Sissy: So I'm told.

Doozy: Hard to believe I'm sleeping with the last Yapochee on earth.

Sissy: We could make another.

Doozy: Good idea.

(*T H E   E N D*)

Daisy litters the bed with thousands of snapshots. Here he is, bouncing a soccer ball. Here he is, eating ice cream. Here he is, riding the red tricycle. Here he is, falling off. Here he is … She could go on like this all day. Here are the three of us. I already look old.

*We've got to be brave. That's all there is to it. Wait. Hope. Be brave.*

I'm not brave. I'm anti-war. I'm anti-everything. I'm anti–yesterday's Girl Scouts peddling cookies at my door.

Those are good cookies. Have one?

The reality is these cookies are so-so. If they were of higher quality people like us would feel obliged to donate more for them, but in the end scheme of things the volume of sales would plummet. I could deliver an hour's lecture on the subject.

Please don't.

———————

At the church square Officers Ryabovitch and Tallis learned they must descend the hill to the river, and follow the bank till they reached the gardens, where they might expect to find a path leading directly to the general's house. All this was well and good and eventually they were upon the specified trail, which much delighted them, for the path was pleasantly maintained, boasting wide fields to either side redolent with quail and hare, and the far woodlands fancifully dressed in splendid red and golden leaves, and a running brook that afforded good company to the already good company shared by their twinned minds. Do you think there will be girls at the general's party, asked Ryabovitch, at a certain precipitous turn. (Here the view stretched interminably downhill, the distant house barely to be seen among a richness of colour as done by Vermeer.) Both paused, exchanging contemplative smiles, and taking advantage of their brief pause to remove the odd pebble that had gravitated into their boots. 'I expect many lovely ladies shall be present,' said Officer Ryabovitch, smirking. 'Together with a cadre of teens for you to dally with.'

'I shall be disappointed if there isn't,' Officer Haley replied. 'I shall grasp the sweet hands of each one, and lend my beggar's ear to their every remark. Though all the while I shall hope to see the divine X leaping from a secret cupboard, clutching school books.'

Ryabovitch laughed at his friend's extravagant remark, and they laced their boots, lay arms across each other's back, and went on again towards what they believed to be the general's house and a party alive with good drink and winsome girls. But after a time, the gentle slope steepened, bogs there were to cross, and a swampy enclave of buzzing insects and menacing snouts protruding from the muck. Confidence was eroded, and they cast suspicious eye upon each other. As if to say, Ryabovitch, you are to blame, for it seems we have lost our way, and Ryabovitch at once crying out, You are the dolt, Haley, since you refused to look where you were going, your mind so set on having your way with the girls, and losing all that time with emptying your boots, which would have us late and the party done, and all the girls retired.

These comments inviting others, each more wrathful than the first, until full rancour ignited. They rolled on the ground, each doing his best to tear the uniform from the other's hide, and blood pouring over both, scornful words in plentiful supply.

In aftermath, dusting themselves, apologies rendered.

My fault, old scout.

No, mine, young lad.

We took the low road.

Not the high.

Shall we go on?

By all means.

They arrived at a scene like unto Monet's Argenteuil garden, and who bursts through the door but Anna Sergeyevna, radiant in a lilac-coloured gown. 'My saviours!' she cried, thrusting upon them manifold kisses. 'I feared you would never come.'

Later, the two steal separately back to camp, where they lay in contemplative appreciation of an evening well spent, perfumed and alight still in fancy uniform, handsome faces bright with cheer and flushed from excess wine.

Voices raised to the rafters as they regaled and challenged each other with exaggerated appreciation of the general's splendid house and grounds, his many servants, the lavish spread of viands, the merry music, Anna's narrow waist, the exquisite warmth of a girl's hand, softness of flesh, the brief, sensational display of a well-turned ankle, the laughter that rang out through the whole of the day, the enchanting intrigue of passion in darkened rooms—of all the fine womanly arms that evening-long encircled them.

'You surprise me,' Emmitt tells Daisy, 'by turning out to be of overwrought nature. Put those photos away.'

'I haven't *turned out* to be anything I wasn't before. All women are overwrought. Being overwrought is the way we've devised to tolerate men. And married life. Men couldn't stand us any other way. Overwrought is how we get things done. We are life's churn, men the residue. I will not put these photos away. Here is one of you with a snapping turtle. The turtle is the good-looking one.'

Recounting this episode on the phone to Arthur, Emmitt heard Arthur say, 'Dips and dives, a life is, and unscored heights. Meantime, you're both like the football player in the huddle who emerges to weave along the scrimmage line when the fool is supposed to be downfield pulling in the long goal-line pass.'

'You know nothing whatever of football,' Emmitt said. 'You are a screwball poet incapable of tying your own shoelaces.'

Daisy fluttered by, waving snapshots. 'Here's a whole Polaroid batch of you and me, jay-bird naked. I can't imagine why.'

———————

*'Young man, you have not heard the last of this. I've had enough of your lollygagging between sheets. You are herewith grounded! Do you hear me? Grounded!'*

*'Honey, the poor knucklehead is in a coma. He already is grounded.'*

———————

During the night each heard the intrepid whine of an ambulance slowed by the maze of one-way streets. You didn't call, did you? Why would I do that? We have no emergency here. Then why is it stopping at our house? They are checking numbers. It's next door. Is it old Mrs Poindexter? Go see.

It was old Mrs Poindexter. Her son was visiting. He says she fell down the stairs.

Is she badly hurt?

Just shaken.

Did he push her?

I don't know.

He wants the house.

True.

Do you think when we are in an old-age funk

Tallis will want to push us down the stairs? I don't.

Me neither.

You might have employed 'neither' that way five hundred years ago. Now such usage is considered archaic.

'Nay, Horatio. Nor I neither.' Shakespeare.

You're a lying fool. I thought the ambulance was coming for me. That's why I have my boots on.


Mary the maid.

This is, I assume, the Haley residence.

It is, dear.

I am calling for Mr Haley. Is he available?

You sound quite young. At a stretch, I'd say you are too young for Emmitt. He's nearing fifty. If he told you less you will have to accept he lies.

Runs around on you, does he?

Not really. I'm attempting to enliven my day.

The caller laughed. Tell Mr Haley Mrs Poindexter hopes he will visit. At the hospital.

Mrs Poindexter is way too old for him, I should think. May I have your name, dear?

I am Nurse Cee.

Nurse C?

Close enough.


Now why should old Mrs Poindexter expect a visit from you?

I make a soup, a stew, I run over with a bowl. She's not much good any-more at a stove.

What a fine Samaritan you are. I had no idea.

I had her cat put down.

Excuse me?

Fudge. The cat. Fudge was almost as old as Agnes.

Agnes?

Mrs Poindexter. Fudge threw up all over the house. She was mostly blind. Liked waddling about between the legs. I was afraid she'd fall. Bust a hip.

The cat?

She loves my Pearl Bailey macaroni and cheese. She probably hopes I'll show up at the hospital with a bowl.

You put too much butter in your macaroni and cheese. I keep telling you.

But you don't know the odd bit.

The odd bit is that you appear to have a life apart from our own. What odd bit do you have in mind?

Nurse Cee.

Who's she?

The woman who called you. Nurse Cee.

What about Nurse C?

She's gone out with the son a time or two. Agnes is of the opinion Nurse Cee may be her son's girlfriend.

Is that good or bad?

I don't know.

Surely they'd not both push her down the stairs.

Push who?

Your Agnes.

Who's saying anybody pushed anybody down the stairs?

You did.

You said that. Not me.

Why are you putting on your coat? Where are you off to?

The Hardware. Need paint.

What in the world for?

Saying this, her thoughts already have turned elsewhere. A Dostoevsky line has floated in—*The children run about and crawl among us.* She wills herself to visualize Tallis among the many running or crawling. And there he is, tottering, but coming. His first meagre upright steps, her arms waiting.

Nurse Cee is this minute scratching her tummy. It is a habit she wants to cure herself of. She does it when she feels someone is talking about her. She knows any number who might at the moment be asserting words in sabotage of her good name. Foremost among them is William P. Poindexter who diligently insists on pinning her against any wall presenting itself. She finds this funny sometimes, especially as he likes to whisper tidings into an ear as he presses. She can predict what he will next say, which is why she can't refrain from laughing. The laughter undermines his passion and usually he wheels away with hurt feelings disguising a total disgust. This compels her to laugh somewhat more judiciously. She has not been brought up to inflict pain. Which may explain why she may then mash her pelvis against his or seize one of his hands (or both) and thump that hand onto a breast (or both). At this, his eyes, as if propelled by hidden springs, will go bong-bong, and she knows she must move fast, because here he comes again.

She does not act this way with other men, and why she does this with William P. Poindexter is something she must think about, should she ever find the time. It's kind of fun teasing William P. Poindexter; doing so is not yet a malignant curse. Witnesses to these displays might conclude Nancy Cee harbours a playful, or lustful, or slavishly sluttish nature. But how wrong they'd be. She's quite prim—prudish, in fact, very much the image of her adoring, and adored, grandmother. The men Nancy has slept with may be counted on one finger. And half of another, to be strictly truthful. That half has to do with something that happened to her in a limousine, on the way to that very grandmother's ninety-seventh birthday party. William P. is not to be seen on either of these fingers. Her view is that William P. is a man of two halves: one half narcissistic, the other his narcissistic brother. Has he spent his life pressing women against whatever? Could be. Not against sheets, certainly. When Rebecca Whitehall is so ensnared in Sheila Shott's books she has Rebecca thinking *Oh God save me from this!* Nurse Cee would not spell out the O. Like: *O my God, not again!* It's the one fault she finds with Sheila. Refuge Nancy finds in blaming the books' copy editors. *Oh* demands a comma or exclamation after it. *Oh! Oh! Oh!* she finds herself murmuring, at any approach of William P. Poindexter.

'You want to turn him now? God, look at his back. This cream isn't worth spit.'

'Wash between his toes. Have you washed between his toes?'

'I never do, according to you.'

'Anna Sergeyevna loves kissing. She received few as a child and fewer still from her husband. Moscow-lover kisses were heavenly, though random. My Toronto kisses are her best ever.'

'Zan likes kissing.'

'Baloney. She hardly knows you exist.'

'What are you saying? A moment ago she was washing between my toes.'

Daisy Haley, as on every other day, was sitting by her son's bedside, sick with despair, exhausted by the pain of grief, as if pain had been ushered in by the House of Usher: I must have drifted off. I was so worn out, you see. A ghostly, wonderful presence strode in. I was bathed in a golden light. Suffused with the most benevolent warmth. But when I raised my head, I saw there was no ceiling. The roof had lifted off. I could see through the walls. Dancers were performing a ballet. In the snow. I did a double take, thinking I'd recognized someone there. Tallis. He was dancing, too. But I looked to the bed, and there he was. I closed my eyes. I must have moaned. And it was then I felt something graze my cheek. Ever so softly. I opened my eyes and just as I did his hand was pulling away. His face turned to me. With such a smile. Such a heartbreaking, wondrous smile. The arm folding to his chest on the sheet. His eyes closing.

The smile vanishing. Gone again.

*Daisy in The Looking Glass Following A Very Bad Day*

A Toronto mystic, appearing on Jack Webster's TV talk show this morning in Vancouver, claimed she had predicted the boy would stroke his mother's cheek. 'Love can bridge all gaps,' she stated. Webster suffered a broken finger, getting onstage, when he toppled against a lamp. The mystic had predicted this mishap while in the green room. Daisy Haley, in the meanwhile, has turned down an invitation to appear on *Good Morning America*. All offers of marriage, she said, have been refused. He's underage. Try later.

He did stroke her face. She knows it happened and she will not hear otherwise. It has brought her the most wonderful peace. She feels robust, her old self. Never mind the tears. Those, my friend, are tears of joy. I am beside myself with elation. It is a sign. Tallis is coming back. He is coming back to us. No. For once and all, listen to me. To us. This was your imagination. Only your imagination. Stress. Do you hear me? You are having a breakdown. You are sick. You need help. Here, take these pills. Dammit, would you take them? Rest. Close your eyes. Do we have to hog-tie you? You want to be committed? You will be, I promise you, you keep this up. Daisy? Oh, Daisy, show some sense. Me? Show sense? Here is sense for you. I want a full-time person hired. I want that person stationed inside that boy's room any time we are not there ourselves. I insist on this. He comes out of that coma, I tell you. He exits! He came out of it to stroke his mother's face. My face. You're jealous because it wasn't your face. How do I know how he does it? He just does it, how does any-one know how? He leaves his bed during the night. I've seen proof! Pure, exalted truth! Constant vigil! She's raving again. What did I tell you? The grief was too much. She's lost hold on reality.

'Common people. The rabble. The herd.'

'Yes?'

'That's us.'

'I'm common?'

'Uniform as a garden rake. We constitute the aggrieved society. We contend against a hostile agency. Our own government wishes we didn't exist. We are the nation's headache. We are capitalism's nightmare.'

'I am not common.'

'Yet we plow the roads. We waitress tables. We die in our wars. We hope one day for a living wage.'

'I do very well, thank you.'

'Your day will come.'

The girl who likes sometimes to call herself X nightly must tolerate such conversation from the parental unit. Since being jackknifed through the air and bonged on the head she has sensed a modicum of humour lurks within their interminable chatter. They refuse TV's insanity; this is how they entertain each other.

They have dined. Rather well, too. Not chicken, unless dressed up to taste other than chicken. Now Zan sits at the clean kitchen table, ostensibly doing schoolwork.

If I had known of your socialist tendencies, I would have thought long and hard before agreeing to marry you.

You jumped right in. You thought not for one second.

True. But now I do.

Concluding what?

I don't have to tell you my every thought.

True. But I find a deepening understanding of how you think draws me ever closer to heaven.

I don't doubt it. Soon you'll be sitting next to God.

Zan has had enough of this. She is snatching up her coat.

And where do you think you are going, young lady?


… head out to the SuperSave, leap a curb, jump a hedge, strike again! Kill somebody. See whose head is hardest. What she's got to show for it is a small sometimes throbbing wedge of blue up on her forehead. Chipped bones, they say. Ice-pack the mother. A scalp-gash hidden by everyday wiry chopped hair. A pert nose she regards as bent. A slightly cast left eye. Otherwise, she's healed, she's back to normal. Flying colours, every test. But take it easy, young lady. Take it easy for a while. Best to be careful. Cautious. You never know.

*I know.* Zan says this: 'I killed him.' She can have her ears plugged, music pulsing with Lisa 'Left Eye' Lopes's 'Baby-Baby-Baby' and her head suddenly says to her: 'You as much as killed Tallis Haley.' *You're the chain-saw cyclist maniac.*

No way she's ever again getting on a bike.

She can hear the crunch of her shoes in the snow. She is aware of sunlight. Pretty dazzling it is, too. The haze has left her head despite TLC's fine thumping 'Red Light Special'…. Can it be that she's inching free of her dark sack? That grief's claws have dulled? She's alone, for a change. Thank you, God. No one hanging by, clutching at her arm, issuing soggy concern, pathetic advice. They've been dogging her footsteps, those mushy, soggy parents, hour after besieged hour. 'How's the kid?' If she hears these words again, she will kill herself. No way. No way she's going to put up with any more of the parental unit's perpetual hand-wringing, their weepy looks. Get off my case!

Get stuffed!

Get a life!

Go feed the world's starving people!

Get a divorce!

She has told them that. Today she stands on Bloor, in snowy slush outside
the SuperSave, clearing her head of all that muck. Mush, muck and drivel. A
walk. Mom. Would you mind? She has slammed the door, snatched up her red
beret and hit the road. She has hit it, and got one miserable block. One hundred and twenty-eight steps. Avoiding all sidewalk cracks. Hit a crack, go back.
She is here at SuperSave, eyeing the melon display—for ten minutes eyeing the
melons, uneasy of mind, definitely something scratchy inside, having a go at
her stomach walls. She wants to puke. Yes, she would very much like to puke,
even if it is only on these melons. It gnaws at her the cruel words she's hung on
her dopey, weird, slop-slinging parents. Though that is not what is bothering
her. Garbage flung at ridiculous parents is nothing to stew about. Nothing new
on that front. So, what is it, then? Why not confess to the crap that is clawing
her insides? What it is is knowing—but not knowing why—she has arrived at
the Bloor SuperSave bypassing with leery eye dreary 2x8. She has circled
around the scene of the crime. Oh, yes, she is no idiot, she has deliberately
avoided sight of the place. No more of that stupid vigil of dismal 2x8, in
weather so cold it gives the ears nosebleed. 2x8 Major can rot. It can go to hell.
She is over feeling that guilt. Over the pain. Out of the nightmare. The nightmare is done, splat, kersplatted! She is not going to mourn the rest of her life
over that nitwit boy. If his goose is cooked, then let it cook. Good lord, it was a
fluky accident, it was fate, it was definitely, definitely, not her fault. The bike's
fault, the cat's fault, the honking car. And wasn't that freak Ormsby running
towards her, waving his arms, pants about to fall off him. And some U of T
birdbrain on a porch kissing some girl. And nitwit's nose in a book when it's
clear he'd seen her. Seen his eyes slanting her way. Maybe it was those slanting
eyes to blame. Otherwise wouldn't she have paid attention to the blaring car
horn? No, no one in her right mind is going to fault her. Let them try. Let them
go ahead and try. Just let one freaked-out butter-belly person utter one word
that would even begin to suggest this X girl was even one smidgen responsible,

or that Tallis Haley now must rack up the rest of his life in abyss hell because stupid Zan couldn't keep her butt glued to the bike seat!

She looks down Major towards the house in question. It will do no harm to assure herself the house in question is still standing. She spins, looks, and lets fly a string of silent curses.

Ludicrous. Absolutely ludicrous. Spotted is Chig, her self-appointed guardian angel, trying to scoot and hide. Dropping from sight behind a muddy Honda Civic. Her self-proclaimed utterly insane father, trailing behind his crazed maniac chain-saw-killer daughter. Keeping watch. Looking to see who the treasured daughter—with her bare hands, perhaps?—will maim today. She flings up her hands in despair—Is the whole world in collapse? Must I shoulder every burden?—and strides through the slush towards this miserable excuse for a parent. A baby. He is such a wet-behind-the-ears guy. Such a baby.

I'm okay, Dad. Wish you didn't worry so much.

There they stand, in the middle of the street, hugging each other.


Daisy?

Yes.

She's there again.

Who?

That girl.

Call the police. That man is way too old for her.


Daisy: Sheila's on the phone. She insists on talking to you.

Rebecca Whitehall: Tell her I'm not available.

Daisy: You're her character, honey. She needs you.

Rebecca: Tell her to use a stand-in. Like in the movies when the star doesn't want to be thrown from a train.

Daisy: I'll tell her. But you two need to work this out between yourselves.


Daisy: She says she's blocked.

Rebecca: Us characters know writers' block to be plain foolishness.

Daisy: Oh, come now.

Rebecca: It's pure laziness. We sit around by the thousands, fiddling with our hair, blowing the nose, filing our nails, waiting to be called. We twitch, beep and peep like newborn birds, we yowl like water buffalo, but do they listen?

Daisy: She won't come to the phone, Sheila. She says to tell you she's pigging it out here with me at 2 x 8 Major.

Sheila: You're eating?

Daisy: Emmitt made us Reubens.

Sheila: Wine?

Daisy: You betcha.

Sheila: The randy bitch knows very well consumption of dairy products makes her acne break out. Her face will resemble a road map of Mars. But for me, she'd be an overweight twit.

Daisy, hanging up, says to Sheila, 'Overweight is good looks misunderstood.' She turns, intending to tell Rebecca Whitehall this intermediary business is giving her a headache. But the space occupied by Rebecca a moment before is now empty. The unfinished Reuben, showing the imprint of an aggressive bite, a crumpled napkin, is there on the table. Rebecca, gulping the last of her wine, with a quick fluffing of her great hair, has been snatched away. Sheila's work, Daisy presumes.

True.

Rebecca was sidetracked, only for a second, as she shot out the front door. A man was mounting the steps. Russian, by appearance. She sensed a peculiar connection. 'Your name, sir?' He clicked his heels. Bowed. 'Officer Ryabovitch, at your service, madam.' 'You live here?' 'For the moment.' 'Goodbye, then.' 'Yes.' By God, she thought, hurrying on, in a huff because that stoop-shouldered, lynx-whiskered man quite obviously held himself superior to her. She had her problems with Sheila, but by God her genre was every bit the match of that high-brow bunch.

*'How lovely, you look, my darling!'*

*Rebecca fixed onto Turner P. Blindstone's bold, gleaming eyes. Such a hand-some man.*

*'Did you like my speech?'*

*'Hemostatic!' Rebecca declared, dancing high on her toes. Turner, for his part, thinking,* Those eyes of my sweetheart could melt steel. One could run a subway on those beams. *His own eyes sparkled magnificently. And why not? It isn't every day an ordinary citizen is invited to address the UN.*

*'You were sensational, my darling. My heart thundered with pride as China and Russia—together with every other nation, stood to give you rousing applause.'*

*'Ah, well, they are with me, you understand, on the new tunnel between England and France. Fourteen billion pounds I stand to make on that deal. After paying off the concrete guys. More, once the tunnel opens. It impresses China and Russia that I could pay off in one sweep of the hand their entire national debt out of the change in my money belt. Though I prefer spending it on you, my exquisite one. Shall we go? Mary is expecting us.'*

*'Mary the maid?'*

*'The queen, my precious pet. Afterwards, I propose we jet away for skinny-dipping in the Black Sea.'*

*Rebecca well remembered the humiliation last suffered at Windsor Castle, when she had stumbled over the queen's legs in the dark—why the queen had been sitting alone at midnight in the darkness of a long hall remained a mystery—and been chased down those same halls by wild animals said to be dogs, which they did not in the least resemble. On the other hand, last season's visit to Turner's grand Romanian estate on the Black Sea had resulted in pleasure elevated to the highest atoll. Here, where the sand was powdery-white as icing sugar they had made repeated love to the tuneful waltz of lapping waves, as little fishes of gay colouration swam excitedly within their own gaily-thrashing limbs.*

*Sheila Shott often said this was her best scene ever, up there with* Gatsby, Moby Dick, *and Molly's soliloquy in that Irish fellow's work. Rebecca acknowledged that, in the throes of passion, she had repeatedly shouted* Yes I will Yes I am Yes I dunno Yes, *but of her own volition, having pissall to do with Sheila's expertise or lack thereof.*

The front door at 2x8 Major was found to be open on a mild Sunday in late February, and then it was that a large dog, unknown by any in the vicinity, and of unknown disposition, made quiet entry. The dog gave every appearance of being on some quest, perhaps nothing more than a search for food, in that first it padded straightforwardly into the kitchen. There it discovered a bowl for some reason abandoned on the table. Ah. Beef, cheese, bread!

The dog chomped these up and for some little while licked the bowl. A noise from above caught its attention. The dog responded with a low growl of no great artifice, while simultaneously wagging its long tail. Shunning the bowl, the dog proceeded the few steps to the back door; the dog examined the backyard through the glass pane, discovering little of interest. A cat looked sombrely back at him, and two young squirrels raced up and down a far wall. The dog made a turn on the floor, then lay down to lick a rear leg, its ears attuned however to the sound still issuing from the upper floor. With sudden ferocity of impulse, the dog bounded up the stairs. In the first room it saw a strange lady fussing over something at a table. That she was dressed somewhat peculiarly the dog did not think to remark upon; it could surmise at a distance that the objects she was moving about held no scent, and thus did not warrant his attention. A second person was moving about in another room, now and then snorting, now and then clearing the throat. The party in question was at a side window, cleaning the glass with a dirty rag. Dust floating up from this rag prompted the dog to sneeze. The man took no notice, which the dog found interesting, though not declaratively.

He continued his quest, now returning to the long hallway of polished wood which, amusingly, made his paws go *click-click*, made him slip and slide. He thought again of the empty kitchen dish, which at some point might again be filled. He could see ahead a window where sunlight flitted, and smelled in his immediate future another human presence. He poked a curious head inside this space: an inert form lay on a bed. This shape did not instantly beguile the dog. First he must go to the window.

This the mutt did. It stretched forepaws upon the sill and looked out upon what proved to be a familiar street. A few sparrows briefly returned its gaze. Otherwise the scope of matters under way there seemed without purpose. Truthfully, the dog did not quite know what to do with itself. Certainly, it was time to quit the window.

The dog did so. And there before its eyes, as though seen for the first time, was the bed and a still boy in the bed, inviting comfort.

It leaped at once onto the bed. It applied a wet tongue to the boy's face, looked to see if the boy's eyes might open.

They did not. Experiencing no great rupture at this failure, the dog pressed cold snout against the boy's neck, tongued an ear, scratched a paw over its own scrotum. The boy's odour was one unfamiliar to the dog's intellect; his stiff posture while asleep demonstrated the firm hand of a disciplined master-in-the-making. For a homeless dog, such might be advantageous. He vowed 'to play his cards right' and stick around long enough to see what news evening winds summoned in. It licked the boy's salty limbs. Finding satisfaction. It'd known the silent response before. Smiling, it stretched out full-length alongside the boy, sliding immediately into twitchy if dreamful sleep in which fat white rabbits snickered on high snow-clad limbs—the dog thinking his day, overall, was proving in everywise detail worthwhile.

How much of her brain was left inside the coma? How much there to begin with. She sees a spangle of rodents nibbling: I like this lobe. I like the other. You are both fools. Those others are good as French cooking. Tallis Haley. The wimpy, crude, starry-eyed grunge. Why couldn't he find another place to sit? Who, these days, except gung-ho Tallis, would sit on the stoop in freezing cold, nose buried in a sea of books? She wonders now, not for the first time, if it wasn't some snitch of white page seen out of the corners of her eye—What is that crazy guy reading?—that made her lose her grip, plummet through air, land noggin against noggin.

What noble deeds our boy might have accomplished, the parental unit will be saying.

What Zan sees when she thinks about this Haley boy, whom she thinks about every odd second, is herself at the head of a terrifying Hells Angels bicycle gang plowing down over everything on the road. They are slooching north now on Spadina, through Chinatown. They take the ring above College,

wheels squeal at Harbord, and here they barroom up
Major. Zoom-zoom! And there sits this clown, reading.
Here we go, girls, she says to her murderous pals.
They hit the gears, give gun to roaring catcall
—and SPLAT!…So long, Haley.

Neighbours complain that suspicious persons enter and exit 2x8 at all hours,
and that, indeed, a deathly pallor at times embraces the dwelling—a terrible
discredit to our fine neighbourhood, people say. Those poor bastards know
not which way to turn. Insomnia depression wit's end collapse into sorrow the
very pits of hell hanging by a thread flag nailed to the mast hands set to the
plow laid on with a trowel cards on the table skating on thin ice a place that lets
no light in the cold breath of reason passes by no scent of flower blink of sunshine every heartbeat measured tears cut glass under the eyelids, all apparently
without end let's change places climb into his body he assume ours, something, anything, end this mercy calling to the Infamous Nothing

Help!

Help!

Help!

'And so. And so, Emmitt, dearest husband, what I feel in sum is that there is
precious trivial difference between what is normally thought of as the real and
the true, and what is normally thought of as a thing made up, invented, fictitious, impossible and untrue. Which is why I am so delighted to have you sitting here with me, sharing this pot of tea in the grip and glean of frosty night.
'We had no hot water this morning. And a wet towel on the floor. Where he
ALWAYS threw his. And his desk messy, where he'd been looking for something. Rebecca Whitehall agrees. One thing she says she has learned from
Sheila is that fiction and life are the same. For instance, herself a little girl from
Saskatchewan, never dreaming she'd one day have a thousand orgasms in a
Romanian field.'

'Spare us Rebecca's orgasms, please. We don't want to excite the boy.'

Emmitt is at U of T's Robarts Library, returning a batch of books found in a Tim Hortons sack under Daisy's desk when he was swinging a mop over the floor. 'A touch overdue,' he admitted. The man he is speaking to arches a distinguished brow. The brow curls higher, each peek at the books. 'You have been out of the country on an extended stay, perhaps?'

'Not exactly.'

'From which there was no easy exit? Easter Island in the southeastern Pacific Ocean, perhaps? St. Helena in the South Atlantic?'

'I know where—'

'Antarctica? Nunavut?' A grimace of distaste distorts the man's face. 'Are these coffee stains, perchance? Volcanic ash? Mayonnaise?'

'Beg pardon?'

The man sniffed. 'Mice droppings? The cereal bowl tipped?'

'You're saying those books are damaged?'

'These *rare* books? Possibly they were abandoned to the elements?'

'Excuse me?'

'Rain? Sleet? Did I somehow fail to notice a recent typhoon struck our area?'

'What are you getting at?'

'Your Daisy I take to be the same Daisy who mutilated a prized *Finnegans.*'

'You know about that?'

'Word percolates. It is inconceivable to me that such a person could have once been among our celebrated faculty.'

'Once! She still is!'

'Not as I hear it.'

Emmitt's shoulders sag. He's giving up. Time for a hasty retreat. A thousand eyes appraising him. Daisy's library card confiscated. Borrowing privileges suspended.

Aw, gee, the embarrassment: trudging home, long woollen coat, picked up at a Stollery's sale, dragging along the snowy walks, rabbit fur hat-flaps snug against the ears, frigid wind blistering the face. Ice needles hang from every eavesdrop and spout, every rooftop and tree limb. Soon, he thinks, to hang from his nose. From the very uppermost heavens they hang, glittering like strung diamonds. Automobiles zag on the roadway like ice boxes flung from the back of sixteen-wheelers.

'Hello, Mr Haley.'

That Zan girl, passing. Kicking up snow. He's touched by the greeting. Wishes her good health.

Daisy: Our son's bedside lamp appears to be broken.

Emmitt: Broken? How?

—The light doesn't come on.

Try the switch.

—I did.

Perhaps the bulb is dead.

—I changed the bulb.

Is it plugged in?

—I will not have him exit to find his lamp doesn't work.

—I see you've disassembled his lamp. To what end?

To fix it.

—What's wrong with it?

Switch is shot.

—What can be so difficult about fixing a lamp?

You are trying my patience, Daze.

—I will not have Tallis waking to find lamp parts scattered all over his bed.

He was always taking things apart. I thought he might enjoy it if I fixed this lamp on his bed.

—I will not have you speaking of him as though he existed in ancient history. He's alive. His heart is ticking. He will get well.

This lamp won't. This lamp is no good. I'm throwing out this lamp.

—Throw me out, too. Throw us all out.

Morning. Daisy Haley enters her son's room, flicks the light switch. His table lamp flashes on. But what is that? The tiny little screwdriver is cupped in her zombie son's hand. Daisy's hands converge on her mouth. She will not scream. Her mind is in conflict. If she did scream, she does not know what emotion that scream would be meant to convey. Her first thought is joy. A second later, dismay. Horror. She does not know what it is she is meant to think. Has Tallis woken during the night and repaired his lamp? Did her husband do so? Did he carefully place the tiny screwdriver in the boy's hand? Out of kindness? Perversity? Wickedness? What mental aberration has manifested itself?

'Emmitt!' she screams. 'Get in here!'

He enters, on the run. Fresh from a shower, towelling his head, another towel draping the hips. He halts at the door, looks first at her face, then at the bed. She notes the precise moment he sees the screwdriver in the boy's hand. His mouth gapes open. He glances at the lamp burning brightly on the bedside table. Now looks back again at the boy's hand. 'What's the joke?' he shouts. 'What have you done?' He whirls away. She hastens after him. They palaver in whispers awhile within their bedroom. Then, together, they are back again. They stand side by side by the boy's bed.

*You did it! I didn't! Did! Didn't! Then, who did?*

*Who repaired the lamp? Who deposited the tool in the boy's hand?*

The bed rocks. They are shaking Tallis Haley and shouting his name. Nothing. Finally, they stand silent, holding on to each other. Silence is around them like a spell.

*He did it. Came out of deep sleep. Fixed the lamp.*

Emmitt is telling the Hardware employees of an episode in London when Daisy convinced him it was time he owned on his head a true English gentleman's hat.

'That little French thing you wear isn't you.'

They were ambling along Old Burlington Street, hatters to right and left. The Herbert Johnson window, as did most hatters along Old Burlington

Street, had a sign: *By appointment to Her Majesty the Queen.* Daisy misread the shop's name, expressing surprise that George Johnston, a favourite Canadian poet, had a hat bin on Old Burlington Street.

The Herbert Johnson gentleman was very rude. '*Bin*, Madamn!'

'Are you knighted, sir?' the gentleman asked.

'Not yet,' Emmitt replied.

Nose elevating. 'Our hats are the high water of hats,' the hatter said. 'One has to be of high station to wear our hats. It offends us to see our hats on a Canadian's head. We find it vile.'

'This put my dander up,' Emmitt told Hardware. 'So I put one and another of his hats on my head. I pranced a bit. Daisy was telling that hatter a thing or two. We ended up with two hats, one for each of us. She still wears hers. Well, until recently, she did. She sits in her workstation, wearing that hat. A man's hat, you see. Quite becoming. I don't know what happened to mine. A fine Anthony Eden umbrella, silver tipped, completes the show. She tells me her prospects when she married me were melancholy. Humanity shuddered, she said, each time she inched close to saying yes. She reserved the right to sue me for reparation of war debts, should we ever divorce. There's much to be said in support of that view.'

'War debts,' said the Hardware woman. 'I must remember to insert reparation of war debts into my vows.'

'You're getting married?'

'Third time. Can't you tell?'

'By how beat-up she looks,' another said. 'Once to me.'

# Women Ignite Sparks at Economic Talks

Toronto's globe-trotting Daisy Haley, in an unexpected appearance today at the World Banking Summit, at The Hague, set fire under numerous delegates when she issued a stern rebuke of international banking practice. Ms Haley delivered a passionate statement in support of a 'universal concept of ethics' that follows 'reverence for life' theories, a philosophy now held outdated. Her speech caused pandemonium among the thousand international bankers in attendance, who had expected Henry Kissinger. 'It

Why Must Women Do All The Work Around Here?

smarted a little,' one Royal Bank delegate said, 'but much was over my head.' A stoic Rebecca Whitehall, fresh from a London detox centre, accompanied Ms Haley. Turner P. Blindstone, director of the summit and head of British relief operations in Bosnia, called the women's appearance an outrage. Whitehall declared the summit 'harrowing'. These bankers come at a pretty woman like fullbacks charging a line, she said. The women next go on to Rio de Janeiro, where ...

In bed beside her, the lamp low, Emmitt watches Daisy breathe. Breathe and twitch. Small bubbles form over her lips. She has always twitched a bit, when dreaming. Thrashed about. Ah. The bubbly eruptions disappearing now.

Sheila Shott, phone in hand, is beside herself. Her agent has refused to take her call. Now her publisher is on the line, putting the screws to her. They've gone all chintzy. No more will they absorb the cost of even a fleabag hotel. 'Your sales have plummeted,' the woman is telling her. 'You've gone from midlist anonymity into slimy basement. *Peyton Place* your books are not. Your fan clubs are dissolving. You're old hat. You're last week. You haven't moved with the times. The F-word has never appeared in a single Sheila Shott book. Turner P. Blindstone is a bore, Rebecca Whitehall erratic. She's a liberal freak. Possibly a socialist. Your sex scenes don't sizzle, your sheets don't tangle. Ho-hum, your readers say. Their hearts don't clutch. We will not be reissuing any of your clammy titles. Peddle your new rubbish elsewhere.

'Fruitcake!' Sheila screams. She slams down the phone. 'Moronic imbecile! You will hear from my lawyer.'

Now what? Has the hotel desk been informed? She's busted, maybe fifty bucks in the purse, no way can she pay the bill. Okay, raid the drinkie unit, sit, pause, think. A back door? Classy joints like Four Seasons protect the back doors. The hounds of hell guard those doors. This drinkie is nice, thank you, I believe I'll have another. All right, what would my heroine do? One, she'd empty the little drinkie unit's drinkies into her purse. There, that's done. Good, now I'm a thief. It's a busy, hustling joint, surely I can slip by the desk, the doormen, hop into a waiting cab. They do not get many take-chargers like Sheila Shott. I'm ready, my grip packed—stockings sweaters notebooks undies money shoes toothbrush now where is my coat? Oh. On me. How quaint!

No one can say being a woman has held her back. She slings gear over her shoulder, checks her face in the bathroom mirror. Great! I am so stunning. Utterly fantastic. Stuffs into her purse the soaps, the shampoos, the entire cute basket into her bag. The hair dryer won't fit and is furthermore anchored to the wall. All right, this pretty hand towel.

"Bat Torner, please..."

It was all untrue and a terrible trick that was being played on everyone. He was a boy full of life one minute and the next limp in his father's arms. Head against his father's chest, the father stroking his face. Shaking. No one yet to rush up and look after the other one, no one concerned with her. Because who was she and what did she matter, and wasn't her mistake the cause? She was the unknown object suddenly flung through air. She was not yet the concern. The concern, and why he thought of her as the unknown, is that he had the idea she needed help more than he did himself. She needed looking after. No one was doing that. He thought his father should go do this, but his father was holding him. He wanted to tell his father to be careful—not to shake so much—and he had every reason to think he had told his father this, but Father was not listening or surely he would have gone to see about the girl. He knows that girl. Okay, not true, he's only seen her around. She's captured my interest, let's say. I'm fine. Don't bother with me. Go help the girl.

One memory that Daisy has is that he had stood by their bed the night prior to the event, saying nothing, staring at them intently as a stray cat. Wanting assurance they were asleep. Later, she heard him downstairs, going through the refrigerator. So he had eaten that last night, a wedge of key lime pie bought that very day. On the counter in the morning were the saucer, with its dry crumbles, the milk jug and what was left in it that had gone to rot because he left it out. She remembers thinking, gone to rot. And thinking, to see this proof that next morning of his secret raid, oh it grows on trees, that's what he thinks, and a good mother says nothing to the father, just pours this soured mess down the drain and goes on to something else. She remembers that. And remembers later in the day looking in the fridge for a bite of lunch and finding the fridge bare. Cleaned out. Then to find the same thief has been at her larder. But the funny thing about her remembering, funny to her mind, is that she did not associate this discovery of missing food with the nocturnal activity, that previous evening, of her son. She still doesn't. Or at any rate not in the same way. As Rebecca says, she has *moved on*. That night, she heard him out back, by the garage, and heard other voices as well. They were trying to be quiet. She could tell that by the furtive sounds. They were being quiet like cats are quiet, cats up to no good. It had even sounded to her ears as though some of the people making those noises were tipsy. And she had thought: well, surely not Tallis. Surely my boy does not drink. Why isn't he in bed?

She had called out the window, and everything back there had gone silent.

They must have seen her coming. Anyway, whoever had been there had disappeared. Tallis was back in bed. And she was the party looking at someone pretending sleep.

Sheila Shott strides into 2x8, a comet streaking past assembled parties. Business first, she croons. Your loo. Then the girlie talk. She's like this, a habit nurtured since friendship's day one: keep the girls off balance. I'm dismissing you, be right back. Rudeness, a Sheila Shott trademark. Prepare yourselves, ladies, for the tornado Sheila is. She blows into her publisher's office, don't a dozen arms fly up, chairs spin as every employee leaps to the feet, big-wigs' doors burst open, big-wigs come running? Settle down, darlings, first the loo. Well, once it was that way, in dreams if not in reality. She'd done her loo business, washed the hands, given brief appraisal to the inspiring face the mirror reflects. Not a knockout precisely, not a face yet found adorning the *People* magazine cover, though on the whole an exemplary face, an honest face notable for high cheekbones, the Julia Roberts wave of lips, the fine Romanish nose despite the barely visible bump thanks to a dopey incident involving a child's high chair.

Time to get down to the nubs of what has brought her here. At ease, Rebecca, I have no further interest in you. I've been wasting my talents on you. You're old hat, last week's news. I was thinking that, strolling along Bloor, watching the university jocks go at it. I wanted to suit-up, knock heads with them. From here on I'm launching my spears at the heavy stuff. Literature. Rejuvenate a declining market. I've got big guns, heavy artillery, from here on I'm going after big game. Here's the deal, Daisy. Bed in your basement, a desk. A spare coffeepot? An inspiring abode steers one to truth. Readers will go gaga. Their eyes bug out.

Stay here? Daisy's mouth is wide open, saying this.

Till I get my legs beneath me. I'll be but a ghost. You feel chilly air on your backside it's me passing through. You'll hardly know I'm alive. I feel such artistic rejuvenation my arteries may burst. A molehill today, Kilimanjaro tomorrow. Hell, I may even take on the poets. Listen:

They will feel my arrows
Quivering in the bulk of spiny backsides
As they wrestle penny the page payment
Over floors worn smooth
By neglected pioneers. Now to arrive
Me with filled pail,
Brushstrokes to alter eternity.

Isn't that the greatest poem? Your expansive eyes, gaping mouth, tell me you love it. Shoo, shoo. Romantic ballads step aside. No more spiff to rivet a maid's spine. A month in your basement and I'll bring forth poetic word that will banish any view you may possess of the beauty of radiant sky on starry night. See? I'm already speaking the lofty language previously reserved for immortal bards. Do you know why? Can't you tell? I've fallen in love.

*Help!*                                    ('Sheila living in my house would be the end.')

---

The house at 2 x 8 Major was pitched into widening chaos later in the day. The elderly Hungarian man living across the street intercepted Emmitt at the Hardware. They were in the Paints section, examining brushes—three for a dollar or one of quality at ten.

'That boy of yours.'

'Yes, Mr Kuimets.'

'Often see him. At your window.'

'See him?'

'At your window. He waves.'

'Waves?'

'Lifts a hand.'

'You sure?'

'Other night, shouted at me.'

'Shouted what?'

'Said he was dying for goulash. Bowl of goulash.'

'You're joking. Goulash?'

'From Country Style.'

'The restaurant on Bloor?'

'Good goulash, Country Style. Happened we had a pot on the stove.'

'Goulash?'

'Wife's goulash. Her goulash also good. She came out. Said, "Who you talking to?" Him, I said. Pointed to window.'

'She saw him, too?'

'No, no, no!'

'No?'

'Saw nobody. Said I was *vak bolond*.'

'Meaning what?'

'Meaning I was blind fool. No one at window. Pitch-black up there. So we had our goulash. In kitchen. Good goulash. You like goulash?'

'Sure. Goulash is good.'

'Hungarian paprika essential for good goulash. Otherwise, waste of time. Another thing.'

'Yes?'

'Where went naked woman once seen your house? Now see only scary woman in housecoat.'

'Daisy, you mean?'

'Another thing. Your boy.'

'Yes?'

'In Budapest we say *Lasu viz partot mos*. Still waters run deep.'

---

At school, Mr Evers, teacher of the strychnine class, said to Zan, 'I've been alert for that beacon of light from the cesspool. It isn't you.' What they meant in calling it the Free School was that teachers could hang you by the neck anytime they wanted to.

'I'll never amount to much, will I, sir?'

They loved the 'sir' touch. Undermining students, in her opinion, was what they did best. All right, confess: some teachers were inspiring. Same as the parental unit, once every blue moon, demonstrated the potential.

Home, Zan informed this unit—afloat in cocktails—she required twenty-five dollars for school. They surrendered this amount after a slew of questions—why, dominating. Because. Because is not why. Oh, give it to her, Chig, before she falls into another coma. Fine. Sign this receipt. $25 *received from Chig for undisclosed purpose.* I will not sign that. You can't make me. Then you don't get the cash. Is this receipt a kind of IOU? Before I reach the age of consent I'll owe the two of you a million dollars. What's this 'consent' crap? You already owe us a million.

The twenty-five Zan turned over to a young misfit repairing potholes on Sussex Avenue. She required, in exchange, his orange *WORKS DEPT* vest. He was a teenage misfit, he said, in his first job. 'Other than KFC,' he said. 'Flabby Jacks. Some others.'

'Where's Flabby Jacks?'

'Yukon,' he said. 'You probably know my dad. Hangs out around here. Ormsby.'

'You're Ormsby's kid?'

'Sure. Got a sister, too. Women seem to like my Dad. He tells me the CBS woman, Lesley Stahl, gave him the come-hither look.'

'How'd a misfit like you get a city job?'

'Influence. Ormsby did it. Ten zillion potholes in this city. To date, I've done four hundred forty. You're pretty. But skinny. Tall as me. How much do you weigh? Why do you want my vest?'

'Tree work.'

For days she'd been eyeing a certain maple tree standing in the Kuimets yard.

Neighbours paused on the sidewalk to inquire why she was sitting high in the tree in that ugly jacket. She told an outright lie, that she was employed on city business. She had on her person an array of tools, in abet of this fabrication. 'What city business?' they asked. 'Maple-leaf blight,' she said. 'Quebec infestation of prairie leaf-moth.' 'That maple has no leaves,' they said. 'You lie. This is more of your Haley folly. But don't worry. We love romance. We won't rat you out.'

The view into the beloved's room proved to be sterling. Old Mr Kuimets nightly sat in a rocker on his porch, dwarfed by a thick hooded coat and sipping through a straw at something in a mug, occasionally calling inside to inform the wife that the X girl hadn't yet broken her neck.

What she saw through the target window was fascinating. Tallis was in bed under white sheets. Lots of white pillows. Lots of shadowy movement as people came and went. The parental unit, one or the other, sometimes both, usually occupied chairs by the bed. Then the father was sitting on the bed, in apparent deep study of a lamp he'd taken apart and was now fixing. She saw him plug in the lamp, turn the switch, and the lamp not come on. He screwed in another bulb and still it didn't. He again disassembled the lamp. Sometimes he put the pieces on what looked like an ironing board and other times he scattered parts over her beloved's bed. He employed a good many gestures she thought excessive. He seemed always to be talking to someone; more likely to himself. He obviously was not gifted in the fix-it department. If she succeeded in hitting up the parental unit for another twenty, tomorrow she'd troop down to Honest Ed's, buy her beloved a working lamp. Drop it off on the porch, bang on the door and run. That idea made her eyes moisten: her lamp by the beloved's bed. One day they might be beside each other in that bed, reading. Tallis would roll over and say, How remiss of me never to thank you for our lovely lamp from Honest Ed's. Rapturously overwhelmed by her beauty, he would have no recourse but to rapturously kiss her.

The days she afterwards spent in bed, suffering what at first was thought to be pneumonia—mild case of frostbite, too—before being downgraded to the common cold, were found to be rewarding. She liked being pampered, and could now brag to friends of her police record. She'd picked up vital information about a great many things, some entirely relevant to her beloved. She extracted from a secret niche in the floor, her diary.

*Dear Diary: I want to tell the boy I love about myself. Even stuff I hate to admit. Stuff I wouldn't breathe to any other mortal. I'm a touch skinny, a touch taller than most my age. The parental unit demand I square my shoulders back. They smack my butt should I not. I used to be pigeon-toed. I grew out of the pigeon-toes concept of being. This was the same period I stopped being horrid to the parental unit. This didn't stop them being horrid to me. How many times have they screamed at me, What idiot didn't fill the ice tray? What idiot forgot to close the door? What idiot didn't pick up her clothes? Like they can't come up with my name? These merely the quaint everyday misdeeds, not like the time I allegedly ruined, demolished, diabolically injured the master's precious private Bang & oh-my-god Olufsen inviolate turntable by playing* Stuffed Bird *on his Holy Instrument reserved strictly for his inimitable Lily Pons. I don't do* Stuffed Bird *anymore. XXX. More later should I live.*

*Ormsby's misfit boy (he's nice) begs me to go to the Yukon with him. He's made pots of pothole money. My heart belongs to another. YOU! My birthday came and went and me and Seong tipped our Gatorade to yours. I saw you being washed. You have a beautiful chest. I nearly fell from the tree.*

Emmitt had brought the ironing board, and the iron, into the son's room. He'd meant to iron a few shirts, the tablecloth, napkins, doilies, blouses, skirts, pillowcases, hell, why not the sheets. Big king bastards, take all day. Daisy refused to remove for the wash the decaying robe adhering to her body night and day.

---

Ryabovitch was mystified. 'What is the fellow doing?'

'Who?'

'It's a railway station in here. Smacks me as uncivilized. I may have to go out.'

'Go where? Shopping again?'

Since escaping Chekhov's tale, a transformation had occurred. Ryabovitch had cast off his round shoulders and meek mien. He'd shed the unbecoming spectacles the author had made him wear, opting for a spectacular design he'd heard were called *shades*. He wore a blue velvet suit— Ermenegildo Zegna, he proudly said. Bow tie over stripy blue-white shirt, black pointy shoes elevated in the heel, these often topped-off by a white silk scarf that he liked twirling from a ringed hand. He'd been passing Harry Rosen on Bloor, had walked in. After a leisurely cappuccino in Harry's upstairs den, he'd sauntered out like a gay blade, hardly aware of the chorus of shouts— *Stop! Stop!*—pursuing him. He couldn't stop. He had a date with Anna Sergeyevna. They were off to see *Miss Saigon* at the Princess of Wales Theatre.

Shirts. Emmitt preferred beginning with the front, then the back, next the sleeves, finally the collar. Cuffs again, for good measure. He said to himself as he always did, Why don't I take these to the cleaners, as sane men do? Because he wasn't sane. Not since calamity struck. Because ironing was punishment well deserved. Because he didn't mind ironing: focusing on the task, you could shuck off worse thoughts, you could press the red button and watch clouds of steam puffing up. Put the shirt on a hanger, the hanger on a door knob, start another one. Front side, back side, sleeves, collar, there! Another one. All while scoping out the son: *Hey, you! Lazybones! I could use a little help over here.*

'There she goes again.'

'Who?'

'Your exalted one.'

'Where is she going?'

'Store.'

'Why?'

'Something to wipe her nose.'

'She has a runny nose?'

'She walks low to the curb. Thinking of you. Thinking of you casts her down. Did I mention she was several nights up a tree? What is troubling that dog?'

'What dog?'

'The dog licking your face.'

'Nothing is licking my face.'

Closet suitcases mutter among themselves like elves left out in rain. Fill me, fill me, is the cry. A shoe, left alone by itself, cries woefully through the night. It was never held by its mother and has heard too many stories about the evil that dogs enact upon innocent leather. A four-year old down the street is being treated for scalp lesions by iodine that forgets her name. It's havoc all over, including in here, where Daisy holds her son so tight a Yapochee on a distant plain dares not breathe.

'I can't breathe, Pierre. Are you breathing?'

'Once in a while.'

Ryabovitch disappears from time to time. The boy looks for him and he isn't there. Here he is today, cleaning his dark shades, strutting about in the uniform recently returned from the cleaners. Saying, 'How do I look?'

'Where are you going?'

'It might surprise you to learn I am not the only Russian in this city. I have friends, you know. A quick polish to these boots and I am off.'

'Take me with you.'

'Not looking like that.'

'I'll dress.'

And there they go.

'Will I know anyone at your party?'

'Doubtful. Some of Babel's people usually show up. Isaac's, I mean. The Tolstoy crew may drop in. Old Ivan Ilych, though he doesn't get out much any-more. Still has that pain in the side. Not happy about it, either. Naturally, since it killed him. A few Dostoevsky-ites, on the whole a gloomy lot best avoided.'

'Will any authors be present?'

Ryabovitch laughed. His nose took the air. 'You should surely be aware that we don't mix. Authors are not invited and if any materialize they'd likely be shot.'

The meeting place was poorly lit. Not shabby, exactly, but deeply underground, somewhat spartan, and strangely ventilated. A pretty woman, no longer in her youth and scarred by unhappiness, seemed to have the floor.

'Who is that?'

'My dear boy, you do surprise me. She has visited us many times at 2×8. That's Anna.'

'Anna Sergeyevna?'

Anna wasn't how he had pictured her. He recalled with fondness their initial meeting: *People were telling one another that a newcomer had been seen on the promenade—a lady with a lapdog.* And there the lapdog tonight was, pacing at Anna's heels. Rather more sizeable than he had imagined. Life's hardship had taken a toll on the natural beauty of the woman. Love, coming late, had restored some of that. She wore both on her face. He was, what?—a mere fifteen or sixteen when last possessing a thinking mind—so what did he know? Next to nothing. Hard times didn't appear to have wrought any hardship on her body, which remained that of a young woman comfortable in society. It was mostly in the beautiful eyes—she was looking at them—that one saw the deep mix of suffering and pleasure.

'Would you like to meet her?' asked Ryabovitch. 'Follow me.'

Absolutely not. He'd be too embarrassed. He knew too much about her. He wouldn't know what to say. Funny he didn't feel that way about Ryabovitch, or for instance old Ivan Ilych, on a wheelchair over in a far corner surrounded by a clutch of admirers. He couldn't resist wondering why Anna Sergeyevna had allowed herself to marry so badly in the first place. Stories of adultery, painful stories of late-arriving true love confused him. In fact, made him kind of angry. He knew with utter certainty in his own life, which very likely would contain moments of desperation and conflict, he would never ever act the foolish way so many of these characters in books did. What? He's head over heels in love with, for instance, Zan, one day, and the next day he's hot on the heels of some redhead living down the street! No way! Not him! No chance! Never happen! Not even if some guru-genius like Chekhov got hold of him. He'd be forced to say to Chekhov's face, You hold on. You just wait a minute.

'What is that group bunched around the beer tub?' Tallis asked. 'Noisy, aren't they?'

'Gate-crashers,' Ryabovitch sourly replied. 'The Dublin brigade. Louts, one and all. They don't have much to do with us nor us with them. Say nothing against their author or you'll get a punch in the snout. They see themselves as big-timer world-beaters, because of ... well, because of the fame their master technician gave them. The Joyce guy. Don't get me started on *him*. The whole lot is enraged tonight because a rumour is afloat that your mother set fire to a *Finnegans*.'

'Daisy! Set fire to *what*?'

'Took *Finnegans* out to the backyard and threw it on the barbecue.'

'Daisy!'

'Like you'd cook a steak. That's the rumour. Some over there claim they are in that book. The blowsy fellow running on at the mouth is J. J. O'Molloy. He'll try hitting you up for a loan. Don't bite. That's marvellous Molly Bloom holding herself aloof under the blue light. Handsome devil. If she starts a sentence, don't wait around for its ending.'

'How do you know those people?'

Ryabovitch is offended. 'I'm not the ignoramus I was painted to be.' A second later Tallis sees tears flush Ryabovitch's eyes. He's embracing the boy, kissing both cheeks. Now stalking off into the milling crowd. Tallis has the oddest feeling: he will never again see this good friend.

A very pretty woman has sidled up to him. 'My God, Tallis,' she exclaims. 'You could have knocked me over with a feather, when I saw you at this shindig. What has got you out of bed? You're supposed to be in a coma. Do your parents know? My name's Rebecca Whitehall. I'm hitting the bright spots. Slumming, actually. Would you like to dance with me?'

'I've kind of been mothballed.'

'Oh, come on. Let's whirl.'

———————

—Good morning!

—You think so?

Sometimes, crushed by grief, erosive woe, melancholy that strides a wicked field, a husband may be forgiven for thinking his wife impossible to live with. He was sufficiently trained to know enough not to say so; he didn't have to. The look on his face told Daisy everything she didn't want to know. Doors were slammed. House lights remained dim.

—Good morning!

—Will you please be quiet, please.

The duty of a dumb house is to reflect the occupants' mood. So some say. On such days Daisy might allow herself to think the unforgiveable: the cause for her bleakness lay not with Emmitt, nor with the poor girl who had pulped her son, but with that son's very self. Didn't she remember? Yes, by God, just think how impossible he was from the start. In the womb, upon delivery, every second since. Jumping up and down in his Jolly Jumper, hadn't he brought down the ceiling? On his head? And blackened the left eye, as she recalled. Dented his lovely nose. Could be that was his father's fault. But hadn't Tallis Haley been content to crawl on the floor way past the time anyone would designate a normal period! And want to breast-feed, seemed like, into his old age! And not learned to tie a proper bow in his shoelaces until practically in his teens. If he yet could. Shirt buttons misaligned, socks mismatched, belt missing the loops, hair a mile long one month, butchered the next. Then what, I ask you. Then what. Then you can't get a word out of him, about anything. You want to know why my hair turned grey, that's why. I come out on the back porch one day, and he's up on the roof, dancing. In a sword fight with Rasputin, he says. Deadliest of enemies. He's six years old. Rasputin, where does he get these names? Get down from there this minute, you'll break a leg. *Argh*, he's down, wriggling like a trapped fish. *Argh, Rasputin got me in the knee cap, I'm done for!* Hanging from the gutter, fifty feet up, he says this, the silly squirt. Perverse. Like his father.

Maybe a little music to cheer me up. Maybe 'Little Girl Blue'. Chet Baker. Chet's sad song will cheer me up. First, one of these pills. Two, three? Why not a handful?

———

Emmitt returns from the 24-Hour, singing snatches of 'The Old Chisholm Trail'. Daisy hopes to God he's brought something she can eat.

'Tell me.'

'Tell you what?'

'How many beautiful women did you lust after today? On the street.'

'I didn't count them.'

'How many?'

'Four, going. Three, coming back. The young don't dress for beauty anymore.'

'Is that a fact?'

'Different story in summer, of course. Nudes on parade. Kid wake up?'

'Have I told you I like this house?'

'Why is that?'

'It has us in it. We had a visitor.'

'Who?'

'That girl. The X creature.'

'What did she want?'

'She'd disguised herself. Wig, hat, long black Sally Ann dress. Old-biddy stockings and shoes. Said she was seeking housecleaning work.'

'Did you hire her?'

'No, I laughed. The first time I've laughed in a hundred years. I asked if she could provide references. She clearly hadn't thought of that. So I laughed some more. She was pathetic. I think I saw a tear or two. I almost liked her. I even felt the need for forgiveness sweeping over me. Should we forgive her, Emmitt?'

---

Sheila Shott has barricaded herself inside what she's taken to calling the basement parlour. Daisy has never liked this word. 'It is not a parlour!' She shouts this at Sheila from the other side of the locked door. Sheila did the locking. She's been inside the *parlour* for the past several hours. Crying out her eyes. No one may come in. What Daisy and Emmitt have been subjected to over these hours is Sheila Shott's insane weeping, caterwauling shrieks, zany outbursts such as a wounded animal might produce. *What is the matter with you? Have you lost all sense?* Such as that, they have yelled. *Yes, yes, yes!* has come the anguished reply. *I've gone totally bananas. Slide a knife under the door so that I may kill myself. Why didn't you warn me poetry is* difficult.

'I'll slide Edgar A. Guest under the door. Very popular in his day. He may be your speed.'

'Do that. You have mice down here.'

Emmitt has searched the house for a key to the door. He knows this to be useless. There has never since the Middle Ages been a key to that door.

Finally, the door opens a crack. Cautiously, Daisy and Emmitt peep inside. Sheila is seated on her fanny on the floor, quietly sobbing. She looks, to their minds, a hundred years old. Not as old as they themselves feel. A hand shades Sheila's eyes as she blinks up at them. Her voice is cast so low they find they must drop to the floor and sit beside her. 'How long have we known each other?' she is saying. 'Since year one, seems like. I have not been a good friend to you. I have been, in fact, a terrible friend. An awful friend. A fraud. A false friend. Yes, that's the word. A false friend. All this time, to you, my dearest bosom buddies, I've presented myself as something other than I am. Big-time, happy romance novelist, on top of the world. When, in fact, I've kept vital truths—secrets—from you. I—'

'What are you saying?'

'I have not been a model citizen.'

'Unforgiveable. Stop weeping. What else?'

'You'll hate me. Never speak to me again.'

'Shut up and tell us.'

'I was married. You didn't know that, did you? I have a child. You didn't know that. All that time you've thought I was away in East Asia, in France— wherever—I've been visiting her. She lives with her father. I had her about the same time you had Tallis. She's a beautiful lovely fabulous girl.'

'Truly?'

'Yes!'

'We don't believe you.'

'It's true.'

'You're too vain, narcissistic, spoiled, and self-absorbed to be a mother.'

'I am not!'

'What is this supposed-child's name? Who is this alleged husband?'

'Former husband, please. Who he is is none of your business. His name is Turner, if you must know. He is a debilitating influence. Turner's idea of wit is to declaim 'Behold, the hour is at hand,' and fall to the floor in a dead faint. He has never been beyond the nub of his scrap-heap town, and is dumb as a poisoned stump.'

'If so, why did you hook up with him?'

'Because that's what people do. We race across a busy street to save three seconds, and a moron in an automobile knocks us into Saint Elsewhere. Because we want love, whatever the peril, and don't want to waste a lifetime waiting for it. Does that satisfy you?'

'Somewhat. Though it's unctuous drivel. The child? What is her name?'

'Tallulah. Tallulah is a darling child. You will love her. Do you think in your hearts you ever can forgive me?'

'Not without full disclosure,' said Daisy.

'Every gruelling detail,' offered Emmitt.

'Go now. Inspiration knocks. Don't forget the Edgar man.'

---

A knock on the front door. Emmitt responded.

'No one there,' he said, returning. He held in his hands a lamp. Cheap. Sixty-watt bulb. $13.95. Honest Ed's. 'Saw the legs of that girl, running. How did she know we needed a lamp?'

Sheila was put to bed in *the parlour*, on the living room couch that Daisy had once called a chesterfield but now called a sofa. She clutches Daisy's hand: 'Do you think Arthur would mind? My having a child?'

'Arthur?'

'Inasmuch as I may in the near future be having his?'

'Oh my God,' squeals Daisy. 'How much torture can a woman take!'

A phone call. *My name is Mary. I am the maid. Who is calling, please?*

'It's Flute, you dunce. Did you yet receive the lawyer's cheque?'

'I did not.'

'Those weasel lawyers. I've a mind to put Philip Marlowe on the case. Bye.'

She was gone.

Last look-in on the boy, prior to brief sleep. During the day, Daisy had found time to bestow upon him a home permanent. His head was lit with radiant curls. Little Orphan Annie, Emmitt thought. Rather beautiful.

------------

Zan was keen to understand the wisdom of her mother's assertions: 'Boys want to know what you're going to do about it. If they're not the kind to grab you at first sighting, they remain in a petrified state until you let the cat out of the bag. Look at your father. He's certain he rules the roost despite his chickens laying no eggs. What's this moping about: some boy has his hooks into you? Stop blushing, I can see it's true. You're too young to be blitzed by love. Or infatuation, that wizard's pill. If the little turd ignores you, doesn't turn his head when you pass, then it's up to the girl to rearrange his mindset. You don't have hips, so that won't work. No occasion yet, I suppose, to accidentally show a leg. Knee cuts in scraggly jeans won't do it. Listen: *She married for love but was unhappy* is the saddest story ever told. But if you say *She fell in love and was miserable,* you have a different story. In that instance *she* just sounds stupid. She's brought misery upon herself. See? I'm suggesting you not be stupid.' With that, Zan's mother ceased her spiel. Advice from the mother tongue was rare in the household, no less than the rarity of Zan's attention to such. Mother had to go out now. Mother was late for a meeting. Didn't Mother look *chic!* My haircut, silly, how astounding no one noticed. Zan, dear, you are to put the roast in the oven at six o'clock. 350 degrees, I should think. Cook exactly two hours twenty-nine minutes. Ladling frequently. The table is set. Your father will want wine, which I have already breathing, since the idiot is hopeless with a corkscrew. You may have a single glass. Mother will be home late. She has left the porch light on. See that it stays so. What is that boy's name you're so hopped up about? He doesn't deserve you, remember that. "Joy of Man's Desiring", the song, doesn't begin to hit the high spots. Let's hope he's not a Popeye.'

'The sailor man?'

'No, darling. Mr Faulkner's Popeye.'

'What did he do?'

'It hardly bears telling. Bye. You are such an innocent. Such a sweetie.'

Mother gone, Sweetie climbed the rope ladder to the backyard treehouse, Chig's ancient foray into the building trades. Dexterity was required. But the house, sitting at an odd angle, was secure. As the tree grew, limbs fused with the walls, poked through windows, popped through roof and floor. Elevation had increased right along with that of the tree. Now she was above most rooftops, up there with CN Tower. As a kid she'd knelt up here eating Cheese Nips while baking chocolate chip cookies on a stove the size of her thumb. What she saw now was mostly the winter rubble of gardens. The sky was muddy; a Spadina streetcar was rattling south to Union Station. The day cold, though not unbearable.

*She fell in love and was miserable.*

Captured her perfectly.

'Your mom overly saturates,' said her father, tapping wineglasses. 'But this roast is excellent.'

'I burnt it.'

'Fine Yorkshire pudding. You do these?'

'I burnt them.'

'I prophesy there will be no baseball in heaven. You think?'

'Golf?'

'Certainly.'

'Baseball?'

'Maybe slow-pitch.'

'Poker?'

'Day and night. Had no idea you could cook.'

'Everything's burnt.'

'Mice in the walls when I grew up. Feasting on broken latticework. Plaster. How they built walls, in my day. Not a proper wall, you didn't have mice. How's school? Member in good standing of that blessed tribe of idlers known as the student body? Fetch the wine, please. Is there a PTA at your school? I harbour deep enthusiasm for such magnificent entities. But maybe PTAs are defunct. Defunct, what once was the very nadir of a nation's rise.'

'Don't squint at me. I know what nadir means. Not sure you do.'

'In my youth parents were released from jail so they might attend the annual meeting. Or the meetings were held at the jail, since that's where so many of the students were. What's this I hear about you being in love? Who's the rake?'

'I'll get you the wine.'

He rattled on. Some evenings were like that. Sometimes he was actually funny; mostly she sat with braced jaw, rolling her eyes. Parents. They really were pathetic.


Going to sleep that night, no mice gnawing in the walls, she said aloud to those walls, *She fell in love and was unhappy.* That was a sad story and the other wasn't? 'I don't get it,' she said. The sad story makes a better story than one about a stupid girl? What am I missing? What did my mother possibly mean? *Save me*, she thought. There had been days when Winnie-the-Pooh proved difficult.

She heard the front door click open, click shut. She listened for the click of heels on the hardwood floor.

No clicks. Mother has removed her shoes. Now she's before the hall mirror, brushing back her hair. Now it's a peep into the kitchen to troubleshoot. Did the wretches wash up? Sink and counter clean? Good, they are. Check the wine rack. Depleted by two. *Not* good. Must put my foot down.

Zan's psychic friend Glandola's line was that children either knew the parental unit too well, or not at all: either way, you faced disaster.

Zan's mother's ex, noted antique dealer with a clip-shop on Avenue Road, drops by, hauling into the girl's room an exquisite French desk he claims had been a pretty Parisian girl's in the long ago. When knee-high, Brigitte Bardot drew doodles at this desk, he tells Zan.

'Who's she?'

Her mother's ex is a breezy fellow, liked by all.

'Where do you want it?'

'By the window.'

He polishes the surface with a soft cloth. 'Inlaid,' he says. 'Secret drawers. Glorious shading. Heirloom. What's this I hear about your being in love?'

'How did you become my mother's ex?' Zan wants to know. She wants to know *Did they fall in love and were unhappy* or *Did they and were miserable.*

'Hard times. Didn't have a penny. In New Mexico, this was. Laura was selling everything—herself last, to build up the bidding. I wanted her Olds and put my bid in a sealed envelope. We went for a drive in the Olds. To a drive-in in a cornfield and had one popcorn bag to share. A soft drink culled from an infinite variety. The movie unintelligible. Unintelligible but great. *Invasion of the Killer Tomatoes,* or some such. Every speaker at that drive-in shot. We didn't mind during the kissing. Not kissing, the squawks an irritant.'

'Excuse me, you were kissing my mother!'

'We were "besieged by the infinitely unlikely". That's an Aldous Huxley quote. Goodbye kisses, we called them. About one thousand cars with squawking speakers, in that cornfield. Rowdy gangs tramped past, banging on the Olds' roof, jumping on the bumpers. Kiss me, kiss us all, kiss my foot, these goons shouting.

'Much kissing, everybody shouting. Double feature, we stayed on. More kissing. I tell you, we were kissing fools. In those days. Everybody was. I kissed the very ground your mother walked upon. No kidding. We sold the Olds to the refreshments guy, an old buddy who drove us back to where Laura was selling everything. Herself last. To heighten the anticipation, you know. A thousand people in that cornfield watched us go. Our last night together and me with certain expectations. But no deal. She put me on the couch that night and in the morning I put in a bid on the couch, her percolator, four cups, saucers, spoons, what was left of the cream she wasn't pouring in her coffee. The table was a no-go. Wobbly legs, not hers to begin with. She was a renter, the house coming furnished, sort of, the owner standing out by the well with a shotgun over the shoulder.

'We never knew why, he just often was. People arrived, seals were opened, everything soon gone. Goodbye, your mother said to me. You were not the best husband I ever hoped to have, though you could have been worse.

'Letting me off lightly. Last I saw of her that time she was standing on this high knoll holding a stranger's hand—your father, as I do declare. Where she found him, God knows. Quite a dame, your mother. Straight out of Somerset Maugham's *Rain*. I love saying that name, Somerset Maugham. How splendid. Unhappily wed to Syrie Wellcome, another great name. Do you like that desk? That's a beautiful desk. Ludwig Bemelmans wrote his first Madeline book at that desk. You'll look like a French girl, smart and sexy, at that desk. Our own sweet Colette.'

'Who's she?'

'Laura and Chig were heading out to one of those islands in the Strait of Georgia, maybe Salt Spring, if memory serves. There they would raise goats, drink lots of buttermilk, erect with their own hands a driftwood shack held together by the sap of love. Man, was I ever jealous. Still am. I was beat down as a bunny in a briar patch. Love, I'll tell you, it will smash one into smithereens, it will turn one into meatloaf.

'Meatloaf? You're crazy.'

'You just wait. You'll think you and rice pudding are one and the same. But not me. Not back then. I was heroic, a heroic goofball, I stood tall as a redwood, and let your mother go. I'd be your daddy, had she not kicked me out. Out of the kissing loop. You'd have the dimpled cheeks of a poetical creature, were you mine.'

'I have dimples.'

'Yeah, but not *my* dimples. And only when you smile, which I've noticed are in short supply these days. Now tell me about your fella. What's his merit, if any? Are you in love?'

Zan sucks in her cheeks, returning his bland gaze. The next second her features distort, agonizing cries escape her lips. She falls to the floor and rolls about. She rises, pulling at her hair: 'I'm mad with love,' she declares. 'I'm wrecked freight, doomed to become stained fruit, to wallow in squalor, I can't go on. And so on and so forth till the end of time.' She throws herself across the new desk, where for some seconds she wriggles, moans and kicks her legs.

'That's the spirit,' he says. 'Very nicely done. I've experienced the throes of love myself many a time. Thanks to God there has always been another woman to come to my rescue. That nurse creature of yours, for instance, Nancy Cee. Spectacular woman. I'd politely lay my heart in her hand any day in the week. But every time she sees me coming, her eyes narrow, her fists clench, and those tight white nursing shoes she wears on her dainty white feet get ready to kick me into next week. However far-fetched, and despite my youthful countenance and general swagger, it may be that she imagines I'm too old for her. What do you think?'

Downstairs once again, in the brew of a temporary silence, they were witness to a flung-open front door and Zan's mother storming in as if borne aloft by the clatter of high heels and a strong wind. She quickly shed herself of hat, coat and gloves, flinging them onto the sofa-end where her ex just happened to be sitting. 'A glass of wine, please.' This directed at Zan in the kitchen. She'd been there for some time, assiduously attempting extraction of a difficult cork. 'Always underfoot,' she heard Laura say, the voice pitched raucously high, in achievement of the hypocrisy always sought when addressing her ex. 'What brings you over?' she asked. 'You know how nervous your presence makes Chig. If he had a gun I'm sure he would have shot you long ago.'

The ex gave a hearty laugh. 'You know Chig likes me. And why shouldn't he? I'm the party keeping this household afloat.'

Zan delivered the wine. For her mother, the gold-rimmed glass she preferred, for him, a jam jar.

'Your ex has been trying to dig out of me the telephone number of that sexy nurse woman, Nancy Cee.'

'A confirmed rotter,' Laura said, smacking his knee. 'Nancy is hot, but in my estimation not that hot.' She turned to him, smiling as she ran fingers through his hair. 'She's hot enough, though, to eat you alive. We all did. All of us hot women who found you obstructing our path. Gobble, gobble. For us, you were turkey meat. For brief moments your love made us happy, as love is supposed to. You were our sunlight, our blazing star. Then, wham, we saw you as the soulless rotter you truly are.'

'Nonsense. Chig gets nervous because he knows that with a snap of my fingers you'd come running back to me.'

'Ha-ha, how insane you are. I knew you were an insect from the moment I set eyes on you.'

'Ha-ha yourself. The moment you set eyes on me your hands were all over me.'

'Yes, keeping you off. Your hands ever at me, like Jerry Lee Lewis at a piano.'

'What a dreamer. You were hard to stomach then, and still are. Can't a man get a glass of wine in this house?'

'More wine, thank you, Zan. Zan? Oh, look. We've hurt our darling's feelings.'

'Get your own wine,' Zan said, leaving the room. 'The two of you talk like love is nothing but a big joke. I don't find your talk funny.'

'*No, no, no!*' shouted they to her backside.

---

*Lift up your heart and let it sing.*

It is Sunday already, Sunday again, another Sunday, and Daisy is listening to Sunday radio, Gospel Hour, although she is no gospel person. What she has thought is her son might like to hear some rejoicing. *Let your love shine through, let it rock,* the Gospel Hour tells her. It is a Detroit station. Detroit, she thinks, must be a fine place to be, on this Sunday. *Remember your Saviour had bleeding feet.* Daisy remembers this; it isn't something one easily forgets. Now a full choir is singing of the bleeding feet. Some members of this very choir are likely suffering bleeding feet. In many places near and far, she does not doubt feet are bleeding. It is a stupendous choir. She turns the volume way up.

Zan's palmist friend Glandola, talented beyond endurance, no frugality in the chains looping her elegant neck, a spectacular radiance of material beautifully adorning her head, today said: Why don't you use makeup? Try this lip gloss, git in harmony with your essence.

*Get*, Zan said.

Eyes first. What boys look at after breasts. Then lips, to check-see if their presence makes you speechless.

Further, she said: I find I can't do the cards well while engaged in my readership of the *Rubaiyat of Omar Khayyam*. You may well ask, as I did, what is a rubaiyat. A rubaiyat, Zan, is a fourfold quatrain, by which is meant lines four by four customarily rendered in the a-a-b-a rhyming scheme. Would you like to hear one?

No.

A jug of wine
A keg of beer
And thou
Beside me drinking.

Here I've allowed myself liberty with form. Do you like it?

No. When are you doing my hands?

Ah. Your hands. My analysis of your handwriting only revealed the obvious. Show me your hands.

Quite squat, that hand. That hand is unhydrogenated pig fat.

At that, the palmist laughed.

But don't worry. A good meat tenderizer will do the trick.

Whereupon, soul mates, the two girls strolled onwards to school.

My hands don't worry me, Zan said. Last week we didn't have breasts. We were inches shorter. Our hair was rotted fruit peel. They paused by Sally Bird Park, where two school companions of the male variety were fulfilling their aggressive instincts by swatting the earth with long sticks.

Yo! Yo! all said. Today was Make a New Friend Day at school, a hugely unapplauded innovation.

The city sign, *No Winter Upkeep at Sally Bird*, the boys now tried taking it down.

It's in concrete, Zan said, like your brains.

We are inured to insult, they said back. The girls swept snow from the bench and primly sat.

Can you get me a sample of your beloved's handwriting?

Sure.

I'll need a chunk of his hair.

I've got that. I've got a soiled handkerchief of his, too.

Ugh. Won't need that.

What will these items tell you?

The hair specimen will convey what your children will look like. The handwriting speaks to his spiritual latitude weighted by his intellectual resources plus or minus what the blood sample reveals. You have his nail clippings?

I thought you didn't need those.

Changed my mind.

Seriously?

No. You idjit. Quit twitching. Those boys are looking.


On one of those days when thoughts turn to the brave new world, Zan has had a thought she considers part and parcel of that world. She lives within a stone's throw of U of T, this year ranked high in the middle of those institutions of higher learning recognized as best in the world. It had come to her on one of those days that a place of such hallowed worth must surely have a course or courses somewhere in the curriculum on her beloved's dreaded Chekhov. She has investigated. She has thought it might prove highly useful, to her projected romance, if she picked up a jigger of the actual language the author employed. With words skillfully employed, she will knock her beloved for a loop. He will be shocked. He will grip her shoulders. He will stare deeply into her eyes. He will be feverish with interest. She will have to pretend a widespread knowledge not actually possessed, but she can manage that.

Thus, with devoted simplicity—duplicity—she has learned of the existence of an entity called the Department of Slavic Languages and Literatures. Dreaded Chekhov is indeed taught, along with someone called Pushkin and a slew of others. Her Korean friend Seong has set her straight on a deal called *auditing*. 'Forget permission,' he says. 'Few take the roll. No time, too much to teach. Find the classroom, walk in, take a seat. Wear your wig, your Sally Ann dress. Try to look as blandly boring and bored as everyone else.'

She has done so. She now knows as much about the author as the world's leading authorities. Who would ever have guessed the fella also wrote plays? *The Seagull*, goodness, what might that be about? The love of his life, Olga, my goodness. *It has been so long since I tasted champagne*, dying words, my goodness!

Now here she sits among the dozens in a class called Conversational Russian. Another student is beside her, translating for her the instructor's every word: *Teacher asking who your name is. He inquire your origin. He speculate you arrive in wig as KGB spy. He say you lovely. So beautiful. I am good conversation, eh?*

At this very hour Daisy is knotting her way into the 2x8 kitchen, there to find Emmitt slouched at the table, Sheila Shott sitting opposite him, erect and poised. Daisy pulled out a chair, then had second thoughts about sitting. A pause fell as Emmitt and Sheila contemplated the drained look on her face, as with curved posture, she unsteadily crossed the floor: the extended period she stood leaning against the sink, deep sighs reaching their ears in those long seconds before the tap was turned, and finally her cupped hands there to catch the water, the face at last lowering in receipt of this as a string of words escaped her lips, these words unintelligible.

What did she say, what did she say?

# Help me! Help me! HELP!

*Fiuto! Razzola! Fruga!*

*Sniff! Rummage! Seek!*

Zan had imagined setting firecrackers in the alley behind 2x8, to draw the parental unit's attention. Further research has shown there is no need. It is almost incomprehensible what has transpired. Winter is suddenly over. The day is bright and beautiful. She has vowed that nothing will prevent her from entering the beloved's room. What transpires once she's there is yet to be writ. She slips quietly through the front door, her heart thudding. The 2x8 rooms are bathed under soft light; every surface appears to be gleaming. Someone has done a good job here. Possibly the new lodger, said to be an author. Zan can see through to the back garden, where a grouping appears assembled. The air outside has been misty; the mist seems to have seeped into the house.

She makes her way upstairs, undetected.

Don't let's dither.

She enters her beloved's room.

God in heaven, she is going to do it. She expels breath, softly closes the door behind her. Leans dizzily against it.

Too late to back out now.

She has believed she might remove her clothes. Slide in beside him. Now she knows that cannot, may not, occur. He is deep water, the genuine article.

She sits. She finds, beneath the covers, his hand. She has a funny thought: *little feminine feet traipsing over yellow sand.*

She pokes his shoulder. *Little traipsing hand.*

'Wake up, Tallis.'

He blinks. He does.

SECONDARY SOURCE MATERIAL

# FINNEGANS WAKE

ARCHIVE

From: Chandra
Date: Thu, May 24, 2018 at 7:33 PM
Subject: Leon Rooke novel / rare book dealers
To: David Mason

Dear Mr Mason,

I'm an editor with the Porcupine's Quill and have been working with Leon Rooke on his latest novel, *The House on Major Street*, to be published this fall.

The novel features a couple of scenes in which book dealers haggle over a missing rare edition of *Finnegans Wake*. The book dealers are named, and you are one of them (see attached excerpt from the uncopyedited ms.).

This message is to ask your permission to include your name as such in the published novel. Of course, if you have any objection whatsoever, please let me know and I'll ensure your name is removed from the manuscript. If you do approve the inclusion, your participation will be gratefully recognized either on the copyright page or in the acknowledgements. You may respond to me directly via my e-mail or snail-mail address (both are noted below).

If you would like any further details about this, please don't hesitate to ask.

With sincere thanks and very best wishes,

Chandra

**DAVID MASON BOOKS**
*Fine and rare books since 1967*

From: David Mason Books

Date: Mon, May 28, 2018 at 12:40 PM

Subject: Leon Rooke—The House on Major Street

To: Chandra


Dear Chandra— Leon flatters me and of course I'm delighted to be so used by a writer I respect so much. Steve Temple will feel the same I'm sure. Richard Landon, sadly gone now, would be equally flattered by Leon's very accurate picture of his rapacity—except he would sneer at Leon and goad him by saying the Fisher 'already has three copies of it'.

I shall inquire of Leon, next time I see him, just what he means by 'dishevelled' in reference to myself. He only sees me in places where drinking occurs, not in my professional guise where like all greedy dealers I'm always slick and charming. Looks like it's to be a must-read book.

Best wishes to you,

David


P.S.: *Finnegans Wake* was issued in a slipcase (the book slides into it). But a morocco clamshell box is fine—that would mean that an early collector had commissioned one. I add this because writers often get book details wrong. Leon obviously did his homework. It's a $20,000 to $25,000 book now. As it happens I own one, so I don't need his protagonist's copy.


David Mason Books

366 Adelaide Street West, Suite LL05

Toronto, ON  M5V 1R9

Visit our website at: http://www.davidmasonbooks.com

Dear Ms. Wohleber—

Today I received your letter asking my permission to allow my name to be used in Leon Rooke's forthcoming novel *The House on Major Street*. May I cut to the chase and say, sure, Leon is a friend. He may use my name in the story, even describe me as dishevelled (which I am at times). However, I will take the opportunity to make some comments about the incident. It has been my long experience that journalists, novelists and academics, unless they are themselves sophisticated book collectors (rarely), almost never get things quite right. As here. Firstly, the signed, limited edition of *Finnegans Wake* is not all that rare. 425 copies (310 of which were sent for American distribution), is a healthy edition size, it was solidly constructed, and the survival rate has been high. Several nice copies are on offer today online. They would cost you about USD 20K, give or take. It was not issued in a morocco box, but rather a yellow cloth open-ended slipcase. The edition is not so rare that any single copy would be denoted as the 'Portobello copy', or singled out in any other way except if it was owned by someone very special—say Samuel Beckett—which this copy may have been, but which our greedy trio didn't know until they arrived. The edition was indeed signed in green ink by Joyce, but there was never any thumbprint involved. It is basically fantasy to state that it was found in a cheap books bin on Portobello Road. Stories like that abound amongst those who don't really know how things are with rare books. While it would have been possible, of course, it would have been EXTREMELY unlikely, even way back in the 60s. I have always resented such stories as they just keep the punters looking for something for nothing in all the wrong places and keep them out of the places they might have found their treasure—in bookshops.

As for condition, had I known that the copy had been out in the rain / snow and was warped and swollen I doubt I would have wasted TTC fare to come look. I could have wept in private. I would consider such a copy bordering on worthless, certainly not 5–6 figures, just another lost copy (mind, a Beckett note enclosed would overcome the tragedy to a great degree). I expect David Mason would have had much the same attitude. As it happens, it appears that the Thomas Fisher Rare Books Library doesn't have a signed limited copy of FW, but they could have got one for decades any time they wanted to spend the money.

In my experience, Richard Landon, and his wife Marie Korey, would not have shown up in such circumstances. He didn't buy direct from the public. He may well have urged the owner to donate it, and he may have indicated to a dealer to quote it to him if they bought it. But none of the trio were 'haggling'. The copy could not be found, no price was in play.

Again, the scenario is unrealistic. Knowledgeable booksellers and librarians would not be scrambling to buy a ruined copy when they could buy a proper copy any day of the week if they had the coin.

Now, if it was a different book, a genuine screaming rarity of mega importance, such as the Caxton Fisher just acquired, then one makes allowances and thinks about conservation techniques. But not for a ruined signed limited FW.

Feel free to pass this on to Leon. I understand he is writing fiction—meta or otherwise—so I give him free hand to operate.

Sincerely,

Steven Temple

STEVEN TEMPLE BOOKS
PO BOX 45
WELLAND ON L3B 5N9
CANADA
416.703.9908
905.734.4146
books@steventemplebooks.com

From: Chandra

Sent: June 14, 2018 7:33 PM

To: Steven Temple

Subject: Leon Rooke novel/rare book dealers


Dear Steven— Thank you very much for your detailed letter of May 29. I meant to write back to you before this but got off track due to some deadlines.

Leon, Tim, and I are all aware that the book-dealer scenes in *House on Major Street* are 100 percent unrealistic, but that's meant to be the fun/absurdity of it (this likely did not come across well in the too-brief excerpts I sent you). However, we all also know that many readers may not know just how unrealistic the scenes are, and in what ways they are unrealistic.

To that end (plus, for some extra-meta-fictional content), we would actually love to print your letter at the back of the book, together with David Mason's note responding to the letter I sent him (essentially the same as the one I sent you) and possibly also with a note from Marie Korey. (Marie has given the 'okay' for Richard Landon's name to be included in the novel.)

Would you give permission for the letter you sent me to be printed at the back of the book? Or for some portion of it to be printed? (Or even a rewriting/new version of it, if you prefer; I understand, of course, that you didn't write the letter thinking it would be made public.) And certainly we will all understand if you don't wish for the letter to be printed at all.

Either way, thank you very much for taking the time to pen such a measured and thoughtful response, and thanks for agreeing to allow your name to be used in the scenes. The Porcupine's Quill will send you a copy of the novel once it's been printed, likely late this fall (the official publication date is December).

Yours sincerely,

Chandra

From: Steven Temple

Date: Thu, Jun 14, 2018 at 8:20 PM

Subject: Re: Leon Rooke novel / rare book dealers

To: Chandra


tell leon i want a copy inscribed to me, and then go ahead
and print the letter as is


STEVEN TEMPLE BOOKS

PO BOX 45

WELLAND ON L3B 5N9


phone: 416.703.9908

email: books@steventemplebooks.com


member: IOBA (Independent Online Booksellers Association)


PLEASE VISIT MY NON-SMOKING, GLUTEN-FREE WEBSITE AND SAVE 10%:

www.steventemplebooks.com


Literary first editions. General out of print & rare books.

Established in 1974. I L A B bookseller 1975-2015


'Antiquarian books are a thing of the past.' —S. Temple

'The trouble with the world is that the stupid are cocksure and the intelligent
are full of doubt.' —Bertrand Russell

*'Mit der Dummheit kämpfen Götter selbst vergebens.'* —Schiller

(An excerpt from an audio interview conducted by Nigel Beale for The Biblio File, January 11, 2010. Ref: www.thebibliofile.ca. This passage was selected by Marie Korey. Thanks to Nigel Beale for kind permission to reprint this excerpt.)

'There's a fair bit of egotism and vanity involved in all this, but that's okay. It's a great game. If you're going to play the game, then book collecting seems to me to be about the best game I know.... That's the game: it's hunting for the stuff. The end of the game is using it.... You can have some fun with it, if you know enough.' —Richard Landon